I stood for a minute, getting my bearings.

Pie in the Sky was dark. So was the rest of the roof, except for a few dim safety lights marking the edge of the low adobe wall serving as a railing. I walked over and peeked at the crowd below. A group of women spotted me, raised their fists, and booed. I ducked. No devil yet. Backing away, I remembered the tiny flashlight on my key chain. The light provided a narrow, dim path. Where was Satan? Had Barton forgotten? Was he napping on the job?

I tried again. "Yoo-hoo, Devil? Satan?"

The only answer was a low howl of wind passing through chimney pipes. A scent I didn't recognize caught my attention. It wasn't piñon smoke or the remnant sweetness of sugary pies and buttery crusts. No, this scent was more elemental. It reminded me of the hot spring my friend Cass and I visited in the fall, where the water was slippery with sulfur. There, the scent signaled spa indulgence. This smell was reminiscent of rotten eggs. *Or*, I thought with a shiver, *the devil*.

By Ann Myers

BREAD OF THE DEAD
CINCO DE MAYHEM
FELIZ NAVIDEAD

ANN MYERS

Feliz Navidead

A SANTA FE CAFÉ MYSTERY

wm

WILLIAM MORROW

An Imprint of HarperCollinsPublishers

FELIZ NAVIDEAD. Copyright © 2016 by Ann Perramond. All rights reserved. Printed in the United States of America. No part of this book may be used or reproduced in any manner whatsoever without written permission except in the case of brief quotations embodied in critical articles and reviews. For information, address HarperCollins Publishers, 195 Broadway, New York, NY 10007.

First William Morrow mass market printing: November 2016

ISBN 978–0–06–238231–3

William Morrow® and HarperCollins® are registered trademarks of HarperCollins Publishers.

16 17 18 19 20   QGM   10 9 8 7 6 5 4 3 2 1

Acknowledgments

I wish to thank all those who helped and supported me in writing this book. Many thanks to my wonderful agent, Christina Hogrebe, and the Jane Rotrosen Agency for believing in the Santa Fe Café Mystery series and finding it such a wonderful home at William Morrow/HarperCollins. To Emily Krump, my fabulous editor, thank you so much for your insight and guidance. I am humbled to have an amazing team from HarperCollins behind me, including publisher Liate Stehlik; marketing director, Shawn Nicholls; Karen Davy and Greg Plonowski in production; and publicist, Emily Homonoff.

I am forever grateful to my family, my most enthusiastic and steadfast supporters, especially my husband Eric, for everything, and my grandmother Mary, who still has a kid's love for Christmas.

Rita, Flori, and their friends, as well as some aspects of their Las Posadas performance, are flights of fiction. Like Rita, however, I am entranced by Santa Fe, a truly special place. Thanks to friends and acquaintances in New Mexico who have made it even more special.

Chapter 1

Mom stopped mid-stroll, thumping one hand to her chest, gripping a hip-high adobe wall with the other. "I need to catch my breath, Rita," she declared, rather accusatorily.

I murmured, "Of course," and issued my best good-daughter sympathetic smile. I did, truly, sympathize. At seven thousand feet above sea level, Santa Fe, New Mexico, can literally take your breath away, and my mother had flown in only a few hours earlier from the midwestern lowlands. Adjusting to high altitudes takes time. About a week, the experts say, although I've called Santa Fe home for over three years and still blame the paltry oxygen when I pant through my morning jog and puff under overladen burrito platters at Tres Amigas Café, where I'm a chef and co-*amiga*. I've even postulated that the thin air makes my thighs look larger. Lack of atmospheric compression, that unscientifically tested theory goes. The more likely culprit is my steady diet of cheesy *chiles rellenos*, blue corn waffles, green chile cheeseburgers, and other New Mexican delicacies.

Mom took deep breaths beside me. I wasn't too worried. If Mom was at risk of anything, it was overacting. I strongly suspected she was making a point, something she likes to do indirectly and with drama. Things Mom doesn't like? High altitudes, dry climates, hot chiles, and disturbance of her holiday routine. I knew she wasn't thrilled to spend Christmas away from home. My goal was to win her over, and lucky for me, I had Santa Fe's holiday charm on my side.

I leaned against the wall, enjoying the warmth of solar-heated adobe on my back. A group of carolers strolled by, harmonizing a bilingual version of "Feliz Navidad." String lights and pine boughs decorated the porticos along Palace Avenue, and piñon smoke perfumed the air. To my eyes, the self-proclaimed "City Different" looked as pretty as a Christmas card. Once Mom got over the initial shock of leaving her comfort zone, she'd come around. I hoped . . .

Mom reached for a water bottle in her dual-holstered hip pack. "Hydration," she said, repeating a caution she'd first raised nearly two decades ago, when I embarked for culinary school in Denver and its mere mile-high elevation. In between sips, she reminded me that proper water intake was the key to fending off altitude-induced illnesses ranging from headaches to poor judgment.

She tilted her chin up and assessed me through narrowed eyes. "You're not drinking enough, Rita. I can tell. Your cheeks look dry. Your hands too. And your hair . . ." Mom made tsk-tsk sounds. "Perhaps a trim would keep it from getting so staticky. You do look awfully *cute* when it's short."

I patted my shoulder-length locks, recently cut into loose layers that emphasized my natural staticky waves. *I could use a drink.* A tart margarita on the rocks with extra salt would do. My mouth watered. *Behave,* I chastised myself. It wasn't even two in the afternoon, way too early for tequila. Plus, I loved my mother and her cute silver-flecked pixie cut. Most of all, I was delighted that she'd come to visit me and my teenage daughter, Celia. It was nice of Mom. No, more than nice. The visit bordered on maternal sacrifice.

As far as I knew, my mother, Mrs. Helen Baker Lafitte, aged sixty-eight and three quarters, of Bucks Grove, Illinois, had never left home for Christmas before, nor had she wanted to. Mom is a retired high school librarian, a woman of card-catalog order and strict traditions, otherwise known as doing the same thing year after year. Under usual circumstances, Mom keeps our "heirloom" artificial Christmas tree perpetually decorated and stored in the garage until the day after Thanksgiving, when she takes it out, dusts it off, and installs it to the left of the living-room fireplace. She places electric candles in each front window, hangs a wreath on the door, and wraps the holly bush in tasteful, nonflashing white lights. All of her holiday cards are mailed by the twelfth of December.

Food traditions are similarly strict. The Christmas Day lunch begins promptly at noon and is typically attended by my Aunt Sue, Uncle Dave,

Aunt Karen, and younger sister Kathy and her family. Kathy's husband, Dwayne, watches sports in the den, while their three kids hover between completely exhausted and totally wired from their morning gift frenzy. My mother and aunts whip up a feast of roasted turkey and stuffing, scalloped potatoes, sweet potato casserole with mini-marshmallows, Tater Tot hot dish, amazing monkey bread, Aunt Sue's famous (or infamous) Jell-O surprise featuring celery and cheese cubes, and my favorite dish: pie, usually apple, mincemeat, and/or pumpkin. It's a lovely meal, which I truly miss when I can't attend. However, I also love Santa Fe and want to make my own traditions here.

"That's one benefit for your sister," Mom said, polishing off her second water bottle. I swore I heard her stomach slosh. "The beach is at sea level."

"Yep, that's the beach for you," I replied in the perky tone I vowed to maintain for the rest of Mom's visit. "Kath and the kids must be loving it. What a treat! A holiday to remember!"

"I warned Kathy about jellyfish," Mom said darkly. "Rip currents, sharks, sand, mosquitoes. . . . It simply doesn't seem right to be somewhere so *tropical* for Christmas, but Dwayne went and got that package deal." Mom's tone suggested Dwayne had purchased a family-sized case of hives.

I gave Mom another sympathetic smile, along with the extra water bottle she'd stashed in my purse. Of course she was out of sorts. Once the kids learned that they'd get to open their presents early *and* go to Disney World *and* the beach, Mom and the holiday hot dish hadn't stood a chance. I, meanwhile, saw my chance to get Mom to Santa Fe.

I employed some of the guilt she usually ladled on me, telling her truthfully that Celia and I couldn't get away this year between my work and Celia's extracurricular activities. Mom, the master of loving manipulation, countered with how much my Illinois relatives would miss us. I was also single, she needlessly pointed out, implying that I could easily uproot. Furthermore, I lived in a casita, a home with tiny in its very name. She wouldn't want to put me out, she said. Mom then played her wild card, namely Albert Ridgeland, my junior prom date. Wouldn't you know, Mom had said. She'd recently run into Albert and he was divorced just like me, and with his own successful dental clinic and a mostly full head of hair and he sure would love to catch up.

Mom might be indirect, but she's never subtle. Ever since my divorce from Manny Martin, a policeman with soap-opera good looks and accompanying philandering tendencies, Mom's been after me to move back "home." She sends me clippings of employment ads and monitors eligible bachelors. Peeved that Mom had dragged a divorced dentist into the debate, I went for the guilt jugular, reminding Mom that she was retired yet hadn't visited in nearly two years. My tactic worked, possibly too well. Mom was staying for nearly three weeks—to get her money's worth out of the flight—and I'd feel terrible if she didn't have a good time.

I looked over and saw Mom eyeing a brown paper lunch sack perched a few feet down the adobe wall. The bag was open at the top and slightly singed on the sides. I could guess the contents. A votive candle nestled in sand.

Mom stepped over to peek inside. "It's a wonder this entire state doesn't burn down," she declared. "Remember when your middle school band director, Mr. Ludwig, put on that world Christmas festival in the gymnasium? He almost set the bleachers on fire with one of these . . ." She paused. "What do you call them?"

"A *farolito*," I said, proud to show off my local knowledge. "Some people call them *luminarias*, but Santa Feans are very particular about terminology. Here, *luminaria* refers to small bonfires. *Farolitos* are the candles in paper bags. There are electric *farolitos* too. You'll see a lot of those along the rooflines of hotels and businesses. They're pretty but nothing compared to the real ones on Christmas Eve. You'll love it, Mom. You've never seen anything like it."

Mom shuddered, likely imagining Santa Fe bursting into a spontaneous inferno rather than aglow with thousands of flickering lights. I decided not to tell her about the amazing three-dimensional paper lanterns I'd once seen soaring above the adobe city, lifted by the energy of the candles burning inside them. I needed to work on Mom before I exposed her to flying flames or peppers for breakfast.

Mom was rooting around in her hip pack. "I thought I had a granola bar. This time change and

the lack of air are making me light-headed. You
need to keep eating too, Rita."

Eating, I always had covered. I also had a better
idea than a squished fanny-pack snack. "It's the
holidays, Mom. Let's get some pie."

Pie in the Sky isn't the sort of bakery you stum-
ble on while window shopping, unless you've
veered to the top floor of the Inn of the Pajarito. The "Inn of the Little Bird" itself is pretty
immune to stroll-by discovery, although it's only
a block from the Plaza, the historic heart of Santa
Fe. The slender, L-shaped hotel is nestled in a
small courtyard behind an art gallery, a shop selling carved saints, and a boutique specializing in
pricey peasant skirts and turquoise accessories.

Before Pie in the Sky opened a year ago, I'd
known of the Pajarito, but probably couldn't have
given directions to any lost guests. Now I could
find it blindfolded, guided by my bloodhound's
nose for pie.

I led Mom across the courtyard, past a larger-than-
life-sized bronze statue of an Indian brave, and
through the Pajarito's heavy entrance doors. The
doors featured carved reliefs of Native American
dancers, and the main lobby continued the theme,
looking more like a museum of Native American
and Western art than a hotel. From behind an
oversized Christmas tree obscuring the front desk,
a male voice said, "Ho, ho, ho!" The greeting had

a demanding edge to it. So did his troll-under-the-bridge follow-up of "Who goes there? Ho! Ho! Ho!"

"The pie shop is upstairs," I said to Mom. I glanced over her shoulder and spotted a flash of red and two bushy white eyebrows peering through the heavily tinseled tree. Was that Santa spying on us?

"Merry Christmas!" I called out. "We're just going up to Pie in the Sky."

A branch moved aside, revealing coal-black eyes. This time, however, the welcome was more Santa appropriate. "Ah, ladies! Happy holidays! Tell the beautiful pie shop owner that you received a holly, jolly welcome down here at the Pajarito. Make sure you say 'jolly.' That's Christmas at the Pajarito! Merry and jolly!"

And creepy. "Will do!" I said, keeping my finger pressed to the elevator button and willing the antique contraption to hurry. Santa was a bit intense for my taste, and now that I had pie on my mind, I wanted to get there, fast.

Mom had concerns other than the unnerving Mr. Claus. She was sizing up the opulent room. Bronze and marble statues stood on antique sideboards. The cowhide carpets seemed too fine—and cowlike—to step on. So did the Navajo woven rugs, hung as tapestries against pale plaster walls. "Rita, should we be here?" Mom whispered. "We're not guests, and I wouldn't want to guess what this place costs. Clearly too expensive for the likes of us."

I assured her that the hotel welcomed outside visitors. "They want people to come in, Mom.

They have a couple of restaurants, a casual lounge, and a fancy high-end place." The elevator clanked to a stop and its antique accordion cage door creaked open. "Plus, this is the only way to the pie shop," I said, "unless you want to take the back stairs?"

The stairs were steep and winding. I took them sometimes, telling myself that if I arrived out of breath, the pie calories were effectively negated.

Mom answered by entering the elevator. I followed, pressed the button marked 3/PIE, and we were on our way to pie heaven.

"What an odd place for pie," Mom observed as we stepped out and turned toward French doors opening onto a rooftop patio over the hotel's two-story wing. The pie shop occupies a squat, square structure that looks like an adobe tower from the street. The walls facing the hotel feature large windows, and in warmer seasons, guests enjoy the comfortable deck chairs. At any time of year, the views are some of the best in downtown, and the pies are even better.

"Years ago, this little building was a margarita bar," I told Mom. "Then the couple who own the hotel did extensive renovations. Lorena, the wife, thought up the pie shop and does all the baking." I paused, mentally glossing over complicated personal and business situations. "They've recently separated, but she still does the pies, and her husband, Wyatt, runs the hotel. It's out of the way, but such an in-the-know hotspot that she does great business."

Usually Mom demands the details of domestic difficulties so she can offer unsolicited advice on how to fix them. This time, she focused on food and beverage.

"Well, pie is much nicer than margaritas, isn't it?" she said, beating me to the pie shop. I smiled. Mom has a weakness for pie, and Lorena makes some of the best I've ever tasted, including at Midwest fairs. My quest to win over Mom was off to a good start. I slipped into mental list-making mode. If Mom liked Lorena's offerings, we could order a mincemeat or pumpkin pie for Christmas. We'd roast a nice turkey without any exotic mesquite smoke or red chile rubs. I'd even dig my decorative copper molds out of storage and make Aunt Sue's Jell-O, although I didn't know if I could make myself add the cheddar and celery surprises. Mom could have her traditional holiday meal, and maybe she'd even come back some year, bringing my sister and the kids along with her. Santa Fe boasted loads of vacation rental homes, and I bet I could get a good deal through some café customers or friends.

An elbow jab in my ribs brought me back to reality. "Rita!" Mom whispered. "The nice lady said hello."

Mom takes manners seriously. "Sorry," I mumbled, feeling like a chastised kid again. "Hi, Lorena." Lorena Cortez stood behind a glass counter filled with picture-perfect pies. Her dark hair was tied back in a thick, shoulder-length ponytail, and she wore an apron printed with cartoon images of roadrunners chasing pies.

"Take your time," she said cheerfully to Mom. To me, she frowned and asked, "Rita, did you see Santa staking out the elevator?"

"I think it was Santa," I said. "He was hidden behind that huge Christmas tree. Whoever it was, he said to tell you we got a holly, jolly welcome downstairs."

Lorena snorted and jammed her fists into her hips. "Right! Jolly! Let me tell you, don't believe in jolly St. Nick and all his merry, happy holidays talk."

Mom looked up, her face a mirror of the bafflement I felt, only for different reasons. "Chile?" she said, pointing to the lower level of the display case. "Do you mean there's actually hot pepper in that beautiful chocolate cream?" She shuddered.

Lorena put her smile back on. "Yes, ma'am. Genuine Chimayo red chile powder. The Chimayo is an heirloom pepper, sundried and delicious. Don't worry about the heat. There's just a touch, enough to warm your tongue on a chilly winter's day."

Lorena clearly overestimated the fortitude of Mom's taste buds.

"Lorena makes an absolutely fabulous coconut cream," I said, knowing that even a hint of heat could have Mom claiming tongue burn. "Isn't coconut your favorite? Look, it even has a gingersnap crust."

Mom ordered the coconut. I went for the chile-spiked chocolate, which I could never resist. I loved everything about the pie, from the silky chocolate filling to the rich, almost brownie-like crust. Lorena could top it with habaneros and I'd still order it just for that crust. While I was paying, at my insistence, my phone buzzed. The text from Celia reported that she was done with her rehearsal. My artistic daughter was branching out from drawing and painting to acting and had joined a theater group. I was in awe of her bravery. I've done some scary things, like firing up flambés and taking on killers. Never, ever would I willingly get up on stage and act.

I texted Celia back and invited her to pie. "She'll be here in a few minutes," I reported to Mom. "She says she has 'big news' about the Christmas play." My teen sports spiky black-dyed hair, eyeliner that an Egyptian mummy would find a bit much, and an attitude that ranges from bored to surly. She doesn't do effusive, in written, oral, or any other form, so for her to report "big news" must mean massive.

"I bet she got a new role," I said. "We'll definitely have to go see her. The play is called *Las Posadas*, meaning 'The Inns.' It's an outdoor re-enactment of Mary and Joseph's search for lodging and a huge holiday event here. It's the main reason we couldn't leave town this year. Celia's troupe performs every Wednesday and Saturday until Christmas."

Mom and I savored our pies and speculated about Celia's potential roles. Last I knew, Celia was cast as one of the general "townsfolk," responsible for singing carols and uttering a few lines of exultation.

"A new role? A big one?" Mom put down her fork. Her face lit up. "Could she be playing Mary? Wouldn't that be the most important role? Oh my, how exciting! Is there singing? Celia has such a pretty voice. I was so sorry when you let her quit the school choir."

Let wasn't quite the right word. My daughter

had arrived in the world with a strong personality and even stronger willpower. In seventh grade, Celia decided she was done with group music. No more marching band with its itchy uniforms and the saxophone that I loved and Manny annoyingly claimed was too masculine. And definitely no more choir, which overlapped with art club. Mom was right in that I hadn't tried to sway Celia. I'd learned early on to pick my battles.

The pleased look on Mom's face suggested she was already imagining the grandmotherly bragging rights she'd have at her quilting and book groups back home. Before Mom got her hopes too high, I repeated what my elderly boss, Flori, told me.

"The main roles in big events like these often go to members of old-time Santa Fe families," I said. "And by old, I mean centuries. Generations old."

"Think positively, Rita," said Mom, of all people. My mother ranked in the upper tier of worst-case scenario forecasters, right up there with Flori's daughter Linda. I was both disappointed and relieved that Linda was out of town visiting a newborn grandbaby in California. Mom and Linda got along well. A little too well, when it came to whipping up each other's worries.

When Lorena came by, Mom complimented her pie and asked for more water. "We're even higher up at this pie shop," she pointed out in dire tones. "We need to keep up our hydration."

I dutifully downed ice water and forced myself not to eat all my pie before Celia arrived. She burst in a few minutes later, unable to keep her teenage ennui expression in place for long. She grinned at her grandmother. "Gran! You're here!"

Mom stood to kiss Celia on both cheeks and urged her to get a slice of pie. When Celia returned, she carried an extra-large slab of another of my favorites, apple with two surprise ingredients: fire-roasted green chiles and a cheddar cheese crust. Celia offered her grandmother the first bite. Mom surprised me by accepting.

"Mmm . . ." Mom said, after chewing thoughtfully. "This is actually a lovely crust. Your grandfather, Celia, always requested a thick slice of aged cheddar with his apple pie."

I allowed myself another moment of satisfaction. The pie was working its magic. Mom was finding common ground with New Mexico and expanding her horizons. My mind slipped into more planning. I could get us all tickets to some holiday choral concerts, combining sightseeing in beautiful churches with Mom's love of music. We'd block off time to cheer on Celia. Most importantly, I'd keep myself and Flori out of trouble. My beloved boss and I had a propensity for stumbling into—and solving—crimes. Not this holiday! No sleuthing for us. No crime or chaos, just a nice, normal, festive Christmas.

Mom was quizzing Celia about the play. "Now, what is this big news, darling? Does it involve singing? You have the most wonderful voice."

Celia looked up from her pie, eyes gleaming under the heavy mascara. "You'll never guess, Gran. I got the greatest part. The best!" The budding dramatist made us wait while she nibbled a bit of cheesy pie crust. "Okay," she said. "You ready for this? Prepare yourselves . . ."

Mom and I leaned in, caught up in the excitement. "Is it the Holy Mother Mary—" Mom started to say.

"Nope! Better!" Celia raised her fork. "I'm the devil! Awesome, right?"

Mom choked on her coconut cream. "Did you say devil?" she said. The hand covering her mouth only partially hid her look of horror.

"Yep!" Celia triumphantly stabbed a chunk of chile. "That's right. The devil. Lucifer. Beelzebub! The fallen angel himself. There are three, and I'm the second one. So awesome." She took another bite, shaking her head, seemingly in disbelief at her good fortune.

Mom's expression suggested she felt otherwise.

"Celia, that's wonderful!" I said, amping up my praise to cover Mom's stunned silence. Celia bubbled on happily about how she planned to customize the basic horns she'd been given. Red velvet, she thought, with gold flames made of reflective foil.

Mom, thankfully, remained silent, even as Celia pondered whether we could add real flames to her pitchfork. I knew I'd hear Mom's thoughts on a holiday devil later. I focused on savoring both my pie and my daughter's enthusiasm. However, a dark feeling had descended over me and seemingly Lorena too. The pie shop owner cocked her head, scowling at a distant tinkling of jingle bells. My thoughts shifted from Satan to the questionable Santa. Something told me that my quest for a quiet Christmas wouldn't be as easy as pie.

Chapter 2

Celia's a *Las Posadas* devil," I told Flori the next morning. It was Monday just after opening. Frost glazed the café's paned windows, deep-set in thick adobe walls, and a winter storm loomed over the mountains. Inside Tres Amigas Café, however, a fire crackled in the fireplace and comforting scents of fresh coffee and gingerbread muffins filled the air. The little café occupies a historic house that retains its homey feel. Wood beams, dark and cracked with age, cross the ceiling, and the softly rounded Saltillo tiles on the floor remind me of pumpkin pie.

Flori loves holidays, especially Christmas. She'd decorated to the nines, or, if possible, the elevens. Pine swags and red ribbons adorned the windowsills, and paper snowflakes, made by her great-grandkids, fluttered from the beams. The Christmas tree in the front corner brushed the ceiling and practically sagged with locally made ornaments, from chile-pepper garlands to punched-tin doves and angels with wings of golden straw filigree. There were gingerbread men and women too, like Mom made. Flori, however, used a cookie cutter with a Day of the Dead–style skeleton imprint. Some of her great-grandkids had been over last week to give the gingerbread skeletons festive icing hats and green and red femurs.

Flori stood at the stove stirring similarly festive vats of green and red chile sauces. She stopped her synchronized stirring to turn to me. "A devil? How wonderful!" she exclaimed. "Oh, Rita, you must be so proud."

Now this is the reaction I wanted from Mom. After Celia went to bed last night, Mom had shared her thoughts, whether I wanted to hear them or not. Satan, Mom contended, had no place at Christmas. Moreover, even if he did—which he didn't—he should not be played by a nice young lady, particularly her eldest granddaughter. It wasn't right. It wasn't proper, not for Christmas, Mom reiterated. She stopped just short of demanding how she would tell her friends back home.

"Celia's pretty excited," I said, carefully dropping blue corn batter onto the hot waffle iron. The iron hissed and sputtered, like the devils who made *Las Posadas* so special. During the play, Mary and Joseph, the Wise Men, and musicians and singers in period costumes parade slowly through downtown. The procession is somber and reverent, until the expectant couple approaches an inn and asks for shelter. That's when the devil appears, heckling and yelling that there's no room. The crowd responds with

boos and jeers. Celia would love it. Hopefully
Mom would too, once she saw the first performance this Wednesday.

I peeked through the pass-through to see the
café's small dining room filling up fast. Luckily,
our part-time helper, Addie, became full-time
around the holidays. Addie, short for Adelina, is
a local girl who fancies herself the New Mexican
twin of British superstar crooner Adele. The two
share a birthday, as well as a love of belting out
soulful songs.

That, however, is pretty much where similarity ends. For one, the real Adele has moved on
with her hairstyle, switching from a bouffant wig
to a sleek bob. Addie still favors her big blond
hairpieces, and I don't blame her. The wigs add
a certain presence, useful given Addie's other
challenge: her weight. Despite her best efforts to
achieve Adele-like curves, our Addie remains a
stick-thin size four. If only I had *that* problem. The
lack of a natural British accent also plagues Addie,
though that doesn't keep her from trying.

"Ta! Cheerio!" Addie called out brightly, waving
goodbye to some customers. She reached back to
hand me fresh order slips. "Two more specials, me
love," she said, smoothing her Union Jack–print
apron.

"Two orders of *papas fritas*, over-medium eggs,
por favor," I relayed to Juan, our griddle maestro.
I watched in admiration as he turned the golden
potatoes, flipped eggs and corn tortillas, and laid
out bacon for another order. No movement was
wasted by Juan. After one more flip, he scooped
the potatoes onto plates, placed rolled tortillas

on the sides, and handed the dishes to me, along with a rare compliment.

"Tell Celia congratulations," he said. "My uncle once played the devil. It's a big honor. Huge."

I thanked Juan on Celia's behalf and took the plates over to Flori to finish.

"Red or green?" she asked, ladles poised. New Mexico's official state question refers to chile choice and is a phrase I utter so often, it appears in my dreams.

"Christmas," I replied. This time of year, lots of customers ordered "Christmas," or red chile on one side and green on the other. In my humble opinion, Christmas is always the best choice. It's not only pretty, it's like getting two dishes in one.

Flori draped sauces over the potatoes and I brought them back to Juan to top with melty Monterey Jack cheese, a dollop of sour cream, the jiggling eggs, and a sprinkling of chives. The dishes definitely looked good enough to devour. My stomach rumbled. I'd had only coffee and a chunk of muffin this morning, my attempt at a pre-holiday diet. Who was I kidding? I eyed the glorious mountain of goodness. Diets and I never stuck together. I hefted the plates, which counted as exercise, and headed for the dining room.

"Two specials, incoming," I announced. I'm prone to serving disasters, and in situations involving slippery eggs and lava-hot chile, I give customers fair warning I'm within slopping distance.

My neighbor from across the road, Dalia Crawford, looked up and clasped her hands together, sparking a clatter of silver bangles and crystal rings. More crystals in lavender, lemon, and amber hues dangled from her neck, along with two pairs of rhinestone-crusted glasses and a chunk of turquoise in the shape of a bear. Her hair reached the middle of her back, longer than my mother would deem proper for a fifty-something woman, and was woven into a wide braid. Dalia had a tech wizard's fortune but a back-to-the-earth hippie's soul. She followed signs gleaned from the stars, tarot cards, and tea leaves, as well as a medley of Eastern, Western, and Native philosophies and religions. Lately, I'd often spotted smoke rising from the sweat lodge tucked in her back garden. I'd also been the recipient of her well-meaning sage smudgings, prayer wheel chants, and—best of all—homemade jellies, pickles, and baked goods.

Tucking a napkin over floaty layers of cotton blouses, she said to her male dining companion, "This is one of my favorite dishes. You're in for a treat."

"No doubt," he said, beaming more at me than the eggs. I guessed he was in his late thirties, like I joked I still was instead of my true into-my-forties age of forty-two. He was also—objectively speaking—gorgeous. Perfectly coiffed golden locks fell in soft waves just above the collar of his tweedy jacket. His cheekbones were worthy of Greek statues, and mascara models would envy his lashes. If Mom were here she'd be eyeing his ring finger—well-moisturized and lacking any evidence of a ring—unaware that I already had a handsome boyfriend.

My cheeks flushed, both from the man's sexy wink and the guilt of boyfriend nondisclosure.

The flush flared when the door chimed and said boyfriend stepped inside. Jake Strong caught my eye, tipped his Stetson, and showed off some of his best features, those twinkling steel-blue eyes and the adorable crinkle that fanned them when he smiled. My stomach did a happy flutter.

"Barton," Dalia was saying, "You know our new girl devil, Celia Martin? This is her mother and my best-ever neighbor, Rita. . . . ah . . . Oh, Rita, shame on me! I should know this, do you still go by Martin too?"

I shook my head with such force that if I'd been still holding any eggs, they'd be airborne. "Nope, Lafitte." No more Martin for me. That was Manny's name. I was through with it and the philandering cop.

Barton smiled. "Lafitte. What a lovely name. I knew a gentleman in New Orleans by that name once. He had your beautiful eyes. Deep and expressive."

I started to worry that my blush would stick permanently as I denied knowing any Louisiana Lafittes.

Dalia saved me by continuing her introductions. "Rita, this is Barton Hunter. He's a specialist on Native American artifact repatriation and has come all the way from out East to help my sister Judith rid herself of that awful, terrible, toxic collection our grandfather left her. You know Judith, don't you, Rita? She organizes *Las Posadas* and lives a few blocks down from us on Canyon Road?" Dalia shook her head and mumbled some more horribles and terribles as she dug into her breakfast.

I frowned, wondering what kind of horrible, terrible collection Judith inherited. Something else baffled me even more. "Judith Crundall's *your* sister?" I blurted out. I knew Judith Crundall casually and had heard others talk about her. Some cruelly—or fearfully—called her an old battle-ax. Judith was no-nonsense and strict, a woman who suffered no fools or incorrect café orders. She kind of intimidated me sometimes, but I admired her too. She spoke her mind and stuck up for good causes and supported events like *Las Posadas*. In both demeanor and dress, though, I could hardly imagine two less likely sisters than her and Dalia.

Dalia poured hot water from a teapot into her mug and dunked in the bag of roasted-barley tea she'd brought herself. "Funny, isn't it? Daddy always said we shared the Crundall nose and that's it." She pointed to the tip in her prominent sniffer. "We're only half sisters, and I'm fifteen years younger. Our father left her mother for mine. Scandalous for the old-money Crundalls, him running off to a commune up in the hills with a younger woman. Judith's side of the family got all the money and property so they couldn't complain too much, though. And they got that awful collection. May the heavens help them." She closed her eyes and breathed in barley vapors.

In response to my wrinkled brow, Barton spoke up. "It's a stunning collection in its own way. William Harold Crundall the First, Judith and Dalia's grandfather, was an archeologist who collected Native American objects. Some of them . . . well . . . let's say they've fallen out of favor."

"He robbed churches and graves," Dalia said darkly. "He stole people's most sacred objects and even their relatives." Clutching her crystals, she said, "We shouldn't talk about this over breakfast. Bad for digestion. Thankfully, Barton and his assistant, wherever that dear girl is—"

"Late as usual," he said with a sigh, glancing at his watch. "I told her nine o'clock sharp."

Dalia, not a stickler for minutes or days, waved off the assistant's tardiness. "She's from Albuquerque. On New Mexican time. In any case, she and Barton will sort out all those poor, pillaged objects and send them back to their rightful owners. The spirits will smile on us and Judith will heal."

Dalia dug into her eggs. I glanced over and saw Jake hanging his hat on a chair by the fireplace. I was curious about the Crundall half sisters and their collection, but decided I'd learn more from Flori. I made motions to go. "Enjoy your breakfasts. Dalia, when you see Judith, please tell her how thrilled Celia is," I said. "It's quite an honor to play the devil."

Barton nodded seriously. "I'll say. I'm even more honored. Ms. Crundall has me—a complete outsider—playing the first devil. I don't know if I'm up for it, honestly. I'm no actor, and your daughter follows me in the performance. I fear she'll show me up. I'm going to have to up my devil game."

Addie, making the rounds with her coffeepot, refilled his cup. She giggled when he turned his smile and charm on her.

"Dalia told me the food here was lovely," Barton said. "She failed to mention the beautiful staff."

Flustered out of her usual faux British, Addie stuttered, "*Gracias*. I mean, thanks. Oh my . . ."

I decided it was time for both of us to leave. I again wished them a good meal and Barton good luck.

"I'll need it," he said, his smooth face looking perfectly unworried.

"Dishy!" Addie whispered loudly when we were a few tables away. "In all my years!"

"All your twenty-some years?" I joked.

"Every one of them," she said. She handed me the coffeepot and a mug. "Off you go, now. Off to your dishy solicitor."

Ever the Western gentleman, the definitely dishy Jake Strong rose to greet me. "Don't suppose you have time to rest your feet," he said with a smile. Jake's taller than me by several inches and older by a little over a year. He'd never be called pretty. Ruggedly handsome describes Jake, with appealing soft edges. He bent down and landed a discreet kiss on my cheek.

I scanned the room, taking in half-filled water glasses, empty plates, and bills to collect.

"I didn't think so," he said, reading my thoughts. "A man has to hope." He sat back down and stretched out long legs, clad in dark jeans and polished black cowboy boots.

"It's so busy lately," I said, feeling guilty for more than turning down his breakfast offer. "We're overrun for a Monday morning. I suppose it's all the holiday visitors already in town."

Jake sipped his coffee and perused the menu that he surely had memorized. Steak and eggs or *chiles rellenos* were his usual choices. He patted his flat belly. "Wish I was busy. I'm not saying we need some crime around here, but my schedule's so open, my secretary has me stringing popcorn wreaths. Gifts for the sparrows, she says." He groaned. "We're supposed to start making suet bells out of peanut butter and beef fat if I don't get work soon."

I couldn't hide my grin, imagining Jake's sleek office, a repurposed adobe home down the block, besieged by birds. Jake's clientele was usually more serious and well funded. He specialized in criminal defense and was renowned for getting his clients off the hook. Even the guilty ones, my policeman ex grumbled. Jake would say he provided the right to due process, and I agreed. I'd seen him help innocent people, including some of my friends.

"Suet bells sound kind of fun," I said. I loved Christmas crafts, if only I had time to do them.

He shrugged. "Yeah, well, I've got 'Rudolph, the Red-Nosed Reindeer' stuck in my head and popcorn clogging my keyboard. I'd rather have a challenge. A little major theft. A tidy murder . . ."

"You do *not* mean that!" I said. "And don't even mention murder. You know my mother's in town, and I'm throwing a quiet, crime-free Christmas!"

Jake chuckled. "I do wish one and all a peaceful holiday. I suppose I could use a vacation, especially if I can get some time with you."

"I'd love that too." I didn't see it happening. Not with Mom sleeping in my room and me on the foldout sofa of my minuscule casita. Sneaking out like the rebellious teenager I never was didn't seem likely either. Jake ordered *chiles rellenos* with over-medium eggs, spicy green chile, and extra-crispy hash browns.

"Oh, and one more thing," he said as I was turning to go retrieve table one's check. "When do I get to meet your lovely mother?"

I froze and stammered something about Mom's jet lag and dehydration. "Soon, though," I said, mercifully saved by the rude finger-snapping man at table one. "Ah . . . once she gets settled in and drinks more water and . . . well, she can't wait to meet you."

As I grabbed the bill from table one, Lorena Cortez came to mind. *Don't believe in jolly St. Nick*, she'd said. I hoped she was right. Otherwise, Santa would know I'd been very naughty.

Later during the midmorning lull, Juan went out to run an errand, and I helped Flori make *bizcochitos* to feed a crowd. The anise-spiced shortbread cookies are *the* signature sweet of Santa Fe holiday spreads. Flori was making her grandmother's recipe, which called for sugar and spice and lard. Lots of lard.

"What about vegetarians?" I asked, measuring out fragrant cinnamon and anise seed. "Or vegans."

"Vegans?" Flori's head lopped to one shoulder, as if toppled by incomprehension. She could pretend, but I knew she was aware of vegans. When she served *bizcochitos* at the café, she made two kinds and labeled the cookie jars "award-winning traditional recipe handed down for generations" and "no lard."

"This is different," she said after I reminded her of her own two-jar strategy. "*Las Posadas* actors are local. They'll know that lard is necessary for proper taste and texture. My mother and grandmother and her grandmother before her used lard. That's how it's done. I bet when the legislature voted in the *bizcochito* as state cookie, they *specified* lard. I bet it's a law."

Who was I to question centuries of *bizcochito* knowledge or the state legislature? Some other states also have official cookies. I knew at least two states chose good old chocolate chip cookies, which I'm sure garner opinions about crispy versus chewy (chewy all the way, and eaten melty, straight out of the oven, I say). But that's nothing compared to the New Mexican passions aroused by the *bizcochito*. Flori told me that during the legislative debate, representatives took to the floor, holding forth on their favored spelling: *biscochito* or *bizcochito*? The "z" spelling came out on top, but the matter will never be settled.

"You're right," I said, admitting defeat. "Locals will know the usual recipe."

"Absolutely," Flori said. "And if they have any doubts, they'll know I used lard the second they taste the exceptional tenderness."

I supposed that vegetarians and/or lard avoiders knew what they were up against in holiday cookies, tamales, beans, and other delicacies around here.

"Anyway," Flori said. "We're donating them, aren't we? *Bizcochito* beggars shouldn't be choosers."

Flori was making the cookies for the gathering of actors and fans following the first *Las Posadas* performance. I reached for a round of dough and started rolling it out.

Flori passed me a diamond-shaped cookie cutter. "So you met the hunky devil Judith Crundall recruited?" she asked with a devilish grin. My elderly friend is an incorrigible flirt and appreciator of handsome men, some of whom she has been known to pinch on the tush.

"Behave," I said, jokingly. "What do you know about Judith Crundall's collection?"

Flori's grin faded. "Nasty business. From what I hear, the Crundall collection includes actual bones. Skulls. Objects taken from Native graves. Sacred items for ceremonies that no outsider has a right to touch, let alone own. Judith is doing the right thing, having it all sent back. She's not asking for a dime either." Flori patted together another ball of dough. "She has enough money, and it's probably payment enough to watch that hunky consultant all day. He's not as manly as your Jake Strong, but he'll look nice in tight red devil pants."

"He'd better watch out for you," I said. Flori didn't fool me. She only had eyes for the love of her life, her husband of over sixty years, Bernard. Flori chatted on about Judith's current health problems, something undiagnosable involving pain and weariness and endless doctors. I felt sorry for Judith, but I admit, I zoned out a little, fixated on my own minor problem of telling Mom about Jake.

"So, how are your mother and Jake getting along?" Flori asked, startling me back to attention. I realized I'd been about to mix up a bowl of cinnamon salt instead of cinnamon sugar for coating the cookies.

I tried to change the subject. "Ha! I almost used salt instead of sugar. Can you imagine?"

Flori eyed me through her Harry Potter–style spectacles. A month ago, I'd confessed. I'd told Flori—and only Flori—about keeping Jake a secret from my Illinois family.

"You haven't said anything yet, have you?" she said.

Denial was futile. Flori was right, and she can easily sniff out my inept lies. She also claimed to have a sixth sense. At times like this, I believed her.

My elderly friend shook a jar of cinnamon at me. "I knew it. I saw you scuttling off from Jake's table this morning and I just knew. Rita, you have a hot, successful boyfriend. Go yell it from the bell towers. Ooo . . . there's an idea. We'll get a bull-horn and go up to La Fonda's rooftop and make sure your mother's walking down below and—"

I let Flori have her fun. She's bold and would actually make bullhorn announcements from landmark hotels if I let her. My hesitation was hard to explain to the bold. Heck, it was hard to explain to myself. "I waited too long," I said. "You know when someone sends you a Christmas letter and you mean to write back, and then all of a sudden it's February and you feel bad, so you put it off. Then it's June and you still haven't written, so you decide to write something extra-special but you wait some more and it's way too late?" I paused to take a breath. Waiting too long was part of my problem. Another part was feeling protective of my feelings and the budding relationship.

Initially, I'd resisted the handsome lawyer's romantic intentions, taking time to figure out my post-divorce life. Then, as our relationship deepened, I worried that potentially skeptical people, like Mom, might squelch the spark. I'd wanted to nurture the relationship and keep it to myself. Now I'd waited way too long.

"*I* could tell her," Flori offered. "We could get together and knit. My knitting's progressing very well, you'll be pleased to know. That Senior Center class has been quite helpful."

When most elderly ladies mention knitting progress, you imagine an incoming bounty of mittens, socks, and throw blankets. Not so with Flori.

"Miriam and I are ready to hit a lamppost," Flori continued. "We made long panels, like for sweater sleeves. As soon as this pesky full moon goes away, we'll get out there in the dark and stitch that post right up. We have a bunch of pom-poms to tack on too. Pretty and quick. Good for our purposes." She chuckled.

I grimaced. I'd always thought the Senior Center should offer knitting classes. Of course, I should have known that the organization which introduced bifocal wearers to deadly tai chi, Taser take-downs, and carnivorous plant cultivation wouldn't offer peaceful textile crafts. Flori and her classmates were training to be rogue knitters, also known as graffiti knitters, yarn bombers, and fiber-art taggers. They worked at night, or in those early hours that only shift workers, insomniacs, and those over seventy tend to see. Their mission was to adorn public objects in colorful knits. Flori said that the more surprising and whimsical, the better. With Addie's Googling help, Flori had shown me examples of graffiti knitting legend: a double-decker bus decked out in a rainbow sweater, a redwood grove sporting turtlenecks, and a flock of abashed sheep in wooly jumpers.

Flori and her friend/co-conspirator Miriam were starting small. They'd outfitted a statue of New Mexico's legendary territorial governor, Don Diego de Vargas, in knitted slippers and decorated a park bench in festive Christmas colors. Flori contended that rogue knitting counted as exercise. Others, like the police and statue owners, considered it vandalism. A few nights ago, the two had nearly gotten ticketed for knitting onto a street sign. Flori had flirted with the patrolman, while Miriam cut off the evidence and stuffed it down her blouse. Confronted by one flirty, pinch-happy elderly lady and another flaunting a bulging, yarn-padded bosom, the patrolman had let them go with a warning.

"I think Mom's more into quilting recently," I said. My mother could also knit with the pros. She would not, however, approve of messing with statuary or skulking around dark places after midnight. Mom followed the rules and she went to bed promptly at ten.

"I could still tell her about Jake," Flori persisted.

The offer was tempting, if only Flori could be trusted to drop a subtle hint. My elderly friend might get carried away and supply details Mom didn't need to know, like the suppleness of Jake's backside.

"I'll tell her tonight," I promised both myself and Flori. "Or tomorrow. I'll bring up high school, and then she'll mention this dentist she wants to set me up with. It'll be the perfect way to ease into the subject of Jake."

"Or you invite him over for dinner," Flori suggested. "Tell him to wear some nice flannel and tight jeans and that hunky cowboy hat of his. Your mother should be so enamored that she'll demand you flirt with him. Then you can surprise her by saying you're going steady." Flori nodded, pleased with her own plan.

I decided to stick to my original idea. And why was I worrying so much, anyway? Mom would surely love Jake. What wasn't to love? He was professional, handsome, and kind. He had good manners and always polished his boots and belt buckle and wore ties, although sometimes of the bolo variety. On the other hand, Jake represented another reason for me to stay in New Mexico. Mom wouldn't like that. For reasons I didn't understand, Mom also seemed to dislike lawyers. My cousin had dated a noble public defender once. To hear Mom talk about it, the cousin might as well have taken up with a cult member. My late father had worked in tax law. Perhaps if I knew more about him, but he'd passed away when I was in kindergarten and Mom rarely spoke of him.

I realized that Flori was saying something about calling cards. "The best rogue knitters leave their mark. I'm Night Knitter. Miriam's the Silver Purl, spelled P-U-R-L. Get it? Like the stitch? Pretty

snappy. Addie says we need a logo too. I'm thinking thunderbolts in the shape of knitting needles.
What do you think?"

I thought Addie was being way too encouraging. "Isn't it awfully cold for knitting?" I said,
knowing that Flori considered any temperature
less than seventy degrees practically arctic. "What
if your fingers freeze to the needles?"

Flori stirred her red chile. "I know what you're
trying to do, Rita. You're trying to dissuade me.
You don't want your mother to think you're working with a knit bandit, a Zorro with needles.
Ooo . . . that's an idea for our calling cards. There's
no need to worry, though. I'm taking precautions."
She reached under the counter and produced a
fluffy black bundle that looked like a wooly winter
cap. She tugged it over her glasses and revealed a
ski mask decorated in a pretty chain stitch.

"See," she said from behind the mask. "Isn't this
clever? It's convertible. Looks like a regular winter
cap if I roll it up, but when I pull it down I'm the
Night Knitter!"

I groaned.

Flori said, "If you're good, you might get a handy
little knit gift like this for Christmas. Stop worrying about your mother. She'll see that Christmas here is just like her holiday back home, only
a little different." She tugged off her bandit's wear
and added, "Different in a good way."

I was about to answer when a noise somewhere
between a wheeze and a honk erupted on the patio.

"What the . . . ?" I rushed to the window, thinking we'd been hit, but by what? A deflating blimp?
A truck full of wild hogs?

Flori calmly patted her silver bun. "That'll be Juan," she said over the din. "I forgot to tell you. His cousin's donkey will be staying out back for the *Las Posadas* season. He's a star. The donkey, I mean. His name is Mr. Peppers, and Juan brought him a few days early so he could settle in."

"He's staying here?" I asked over an ear-piercing wheeze.

Flori raised her voice, "Mr. Peppers doesn't like to travel. Gives him unmentionable digestive issues. He'll be safe and secure behind the wall. Juan cleared out that little garage in the back to make a manger." She winked conspiratorially. "Just don't tell the zoning commission or historic review board. They'll fine us silly if they find out."

I shuddered. No one wants to get on the wrong side of a Santa Fe zoning board. Hiding a donkey was more risky business. Still, I was curious to meet our four-legged visitor. I followed Flori out the back door. What had sounded like a beast of Godzilla proportions was actually a miniature donkey the size of an overweight St. Bernard. Mr. Peppers wore a Christmas-themed bandana and was accompanied by a black goat with a white stripe down his forehead, a low-slung bulging belly, and nubby horns.

Juan introduced the goat as Sidekick. The donkey tilted his head back, bared yellowed teeth, and mimicked the sound of a train wreck. Different was good, I assured myself. That's what made Santa Fe great. Now if I could only convince Mom.

Chapter 3

Two nights later, I was feeling pretty good about Mom's holiday. Celia had entertained her grandmother with museum visits. Mom had encountered some spicy foods, but her greatest fears hadn't manifested. No chiles had appeared in her breakfast cereal. No one had succumbed to altitude illness either, although Mom risked becoming waterlogged. Now, under twinkling strings of lights and the sparkling Milky Way, Mom scanned the Plaza. Her neck craned, her eyes darted. She was seeking out tall men in cowboy hats. One man, in particular. Jake Strong.

I'd finally mentioned Jake last night, over a relaxing, home-cooked dinner of chicken potpie casserole and lemony green beans. We'd just dug in when Mom, as if on cue, brought up Albert Ridgeland, DDS. I let her describe his whitened teeth and tastefully remodeled dental clinic. That's when I saw my opening and pounced on it. I'd like to think I said, "How nice for Albert. I've been seeing a fine, professional gentleman who remodeled an adobe house down the street from Tres Amigas. It makes a lovely office." In reality, I blurted out something along the lines of "I'm seeing someone, Mom! A lawyer! He has an office! And teeth! Good, straight teeth."

Whatever the exact embarrassing words, they threw Mom into stunned silence. The eye-of-the-storm lull didn't last. "A lawyer?" Mom had said, in the tone one might use to utter, "An unemployed serial killer?"

Mom then set forth a tornado of questions, most of which I either couldn't answer or deflected. Celia provided the juiciest tidbits, telling her gran to expect a hotshot criminal defense lawyer in cowboy boots. Mom had taken a second helping of casserole and held forth on the honest, trustworthy business of tooth care.

"Well, where's that lawyer?" Mom asked now, eyeing a group of ladies decked out in Santa Fe chic. Long, patchwork leather jackets, wooly boots, and enough turquoise jewelry to stock a small boutique. "I hope he hasn't stood us up, Rita. You know how lawyers can be. Especially the kind who defend criminals."

In Jake's case, that meant dependable and courteous. "We're early," I assured Mom, and myself, while surreptitiously checking my watch. We'd spent the afternoon helping Celia refine her devil attire before dropping her off at the *Las Posadas* staging area. We'd then picked up Flori and several trays of *bizcochitos* and delivered them to my neighbor Dalia, who was helping her frail sister and *Las Posadas* benefactor, Judith Crundall.

I'd been shocked to see the feisty society woman confined to a wheelchair in the play's staging area. I'd offered to take her out to the Plaza with Mom and me, but Judith had waved a dismissive hand webbed in prominent blue veins. "I've seen this performance before," she said. She started to say that someone needed to watch over the food, but a rasping cough cut her short.

As we left, I silently gave thanks that my mother, only a few years younger, was in fine health. We walked to the obelisk at the center of the Plaza, where Flori was waiting. She looked ready for a trip to Santa's workshop in a red, puffy snowsuit likely handed down from one of her grandkids. The hood jutted inches over her forehead and was pinned in place by candy-pink earmuffs. A thick white scarf covered the lower half of her face, and her snow boots were suitable for a penguin-spotting expedition.

The meteorologists were predicting temperatures in the mid-thirties with a chance of flurries. I hoped they were right about the snow. I wanted Mom to see the beauty of adobe iced in fluffy white. Santa Fe was pretty in all seasons, but my favorite was a snowy winter.

"Tell me when you hear the singers or Mr. Peppers," Flori said in the booming tones of the hard of hearing.

I raised her left earmuff and said the whole town would hear Mr. Peppers coming. Mom said we were looking for signs of Jake Strong.

Flori's chuckles fogged her glasses. "Helen, you'll recognize Mr. Strong. Look for the hunkiest cowboy in town." She stood on her tiptoes, an effort that still left her shorter than me. Mom once again pointedly checked her watch.

I felt my phone buzz in my pocket. I stepped away to answer.

"Where are you?" I asked Jake, forgetting a polite greeting and barely holding down the stress in my voice.

He apologized over a background din of what sounded like a heavy metal version of "Jingle Bell Rock."

"I'm out at Ida Green's bail bonds place with a client's mother. The mother only speaks Spanish." He raised his own voice, "Which Ida says she can't understand, though I know she does." Lowering the volume, he grumbled, "Ida's a Grinch. I feel awful being late, Rita. It's a charity case of sorts, my secretary's second cousin, a good guy. We're almost done. I promise I'll get there as soon as possible."

I told him not to worry. I had, after all, been married to a cop. As a policeman's spouse, you expected work to intrude on birthdays, holidays, weekends, dinner, and the middle of the night. The worst part was the worrying, but Jake wouldn't be in danger, unless he ate at the diner attached to Ida's bonds place. Ida served up truly criminal cuisine.

"I understand," I said. "So will Mom," I lied.

"See? I told you," Mom said with decidedly un-Christmas-like smugness. "You need a man who will be on time, Rita. Someone who's punctual. If not for you, then for Celia. Teenagers need structure."

I feared she was going to launch into the prompt dental appointments she'd received from Albert

Ridgeland. Luckily, a wheezing honk echoed up San Francisco Street.

"Ooo . . ." Flori said, taking hold of my elbow. "I heard that. Let's move down by the Inn of the Pajarito. That's where the first devil appears."

Part of me wanted to claim the best spot in front of Celia's venue, a second-story restaurant with a balcony facing the Plaza. However, it might be good for Mom to ease into the devil concept. We walked down the street and found a location with views of both Satan's balcony and the procession's arrival. Mr. Peppers honked in the distance, and the crowd tittered and giggled. A few minutes later, the procession turned the corner. The giggles stopped as all eyes fixed on Mary and Joseph. Mary, wrapped in a sky-blue shawl, held her padded belly. Joseph trod as if weary. Behind them walked the three Wise Men and musicians strumming guitars and singing the traditional *Las Posadas* ballad. I wished my rudimentary Spanish would allow me to translate for Mom. When I glanced over, though, I saw she was transfixed. No translation needed.

"How beautiful," she said as the procession neared. She must have been impressed because she forgot about hydration, unpunctual lawyers, and the fire risk of the candles carried by the singers and some spectators.

It was beautiful. If I squinted and blurred out the cell phones, streetlamps, and video cameras, I could imagine we'd stepped back centuries, to Santa Fe's early colonial days. Or even farther to distant Holy Lands where moonlight also cast shadows across adobe buildings. The procession

moved slowly by. A violin player in a colorful
serape was one of the last performers, along with
a woman in all black, except for her brilliant red
hair. Beside her trotted Sidekick the goat, decked
out in a Christmas sweater and a candy cane-
striped harness.

We waved at Sidekick and waited for the true
tail end, Dalia and Mr. Peppers. Dalia could have
passed for a Holy Lands peasant in her layers of
long skirts and shawls. She was walking backward, or at least trying to. She gripped the donkey's
lead with both hands and tugged. Mr. Peppers
leaned the opposite direction, his butt almost in
sitting position. When Dalia saw us, she threw
up one hand in frustration. Mr. Peppers stopped
tugging too, and the release of tension nearly sent
Dalia toppling.

"I don't understand," Dalia said, looking truly
perplexed. "Mr. Peppers and I had a long talk
before we set out. A good talk."

The donkey raised his velvety lips and grinned.

"You're supposed to be carrying the Holy
Mother," Dalia said, addressing the truculent
donkey. To us, she said, with evident exasperation.
"Judith put me in charge, and I said I could handle
it, but Mr. Peppers is not cooperating. He turned
in circles so that Mary couldn't get on his back.
Then he got distracted by popcorn on the sidewalk. Then a Chihuahua spooked him. Then he
stole a man's Broncos hat right off his head and
chewed on it . . ." She sighed. "Someone needs an
attitude adjustment, Mr. Peppers."

Flori chuckled. She ruffled the donkey's fuzzy
head and bristle-broom mane. "You'll be a good

boy and walk now, won't you?" Rather ambigu-
ously, the donkey blew a raspberry, yet bobbed
his head up and down with vigor.

Dalia, usually composed by her spiritual signs
and Zen meditations, tilted her head toward the
singing and let out another exasperated sigh.
"Now what's wrong? Why are they starting that
song over again? It's time for the first devil. He
heckles. The singers and crowd respond. It's
simple!"

She re-gripped the lead. Mr. Peppers threw back
one ear, ready to resist.

Dalia turned to me. "I can't leave him. Rita, will
you—"

If she was going to ask me to hold Mr. Peppers, I'd
have to turn her down. I had a second devil to see.
Her request was abruptly cut off as Mr. Peppers
whipped his head around and snorted. Across the
street, some kids waved and called "Burro, burro!
Come get fry bread!" Mr. Peppers flared his
nostrils, lowered his head, and took off at a trot.

"No, not fry bread! He's on a diet. Put that
away!" Dalia cried. "Rita," she yelled back as
the donkey dragged her across the street. "Will
you go tell Satan he's missed his cue? He should
be on the roof, by Pie in the Sky." Her "Thank
you!" was drowned out by an excited hee-haw as
Mr. Peppers zeroed in on the fried temptation.

A quick cue to the devil, I could do. Sending
Mom and Flori off to follow the singers, I jogged
toward the hotel. Was it *that* hard to get dependable devils, I wondered as I squeezed through the
crowd. A man dressed in a too-tight elf costume
greeted me halfheartedly at the door. A yawn-

ing elf manned the front desk. Otherwise, no one
else was around, not even the questionably jolly
St. Nick. The elevator light indicated that the poky
lift was already on the third floor. Figuring the
stairs would be faster, I bounded up the steep first
flight. By the second, I'd slowed, blaming Mom's
nemesis, altitude.

Outside on the roof, the wind was stronger
and colder than at street level. "Hello?" I called
out. "Satan?" That seemed silly. I wished I knew
Satan's name. Or maybe I did. Wasn't handsome
Barton Hunter going first? I called his name.
"Barton? Mr. Hunter? Anyone here?"

Silence greeted my salutations. I stood for a
minute, getting my bearings. Pie in the Sky was
dark. So was the rest of the roof, except for a few
dim safety lights marking the edge of the low
adobe wall serving as a railing. I walked over and
peeked at the crowd below. A group of women
spotted me, raised their fists, and booed. I ducked
and backed away, fumbling to turn on the tiny
flashlight on my key chain. Where was Satan?
Had Barton forgotten? Was he napping on the job?

I tried again. "Yoo-hoo, Devil? Satan?"

The only answer was a low howl of wind passing
through chimney pipes. I wished I'd worn something warmer than my forest-green wool coat,
which looked nice but wasn't made for standing
around on frigid rooftops. Holding my scarf
close to my neck, I headed toward Pie in the Sky.
The wind carried a strange scent. It wasn't sweet
piñon smoke or the lingering goodness of buttery
pie crusts. No, this scent was more elemental. It
reminded me of a hot-spring spa my friend Cass

and I visited in the fall, where the water was slippery with sulfur. There, the scent signaled relaxing indulgence. This smell was more reminiscent of rotten eggs. *Or*, I thought with a shiver, *the devil*.

For goodness sake, I chided myself. I'd taken on murderers and single motherhood. I wasn't scared of some rotten eggs! I swung the thin flashlight beam and my head from side to side. No devil. I was about to turn back and hurry to Celia's venue when my light swept over a lump by an exhaust fan. I approached, my heart thumping harder with each step. The lump had horns.

"Barton? Is that you? Hey, you missed your cue." The figure leaned against the wall, his legs splayed out straight in front of him. A dark cloak partially covered his red suit. Scarlet horns curved out from a black Stetson that had fallen over his forehead. Tentatively, I reached down and pushed aside the hat. A waxy face stared back at me with unblinking eyes ringed in black makeup. He wasn't Barton, but whoever he was, he was gone. I stared at his unmoving chest and dark stains in the pattern of a devil's pitchfork spreading across his chest.

Stumbling upright, I thought absurdly of Dalia. She was in charge. *She'd know what to do.* She could at least move the procession on to the next hotel. The show would go on and with it, the happy crowd. Down below, the laughing kids and merry adults wouldn't have to know about the horrifying scene above.

I raced to the wall, ducking low so I wouldn't be mistaken for Satan again. Strains of "Silent Night" in Spanish reached me. *Noche de paz, noche de amor.* The singers and spectators held candles and swayed. I spotted Flori in her puffy snow-suit, flanked by Mom and my best friend, Cass. Dalia had wrangled Mr. Peppers into position by Mary and Sidekick. The chubby goat chewed on what looked like a stocking while his redheaded handler checked her phone. The donkey was messing with Mary's robes, picking them up with his teeth to reveal pink sweatpants with the word JUICY scrolled across her bottom.

Dalia's eyes were fixed on the roof. I waved to her, and she responded in the upraised-palm gesture of drivers cut off in traffic. I knew enough not to yell murder into a crowd. Instead, I went for miming. I pantomimed a stabbing knife, chest clutching, and collapse. Two stories below, Dalia tilted her head and raised her palm higher. I pointed toward Flori. She'd get it. Dalia was tapping Flori's shoulder just as a tall figure in a cowboy hat stepped up beside them. Jake and Flori looked up simultaneously as I renewed my miming efforts. Anyone else might have thought I was playing the part of a possessed crazy woman. Flori understood. She reached into her knitting bag, where she kept not only really big needles but also her pepper spray. Jake began pushing through the crowd, heading my way.

I relaxed slightly. Soon my knight in a shining belt buckle would be here. So would the police. I felt a bit foolish for not calling them first. Perhaps Mom was right about high altitudes and poor judgment. I dug my phone from my purse, called 911, and explained to the monotone female voice on the other end that I'd found a dead devil.

"The Christmas Satan, you said, ma'am?" the operator asked, sounding rather bored.

I reworded. "One of the actors in *Las Posadas*. He's . . . well, I think he's been stabbed . . ."

"Yes, ma'am, stay where you are," the voice on the other end said. "Do not, under any circumstances, approach Satan, ma'am."

I suppressed an inappropriate stress giggle. "Okay," I said, cringing at the mirth bubbling in my throat. "No Satan approaching. I'll stay right here."

The operator broke off to summon help. When she came back on she said, "Ma'am, do you see anyone else in the vicinity?"

Here was another concern I should have thought of earlier. The killer might still be here. I spun from the view of the festive crowd and squinted into the darkness. "No," I said, "I'm all alone—"

Except I wasn't. My voice caught, coming out as a wheeze worthy of Mr. Peppers.

The operator took the sound as a sneeze. "Bless you," she said, and proceeded to inform me that the police would be slightly delayed.

"It's 'cause of *Las Posadas*," she explained. "Big crowds downtown, and there's a report of some livestock causing a disturbance in front of the Inn of the Pajarito, right where you are."

My head spun, but not from vertigo or altitude sickness. A figure had appeared, backlit against the French doors leading into the hotel. The silhouette had a round belly, a stocking cap, and a fluffy beard.

"Santa?" I managed in a squeaky voice.

"What?" the operator demanded. "Did you say

Santa? I thought you said 'Satan' earlier. Which is it, ma'am? Satan or Santa? The responding officers need to know."

I wasn't sure. A white-bearded Old St. Nick lurched toward me, brandishing a devil's pitchfork.

Chapter 4

Santa staggered left, right, and forward, steadying himself in between jerky steps with his pitchfork. In other circumstances, I might have called his cheeks rosy, his eyes twinkling. Now I interpreted flares of madness and a glint of mania. Not for the first time, I wished I'd paid more attention at a self-defense workshop Cass and I had attended a while back. I also wished Flori was here with her pepper spray, knitting needles, and martial-arts moves.

All I had was my phone, poor throwing skills, and a good set of screaming lungs.

I held off on a combined action of bellowing while tossing my phone. The phone would likely go way wide, and anyway, I had help on the way. "My lawyer's coming!" I yelled. Realizing this wasn't such a great threat, I amended it to "The police are on the phone!" I prayed that I hadn't inadvertently hung up. I held the phone out at arm's length, like a cross to ward off vampires.

Santa stopped, tugged down his beard, and pushed back his stocking cap. With the fake fluff partially removed, I recognized Wyatt Cortez, owner of the Pajarito and husband of pie maker Lorena.

"Mr. Cortez, it's me, Rita Lafitte," I said, struggling to keep my voice calm. "From Tres Amigas Café? Remember? You like our green chile stew. How about we go get some? You'll have to put down that pitchfork first. The police will be here, and I wouldn't want anyone to get hurt."

He blinked as if he'd only just now recognized me. "Oh, Rita," he said, shaking his head sorrowfully. He dropped the pitchfork. "This isn't mine."

"Whose is it?" I asked, taking a step back.

Wyatt pointed in the general direction of the dead devil. "His! It's all his fault! This was supposed to be the merriest of Christmases. I did everything. I decorated. I wore this beard and hired extra elves. I did it all for Lorena and now . . . now . . ." His words trailed off. "It's all ruined."

Was he confessing? If he was, I hoped the 911 operator was recording it all. I took my eyes off Wyatt long enough to reawaken my phone. He stumbled a few steps backward and slumped against a wall, sinking to a sitting position that eerily resembled that of the nearby corpse. If he was the killer, he'd lost his murderous steam. Best yet, I heard footsteps. That would be Jake or the police. I'd even welcome the sight of my ex, Manny.

Instead, however, spotlights lit up the roof and an elderly woman dressed in a black shawl stepped into the glare. A vortex of wrinkles pinched her face inward, making her resemble an angry apple doll. A hump in her back bent her to Flori's height. She scowled straight at me before flipping another switch. Lights shined over the far side of the rooftop and Pie in the Sky. Wyatt shielded his eyes. I squinted, and by the time I refocused, the woman had scuttled over to Satan's body.

"Ma'am, no, come away from there! You don't want to see that," I said, hurrying toward her.

The woman emitted what could only be described as a cackle and made a sign of the cross. Her words came out as a hiss, carried into the night by a frigid blast of wind. *"El diablo."*

Goose bumps crawled up my arms and across my scalp. When a hand touched my shoulder, I nearly leapt out of my boots. Jake pulled me to him and I allowed myself a moment of comfort. I buried my face as he held my head close.

"Are you okay?" he asked. "You scared me," he said, pausing a beat before adding, "again."

Yes, again. I had a bad tendency of encountering corpses, something else I've failed to fully reveal to Mom. I groaned. I might have made the discovery, but I was *not* getting involved.

Jake took me by the arm and drew me away. "Come on, you're shaking," he said.

"There's an elderly lady. We should get her away from the body." Yet when I looked back, she'd vanished. If she hadn't turned on the lights, I might have worried I imagined her.

Jake guided me to the far wall where I'd acted out death. I peeked over. The musicians had moved up the block and most of the crowd with them. I heard refrains of the singers requesting shelter, followed by heckling, boos, and cheers, and a bellowing hee-haw.

"That must be Celia," I said wistfully. I should be watching my daughter in her premier performance. I felt bad for all sorts of reasons, most of all for the poor dead devil, whoever he was. It didn't help that the first police responder was none other than my ex.

Manny's face was flushed and his chest heaved. Unlike me, he'd never outright pant. He siphoned air through partially open lips before barking at some uniformed cops to "secure the scene." "And make sure no one else gets up here!" he ordered before narrowing his eyes at me.

"Want me to stay with you?" Jake asked.

I did and I didn't. I loved having Jake at my side. On the other hand, Manny turned even more macho-blustery and petulant when Jake was around.

"No, I'm okay," I said. "You should probably go check on Mr. Cortez. I mean Santa over there. He might need a lawyer."

"I'd say so." Jake straightened his jacket and scarf.

Santa would need more than a spiffing up. Under the spotlight, I saw that his beard and cuffs were stained with red.

If I were the betting type, I could have made money predicting Manny's opening line.

"Really, Rita? Another body? At Christmas?" my ex said sourly.

Yep. I'd guessed it. A snarkier, pettier me might have feigned a yawn. Manny had used this line before, only with different seasonal and situational references. I let him continue. Might as well get out his grumbles now.

"Good thing *I* was nearby," he said. "*I* was over on the Plaza, waiting to see our daughter perform."

I folded my arms, indicating I was going to give Manny the silent treatment until he behaved like an adult policeman.

"Fine," he said, after a minute of silence. "Why were you up here in the first place?"

I explained that Dalia had sent me up to cue the devil.

He rolled his eyes at Dalia's name. "Your wacky neighbor's into devils now? No, I don't want to know. Just tell me why she didn't come up here herself."

"She's helping her sister—half sister—Judith Crundall run *Las Posadas*," I said. "Dalia was in charge of the donkey, who saw fry bread and took off. The first devil didn't appear on schedule so she had me check. I was going to run right back down and watch Celia."

Manny grumbled about stepping in donkey droppings outside. Then he asked, "So you turned on these lights and saw him right away?"

"No, I didn't know about the light switches. I had my key-chain flashlight and was looking around. I smelled something right before I found him. Sulfur. I was waiting for the police when an old lady appeared and flicked on the lights."

Manny raised an eyebrow. "An old lady? That wouldn't be your meddling friend Flori, would it?"

Manny never would have dared say that if Flori was around. My octogenarian friend might play the old-lady card to get her way—and discounts— but she hates to be called old and she's no fan of Manny. She once ran him out of Tres Amigas, swinging a tortilla press. I suspect Manny's a little scared of her.

"I think I'd recognize Flori," I said, letting some sarcasm seep in. "This woman was about Flori's age, but she was hunched and dressed in black, with a shawl over her head. She turned on the lights and went straight over to . . ." I felt bad calling the dead man Satan or dead guy. "She went over to the unfortunate deceased and called him the devil. *El diablo.*"

Manny made a show of looking around for the missing woman. "Sulfur? The devil? An old hag in a shawl? You sure you didn't imagine this, Rita? I mean, the air here is already thin for you non-natives."

Through a clenched smile, I assured Manny that I didn't imagine the woman or the smell and I was perfectly adjusted to the altitude. "Why don't I talk to Bunny?" I suggested. "Is she working to-night?" Manny's bodybuilder partner, Bunny, was as serious as her muscles, and she was a whole lot more understanding than my ex.

Manny reported that Bunny had taken time off for a family holiday reunion. "She's on a Caribbean cruise," he added in a disgusted tone.

An image of Bunny doing chin-ups above a clear, blue sea popped to mind. Lucky her. Unlucky me. I told Manny that I'd better go check on our daughter.

"Not yet," Manny said. "I sent a deputy over to guard her, and I may have more questions. I want this wrapped up before those Albuquerque news stations get ahold of it. Wouldn't they eat this up? A holiday murder featuring Satan and Santa in our quaint little capital? Stay here." He stalked off to boss around his colleagues.

I agreed with wrapping this up quickly. The safety of Santa Fe was one of my main talking points to Mom. How was I going to explain a dead devil? I could try to say nothing, like I had in the past. When my dear friend and landlord had been killed, for instance, I'd told Mom of his death. However, I hadn't gone into the details of me finding bodies and confronting killers. A thousand miles makes such omissions easier. It's not like I'd been lying, per se. I was trying not to worry and upset her. I knew Mom wouldn't see it that way.

"Rita? What is going on up here?" Mom stood in the doorway, hands on her hips.

Speak of the devil. I raised my hand in a lame wave.

Beside Mom, Flori slipped off her earmuffs and snowsuit hood. She brandished knitting needles in both fists and had the stance of someone looking for a fight. Dalia and the redheaded woman I'd seen walking Sidekick squeezed past them. The young woman's long hair fell beyond her shoulders, and her geeky-chic black-rimmed glasses slipped to the end of her nose as she scanned the roof. "Is it him?" she asked anxiously. "Is it Barton?"

I wanted to reassure her, yet she'd taken off, evading two patrolmen on her way to the body.

Mom, eyes wide, looked from me to the dead devil and back. I shrugged and gave her my best "sorry" face.

"Get these people out of here!" Manny bellowed. Recognizing Mom, he nodded in greeting. Mom beamed back. She's always had a soft spot for Manny, another result of my failure to communicate. Along with bodies and a boyfriend, I also hadn't told Mom about Manny's chronic philandering. Instead, I'd said we'd "grown apart." It was my fault that Manny remained on Mom's Christmas and birthday card lists.

A stocky female officer with a round face and flushed cheeks took charge of holding back Mom and Flori. Her outstretched arms wouldn't stop Flori if she really wanted to snoop. I bundled my coat tight and went to join them before Flori got any sleuthing ideas.

"What is going on here?" Mom repeated, aiming her most forceful school librarian voice at the woman in uniform.

The deputy put her arms down and raised her shoulders to her chin. "Don't ask me," she said in an apologetic tone. "A murder, I'd say. See this lady coming up here in the green coat? If she finds a body, it's likely a murder." She pointed at me, in case there was any confusion about the body finder in the fashionable but not-warm-enough wool coat.

So much for any hope of glossing over the situation. "Not really—" I said, but Flori was already agreeing.

"Rita has a knack, doesn't she?" Flori said proudly. "A real talent." She tucked her knitting needles back into her snowsuit. Her pink ear-muffs were looped around one arm.

Mom, lips pursed, turned her disapproving gaze to me. "A knack? Bodies? What have you been keeping from me, Rita? It takes me coming all this way to hear you're dating a *criminal lawyer* and, well, now this!" She waved her arms to encompass the rooftop crime scene.

I protested. "I didn't kill him, and it's not like it happens every day, Mom."

"Rita's so modest," Flori said.

The deputy nodded. "Right? She finds 'em pretty regularly, doesn't she? When was the last time? Wasn't it a holiday too? We had a betting pool going at the station about when she'd do it again. I said it'd be sooner." She frowned at me, the inconsiderate chef who should have produced a body for Thanksgiving or Labor Day.

Flori supplied the date of my last corpse en-counter. "Cinco de Mayo," she said. "Early May," she clarified for my mother. "See, it's actually been quite a while since we investigated anything of real importance. Well except for that little missing person case we had over the summer and a few minor tailing jobs in the fall."

The deputy agreed that it had been a while between bodies. "It's not like we get that many murders," she persisted. "So it's exceptional that this lady found another and on a holiday too." She turned to me. "When do you think the next one will be, just between us? You get an inkling, you should call me. Ask for Deputy Davis. I'll tell the switchboard to put you right through."

"No next one," I said quickly under Mom's disapproving scowl.

"Groundhog Day is coming up," Flori said. "Valentine's Day and Easter too, but those are lovely, special holidays. Let's hope nothing bad happens. Oh, and there's Lent. You could give up finding bodies for Lent, Rita."

If any good was coming out of this, it was that my sleuthing was coming out in an already miserable situation. Heck, maybe I should divulge everything to Mom, right here on the rooftop. What would I start with? The real reason Manny and I divorced? The romantic getaway Jake and I planned at his cabin on the Pecos River? The long-overdue library book with holds that I was purposefully keeping until I finished? No, I couldn't go that far. Mom was already upset. She uncapped her water bottle and slugged a gulp like it was whiskey.

"Mom, why don't you and Flori go downstairs?" I said in my best soothing voice. "Call or text Celia and let her know what happened. She'll wonder why she didn't see any of us."

Mom snapped out of her mute horror. "What am I supposed to tell her? That her mother found a dead man? How is the poor child supposed to react?"

"She's probably used to—" Deputy Davis started to say.

"She'll be fine," I interrupted firmly. "She's a strong girl. Go check on her, and I'll meet you all later. This is terrible and tragic, but it won't affect our Christmas." I said the last part with emphasis, hoping Flori caught my drift and didn't say anything more about investigations.

My elderly sleuthing companion winked at me. "Rita's right, Helen dear. We are all way too busy for an investigation. Christmas is for family and rejoicing."

The two patrolmen approached with the red-headed woman and Dalia.

"It's not him," the redhead said, exhaling her words and righting her askew glasses. "Not Barton. I was afraid when I heard . . ." She laughed nervously. "I mean, he's kind of a tough boss but I didn't want him dead."

Dalia patted the woman's arm and introduced her as Shasta Moon, Barton's temporary assistant and an archeology graduate student from Albuquerque.

"Well, who is the poor devil, then?" Flori demanded.

"Yeah, who?" Deputy Davis asked.

Relief was my first reaction to Dalia's answer, followed by guilt for feeling relieved.

"Francisco Ferrara," Dalia said, tugging her layers of woven and lace shawls close. "He works—worked—for my sister doing handyman jobs and gardening around her property. I have no idea why he was here instead of Barton. Perhaps you should try calling Mr. Hunter, Shasta."

I didn't recognize the man's name. That's where my relief came in. No emotional tug of friendship would draw me into this case. Plus, the police seemed to have it wrapped up. Manny himself was dramatically cuffing Wyatt Cortez. My ex glanced our way, checking that we noticed his takedown of a weeping St. Nick.

Mom certainly appreciated his efforts. She

clasped her hands together. "Thank goodness! Manny always knew how to fix things."

I held in my groan. *Manny, a fixer?* The man's only DIY skill involved masses of duct tape.

Dalia was looking too. "Is that Wyatt Cortez they're arresting? Oh, poor Lorena. Well, the arrest likely won't stick if he already has Jake Strong on his side." She smiled and repeated Jake's tagline, "The Strong Defender."

"Jake Strong?" Mom asked. "That's your lawyer friend, Rita? I haven't been properly introduced."

"Yes, well, Jake seems busy," I said. "We should go. We can meet at a better time."

Mom, however, was taking a cue from Mr. Peppers. She bowled past Deputy Davis to take up a position by the hotel doors. I followed.

"Ah, Mom, meet Jake," I said as the unlikely trio of Santa, cop, and cowboy lawyer passed us. A uniformed officer trailed a few steps behind holding Satan's pitchfork, now wrapped in clear evidence plastic.

Jake stepped out of the procession to greet us. "It is my sincere pleasure to meet you, Ms. Lafitte," he said, tipping his Stetson, a move that always sets my heart a-flutter.

Mom looked unmoved, although her Midwest politeness compelled her to issue a tight-lipped "Likewise."

I jumped in with stress-induced perkiness. "Yep, Jake, we're going for hot chocolate, like we planned. I don't suppose, you want to . . ."

I wasn't surprised when he bowed out. "I so wish I could, ladies, but it seems I have a new client." He twisted up the corner of his lip. "Guess I should be careful what I wish for."

Inside the building, the elevator dinged. Jake touched his hat and strode away to keep up with Manny and Wyatt.

Flori and Dalia were chatting, discussing details of the dead man. Shasta had stepped aside and was tapping on her phone. In a scandalized whisper, Mom said to me, "Really, Rita. He's an ambulance chaser?"

"There's no ambulance, yet!" I protested, sticking my proverbial foot in deeper. What's worse than an ambulance chaser? A murder whisperer who shows up before the police and EMTs. I was about to clarify that Jake had rushed to my aid, not to defend a killer.

Mom, however, had already moved on to her main argument. "You should come *home*, Rita. Things like this don't happen in Bucks Grove."

They might if I moved back.

Chapter 5

The next morning, I woke to a sofa bed spring jabbing my ribs and cat claws methodically kneading my head. I squinted at the alarm clock balanced on the sofa arm: 5:59. With a groan, I switched off the alarm moments before it was set to blare. Hugo mewed and rubbed his furry chin on my forehead. His breath smelled fishy. In the kitchen, cupboard doors thumped closed.

Swinging my feet to the chilly floor, I folded up my quilt and the bed, which disappeared into the sofa frame with a sharklike snap. Then I put on slippers, tightened my robe, and prepared to face Mom. Last night over cocoa, Mom had shut down any speculation about the dead devil by Celia and her friends. Talk of the newly deceased was not appropriate for youngsters, Mom contended. Now, however, Mom and I would be alone, and unlike me, she's always sharpest in the morning. My only hope was that she'd hold off grilling me until I had some coffee.

Mom greeted me innocently enough. "How did you sleep, dear? I hope you weren't too uncomfortable on that couch. I wish you'd let me sleep there." Mom was fully dressed, her hair and makeup perfect.

"I slept great!" I lied. I'd never admit that under its common gray cushions, the foldout was a medieval torture device. I wasn't about to mention my nightmares either. In my pre-caffeinated state, I could almost imagine that the events of last night had been a bad dream. Had I really discovered a dead devil and a killer Santa? A warped version of "The Twelve Days of Christmas" popped into my head. *On the first day of Christmas, my true love gives to me, one devil dying . . .*

Mom cut in with another, albeit more minor, nightmare. "We're out of coffee."

I gaped at the empty coffeepot.

My panic was short-lived. Mom held up a wrinkled bag, "I found some whole beans at the back of your cupboard. I didn't want to wake you with the grinder. You needed your rest. I could hardly sleep myself."

Hugo jumped on a kitchen chair beside me, circled, and flopped so that I could pet his soft butterscotch speckled belly. I scooped him up and held him on my shoulder. Here it comes, I thought. *Hang on Hugo.* "You couldn't sleep? Was it the bed?" I asked, delaying the inevitable. "I have a faux featherbed topper if the mattress is too firm." Hugo purred in my ear as if he understood. He loved to pounce on featherbed puffs.

Mom straightened her cardigan and her already rigid back. "The bed is fine. I kept worrying about *you*, Rita. That nice policewoman said you found bodies? Flori says you're a sleuth? You both do this? Doesn't Flori have bad knees? My goodness, she's in her eighties, isn't she? She should be home, retired and knitting."

Oh, Flori was knitting all right. Hugo crawled across my back to my other shoulder, using his claws as climbing hooks. I took it as a message that I should remain sharp. "Flori and I have helped out some folks with problems," I said carefully, neglecting to specify that a few of those folks had been murdered or wrongfully accused of murder. "We happened to be in the right place at the right time." *Or the wrong place at the wrong time.* I was again neglecting key aspects, like being in such places because Flori and I were tailing suspects or luring out killers. I attempted a lighthearted chuckle and reached for the coffee bag. The few tablespoons of ancient beans inside resembled gravel and smelled like dust.

Mom thrust her fists to her hips and shook her head disapprovingly. "Really, Rita! What is going on in this town? It's not right. First you have a devil in the Christmas play—"

"Three devils," I mumbled, placing a wild-eyed Hugo back on his chair. He rolled and batted his paws through the rungs. I stuck my nose in the disappointing coffee bag again. Even if grinding could revive some flavor in the beans, there weren't enough to make a cup. I'd have to run to the store or across the street to Dalia's, though she probably only stocked barley tea.

"Three devils!" Mom said, rolling her eyes

heavenward. "One of whom gets killed and you find him and the police have a betting pool on you . . . Rita, darling, you're a cook! Why haven't you told me about any of this? Your sister tells me *everything*. What else are you keeping from me?"

Before I could respond, Mom answered for me. "A man friend, that's what! How could you not tell me you were dating a lawyer? Here I was, being so encouraging to nice Albert Ridgeland. He's always prompt, and dentistry is such a good, predictable profession. Safe. He even has an RV, Rita, and a summer house on Lake Michigan. Imagine how pleasant . . ."

I'd just tossed the old beans in the trash. Now I imagined fishing out the bag and popping the beans straight. There had to be some caffeine left in them, and goodness knows I needed a boost. I felt like a chastised teenager again. Memories flashed back of the time I crumpled the bumper of Mom's Buick not a week after getting my driver's permit. She'd been upset, but like now, she was mainly worried about my well-being. Then I thought about my teenager. Celia shrugged off problems with a bored "Whatever." "Whatever" wouldn't work on my mother.

I went for my tried-and-true method. Deflection. "I know, how about breakfast at Tres Amigas?" I said, as brightly as I could in the face of Mom's scowl. "We could both use some fresh coffee, and the blue corn waffles are amazing."

Going out for breakfast is not Mom's thing. As I expected, she resisted, but at least she was focused on another subject.

"I don't know what I'd eat," she said. "You know I can't tolerate beans for breakfast or chiles or anything odd."

"We make a lovely granola, Mom, with cinnamon, allspice, cloves, and ginger. It's wonderful. Like a healthy Christmas cookie, and you can add yogurt and fresh fruit."

Mom's scowl softened slightly. "We shouldn't leave Celia here alone, what with all these murders going on."

Any correction that it was "only" one murder at the moment sounded crass. "Celia sleeps late when school's out. She won't get up until ten at the earliest. We'll lock the doors and leave her a note."

I didn't wait for Mom's comeback. With Hugo scuttling at my heels, I bolted down the hall for the shower. Her words followed me. "We have to talk sometime, Rita."

During the drive to Tres Amigas, I took a page from my sister Kathy's playbook and flooded Mom with mundane details, from the age of historic homes to cactus types.

"An artist who makes wonderful mosaics out of tiny bits of paper lives there," I said, pointing to a house mainly hidden by a lumpy adobe wall with thick buttress wings. The lumpiness indicated years of mud layers and was considered a prize feature in my historic east-side neighborhood. I informed Mom that adobe was tradition-

ally replastered every year using straw and a mud
slurry.

"Remember when Celia and I went with my
friend Cass and her son Sky to a replastering
event in Taos Pueblo?" I said, mainly to prove to
Mom that I did, indeed, share information with
her. "Taos Pueblo is amazing. People have lived
there for over a thousand years, and some of the
buildings are four and five stories tall, built all of
adobe and accessed by ladders. The town of Taos
is great too, and the Rio Grande gorge is stunning
up there. You can stand on the bridge and look
straight down eight hundred feet into the chasm."

Mom acknowledged that the ancient Pueblo
sounded "interesting" and "different." "This
whole place is very different," she said. Her tone
suggested that different wasn't the positive attri-
bute the Tourism Office's "City Different" campaign made it out to be.

When we reached Tres Amigas, I mentally patted
myself on the back. My deluge of details and tourism promotion had kept Mom from focusing on
the unfortunate devil. This would blow over, I
told myself. I still had lots more time to convince
Mom to love—or at least like—Santa Fe. I mentally ticked through festive activities. My casita
was too tiny for an indoor Christmas tree, but we
could install one in the yard. Jake could bring by
some of those popcorn strings and birdseed ornaments he and his secretary were making. As Mom
and I got out of the car, I hummed the real version
of "The Twelve Days of Christmas." I was imagining peace and goodwill when I heard my name
called from the front patio.

"Rita, yoo-hoo!" Lorena Cortez stood on the front stoop of Tres Amigas, practically engulfed by an ankle-length feather coat in brilliant turquoise. She held a plastic pie carrier. My heart sank, and not because of the beautiful meringue. I could guess why she was here, bearing gift pie. Determined to head her off, I barged in front of Mom, mouthing, *No*.

The proprietress of Pie in the Sky ignored my rude silent greeting. "Here," she said, thrusting the container into my hands. "Butterscotch with a *bizcochito* crust and vanilla meringue. Consider this my down payment. Rita, I'm hiring you."

"Hiring you?" Mom said, catching up and puffing for breath. "For what?"

My pre-caffeinated brain spun. "Ah . . . hiring me, yes. To make . . . er . . . those cherry empanadas we talked about for your Christmas gift boxes." I winked hard at Lorena, who tilted her head in concern.

"No, I love those little pies, but I mean about Wyatt," Lorena said with a frown. "Are you feeling okay? What's wrong with your eye? Can you smile? People having a stroke can't smile."

Flori saved me from faking a life-affirming smile. She swung the front door open wide. "Fresh, hot coffee," she announced. "Come in out of the cold. Lorena, Rita, will you help me in the kitchen? Helen, I have a lovely seat by the fireplace just for you."

"Let's hear Lorena out," Flori said to me in the kitchen, after we'd set up Mom with coffee, a pitcher of water, and a colorful tourism guide. "It is Christmas, after all."

"Right, Christmas, that's the problem," I whispered, drawing Flori a few steps away from Lorena, who was making small talk with Juan about his hash-brown technique.

Leave the potatoes alone, Juan said. That was the secret. That and the decades of seasoning on Flori's old cast iron griddle.

"I have to think of Mom," I said, nodding toward the dining room. "She's already upset. I should have told her earlier about Jake and the sleuthing, and she still doesn't approve of Christmas devils, especially the dead one." I glanced up and saw Lorena looking our way. Her eyes glistened. I clamped my big mouth shut.

"Francisco," she said. "The devil's name was Francisco. He was my friend. Now he's dead and Wyatt's in trouble. You know Wyatt and I are currently separated, but I can't lose him too, and I'm sure he didn't do it. Please, you've both helped in other cases."

No, I practiced in my head. *So sorry, but we can't. The police will handle it.* I felt for Lorena, I truly did. How awful to have a killer Santa as your estranged spouse, but Flori and I couldn't help that.

"I was up on the roof," I told Lorena, as gently as I could. "Santa—Wyatt—he was dazed and holding a pitchfork when I first saw him. Lorena, there was blood on his clothes. If anyone can help him, it's Jake. He's the best criminal defense lawyer around. I'll testify. I'll say Wyatt looked . . ." Deranged came to mind. Jake could go with an insanity defense. "Ah, he looked disturbed," I said.

"Wyatt's no criminal," Lorena moaned.

"That's why Jake does what he does," I said,

wishing Mom could hear this defense of my favorite defense attorney. "He makes sure that his
clients get the best defense possible and fairest of
trials."

"True," Flori said "And he's fine to look at too.
That sways the jury, I'm sure." She patted Lorena
comfortingly on the shoulder and suggested we
all have a piece of butterscotch pie. "Do you think
your mother would like some pie instead of granola, Rita?"

Mom would disapprove of pie for breakfast.
What she'd really object to, though, was me investigating a murder. "I'm sorry, Lorena," I said,
avoiding her eyes. I scooped granola into two
bowls. I'd have a quick, healthy breakfast with
Mom and get to work. My real work.

"Wait," Lorena said, stepping in front of me.
"There's more. You *will* want to hear this, Rita. I'm
in a meditation group with Dalia Crawford. She
called me last night. She thought I should know
that *Las Posadas* has been getting threats."

"Some people love to make trouble," Flori said.
She bent to cut a thick slice of pie. I noticed the
purple knitting needles holding up her silver bun.
Something black and knitted poked out of her
apron pocket. Had she been out making knitted
trouble?

Lorena fixed bloodshot eyes to mine. "Yes, for
years the play has gotten some angry letters and
general threats. But this year? The threats were
specific. Death threats against the devils." Chills
had already scurried up my arms when she
added, "Rita, isn't your daughter playing a devil?"

Chapter 6

I delivered Mom's granola and apologized that I couldn't eat breakfast with her. "Kitchen emergency," I said, which was kind of true. When I returned, Flori placed a giant wedge of pie and fresh coffee in front of me.

"I'm not promising we can help," I said, my defiance admittedly weakened after several luscious bites of the extraordinary pie. The butterscotch was rich and creamy, with hints of caramel, vanilla, and possibly bourbon. The crust was an entire cookie jar of goodness held together with butter. If I'd been alone with the pie, I would have had another slice.

Lorena assured me that she understood. "I'm not trying to scare you into helping me. I do honestly believe Wyatt is innocent. My husband might be blustery and intense, but he's harmless."

Flori and I exchanged a look. We'd learned from unpleasant experience that anyone can be capable of murder.

"I know what you're thinking," Lorena said. She'd held her puffy coat protectively in her lap. Feathers escaped at the seams and stuck to her black slacks. She squished the coat closer to her chest. "If I'm right, a killer is out there and more people could be in danger."

She let me think about this while I finished my pie and Flori consulted with Addie, who had come in while I was serving Mom the granola.

"We're getting a wee busy out in the dining room," Addie said. From the stack of orders in her hand, I guessed "wee" was an understatement.

I finished my pie and pushed my chair back. "Could you stay and tell us about the letters while we fix up these orders?" I asked Lorena.

"No," she said with a smile. "But, I'll tell you everything I know while I help you cook. You're slammed."

Addie, who had popped out to seat customers, now came bounding back in. "Brits!" she exclaimed excitedly. "Three lovely ladies. They're fab! I told 'em, we have no tea and scones, but we have gingerbread muffins and they said that would be smashing. *Smashing*," she repeated to Juan, who stoically flipped bacon.

Addie made up plates of gingerbread muffins. I handed Lorena an apron, and she tied her hair back in one of Flori's tai-chi scarves, white with a red rising sun symbol. I reminded myself that knitting—even the guerilla kind—was safer than Flori's previous hobby, slow but deadly martial arts.

Lorena snapped on disposable gloves and began to assemble burritos, filling us in on the death threats as she did. "Dalia told me that the devil threats started arriving a couple weeks ago. They creeped her out. They had cutout letters, you know? Like someone found each letter in a magazine or newspaper and pasted it in?"

"We did an activity like that at the Senior Center once," Flori said, easing a batter-coated, cheese-stuffed green chile into a hot frying pan. *Chiles rellenos* were her specialty and one of my favorite dishes. "The workshop was called 'illicit letters.' It was basically a paper mosaic class, but that would have sounded boring."

"It's creepy," I confirmed to Lorena.

"Or creative," Flori insisted, spatula poised over the sizzling chiles.

"Spooky," muttered Juan. He slid crispy hash browns onto a plate, alongside a medium-rare skirt steak and topped both with red chile and two over-easy eggs.

A pang of guilt jabbed me. Steak and eggs made me think of Jake. It was one of his favorite break-fasts. I should have been bellowing his charms to Mom. I would from now on. I needed to find time for my handsome lawyer too.

Lorena tucked in the sides of a plump burrito and wrapped it tight. "Dalia can tell you more. Hopefully she kept those awful letters so she can show the police. They said things like 'Devil = Dead' and 'All devils will die.'"

Flori admitted that this crafts project sounded ominous. "Why didn't Dalia take the notes to the police when she got them?" she asked. "Or did she?"

Lorena shook her head. "She didn't. They were addressed to Judith Crundall, and Judith said they were a childish prank. She said that no bully would make her cancel her Christmas pageant."

Making a mental note to talk to Dalia, I went out to refill coffees and check on Mom. As I approached her table, she stood, smoothing her slacks and patting her always tidy hair.

"I'm in the way," she said, above my protests. "No, no, Rita. Look how busy it's become. There's a young couple waiting for a table. Anyway, I need to get on with my day. You know I don't like to sit around."

"I can drop you off somewhere," I offered. "Or you can take the car home . . ." On her previous visit, Mom had started out for the supermarket and somehow ended up five miles off course and in line for a demolition derby at the rodeo grounds.

Mom claimed to know the way home. She recited the streets, describing them by landmarks and left/right turns instead of their names, some of which involved lengthy Spanish. Just in case, I highlighted the route on the map Mom kept stashed in her purse. We hugged at the door and in a reversal of roles, I was the one fretting. "Call when you get home," I said, stepping out on the chilly *portico*. "I'll be back as soon as I can this afternoon and we can all go do something fun."

Mom promised to call. I watched her make her way down the walkway. I was already formulating more questions for Dalia. *How many death threats? When? How did they arrive? Whom were they addressed to?*

As if sensing my thoughts, Mom turned. "Rita, if that pie woman wanted something other than baked goods, I'll remind you that you are a single mother. You have a responsibility to your daughter, first and foremost."

Mom bustled off before I could answer. I did have a responsibility to my daughter, I thought as Mom maneuvered my car into a slow-motion, five-point U-turn. That's exactly why I *had* to investigate, at least until I knew the police had their man . . . or their killer Santa.

Back in the kitchen, Juan was taking a well-deserved coffee break. Lorena stood at the sink scrubbing a pan and recounting how she and Francisco, the deceased devil, met at a grief support group after her mother passed away.

"Do you know the crazy thing?" she said, scrubbing harder. "The group wasn't very supportive. Some of the members thought Francisco shouldn't be there because he'd caused grief himself. He acknowledged that, but he hurt too."

Juan snorted into his cup of coffee.

Flori said gently, "Lorena dear, remind us of Francisco's troubles. Rita wasn't living here then."

Lorena's hands shook as she tightened her apron ties. "I didn't know Francisco then either. He worked at the community college, teaching history and anthropology. It was Christmastime, about ten years ago, and he'd been to a party. He only had one drink, he told me. Just one. The road was icy or maybe he got distracted or dozed off. Whatever happened, he hit a lady walking along the side. He said he never saw her until it was too late."

I noted Juan's deep frown. Had he known the deceased lady? Lorena noticed too, and spoke directly to him. "I know, such a terrible thing. The victim was a good person. A lot of people loved her. Francisco felt awful. He couldn't handle the guilt. He quit his teaching job and dropped out of everything and isolated himself, except for working odd jobs for Ms. Crundall. It was kind of her to give him a job and a place to stay in her guest cottage. That's how I met him. I volunteered to make pies for the Easter procession, one of Judith's other community events. Francisco was making the backdrop sets and we got to talking. That's why he ended up in *Las Posadas* at the last minute too."

I'd been wondering about that. "Barton Hunter was supposed to play the first devil, wasn't he? He and Dalia came in here the other day and he told me. What happened?"

"Barton's the hot one," Flori said helpfully, when Lorena hesitated. "Judith has him handling her nasty bone collection. I'd hire him, if I had something I wanted handled."

"Flori!" I said.

My elderly friend shrugged. Lorena said she did know the good-looking Mr. Hunter.

"He and Dalia came up to the roof to mark out where he'd stand as the devil. I offered them free pie. I thought it was all fun at the time. He seemed excited."

"Why didn't Barton show up, then?" I asked.

"Migraine," Lorena said, shaking her head. "Poor man. I guess he felt it coming on right before the

play and knew he couldn't jump around on a roof.
My sister gets those, so I understand."

One of my cousins suffered terribly from migraines so I understood too. "Who knew he was
sick?" I asked. Shasta hadn't known when she
raced across the roof, yelling his name. Dalia had
seemed shocked too. How had neither of them
known of the devil switch? I asked Lorena.

"The migraine came on suddenly, like they
do. Barton was at Ms. Crundall's finishing up
some work. He had his costume there, planning
to go straight to the performance. Francisco was
the right size and he'd played the devil before.
Ms. Crundall asked him to help. He called to
tell me after he got in his makeup and outfit. He
wanted me to go see."

"Did you tell Wyatt or anyone at the hotel?" I
asked.

Her horrified expression was answer enough,
but she said, "No! Of course not. Wyatt was acting
all territorial about me and the hotel, even though
I kept telling him that Francisco and I were
friends. *Only friends!* He banned Francisco from
coming in the Pajarito. He watched the elevator to
stop him from coming up to my shop. I told Wyatt
he couldn't do that. The hotel was partly mine too.
Still, I warned Francisco to avoid Wyatt."

"What would Wyatt have done if he saw Francisco come in?" I asked, thinking maybe he'd done
just what the police—and I—thought he did.

Lorena shook her head. "Wyatt was all bluster.
One time, he had his door elf throw Francisco
out. He might have yelled or pitched a fit, but he
would never have gotten violent."

I changed the topic back to Francisco. "How did he seem when he called you?"

"Excited. Kind of nervous too." Her voice cracked. "I told him, 'You'll have your mask on. You can be someone else for the night.' Your old carefree self, that's what I was thinking. If only I'd known."

We worked in a somber silence until a stream of breathless, honking brays erupted out in the makeshift manger. Laughter bubbled from the dining room, and Addie popped her head through the pass-through. "Our British friends wish to see the wee burro. Can we visit, Juan?"

Juan, guardian of his cousin's star donkey, hesitated and then shrugged. In rapid Spanish, he set the ground rules, which thankfully Addie repeated in English.

"Righto. Got it. He's on a diet. Absolutely no fried foods. No cupcakes or muffins. Only carrots. Jolly good. We'll meet you there, Juan." She left to gather the ladies. I took my cleaning rag to the dining room and thought about what Lorena had said. She hadn't convinced me of Wyatt's innocence. On the other hand, I wasn't entirely convinced of his guilt either. I was pondering this, and wiping antiseptic circles around an already clean table, when a finger tapped my shoulder. I jumped.

"Oh dear, I didn't mean to startle you." A woman about Mom's age, with Mom's short haircut and Helen Mirren's glorious accent, proceeded to ask me where her friends had toddled off to.

"Don't worry. They haven't been taken by

aliens," I said. As soon as I uttered the words, I thought that alien abduction might not be the first concern of proper English ladies. However, this was New Mexico. They could be on their way to Roswell and its UFO museum. "They've gone off to see our Christmas donkey and his goat friend," I clarified.

"How utterly lovely!" she said, and I was as charmed as Addie. I told her I'd escort her to the donkey viewing. We went out the front door and around the side. Reaching the back gate, I said, "Right, here we are." I cracked the gate and saw the other ladies and Addie gathered around Juan and Mr. Peppers, a few yards away.

"My, how charming!" my enthusiastic companion exclaimed. "Here, dear one. Donkey, dearest, I have a muffin for you!"

Across the yard, Mr. Peppers raised his huge ears to attention. He cocked his head, sniffed the air, and then, to my horror, barreled straight for us.

I didn't need to understand the exact Spanish for "Shut the gate!" as bellowed by Juan. I was already trying just that. The miniature donkey, however, had the strength of a rhino. Wheezing happily, the furry beast pushed his way through and stopped short of the sidewalk.

"Aren't you a feisty little one," the lady said. She held out the muffin and velvety donkey lips inhaled it. I, meanwhile, was frantically untying my apron, hoping to lasso Peppers with the ties.

"Hold still now," I said soothingly. Out of the corner of my eye, I saw Juan coming up behind him.

The muffin, however, was already gone and the lady was telling Mr. Peppers that she had no more. The donkey flared his nostrils and swung his head. I followed his stare across the street, where two kids—a girl and boy, elementary school age at most—were swinging paper bags splotched in dark, oily stains. I didn't have time to determine that the kids had something even more tempting than the forbidden fry bread. I looped my apron strings around the donkey's thick, furry neck. He smelled the air, stomped a hoof, and charged the youngsters, taking my favorite apron with him.

Chapter 7

The little boy stood frozen except for his stuttering wail as Mr. Peppers barreled at him, wheezing and honking excitedly. I dashed into the street and nearly ended up smashed on the grille of a silver Audi. The car jolted to a halt inches from my knees. In the driver's seat, Jake visibly drew a breath. I regrouped and pointed wildly to the misbehaving Mr. Peppers, who was now trotting after the fleeing boy. The girl was standing her ground, issuing orders.

"Stop and stare!" she yelled. "Look big and scary, like you do with a mountain lion!"

The little boy screamed louder and backed into a patch of tall ornamental grasses.

Jake was out of the car before I could wonder whether donkeys responded to mountain-lion defense tactics. He dashed up the street, hand on his Stetson, in step with Juan, who was ripping his apron off and preparing to rope the miniature fugitive. Mr. Peppers looked over his furry

shoulder and spotted them coming. In one swift
move, the donkey snagged the boy's paper sack in
his teeth and trotted down the street, head high,
heels kicking. Juan and Jake switched directions
and ran after him.

I stayed behind and gathered up the kids. The
girl bristled at my concern.

"We're fine," she said snippily. To her sniffling
companion, she said, "Stop being such a baby." I
guessed he was her younger brother. They had
similar silky dark hair—hers cut in a long bob
with bangs, his flopping across his forehead.

I took the boy by the hand and told him to
hang on to his sister with the other hand. Having
formed this little chain, I cautiously crossed the
street and stood on the sidewalk by Jake's car
to watch the rodeo. A crowd had gathered, including the British ladies, who uttered oohs and
ahhs and held up their cell phones to record the
chaos.

"That mean pony stole my *buñuelo*," the little
boy said.

I asked him his name, but his sister instigated
prisoner-of-war tactics. "No names!" She com-
manded. "And that's no horse, stupid. It's a
donkey."

I told the boy that I was sorry about his *buñuelo*.
A *buñuelo*, as Flori made them, was flat dough,
deep fried, and dusted with cinnamon sugar. If
you don't witness—or can mentally block out—
the frying, *buñuelos* seem light and harmless. That
is, until you've gobbled too many and feel like
you've eaten a doughy bowling ball.

The girl reached inside her grease-spotted bag

and came up with sugary fingers. She methodically licked each one clean, ignoring her stricken
brother.

I was about to tell her to be nice and share her
sugar, when a bump to the back of my knees
nearly sent me crumpling. Sidekick leaned against
my legs. At least the chubby goat wasn't making a
break for it. I moved aside and patted his nubby-
horned head. The boy tentatively touched his
back.

"Good goat," I told Sidekick.

"Good gracious," Flori said, joining us. She
pushed back her glasses and squinted to get a
better look. "Now that is a fine sight."

I assumed she meant Jake, a bona fide urban
cowboy, looking good as he ran down the street,
trying to get ahead of the escaped donkey. Juan,
whom I'd never seen hurry let alone sprint, was
gaining ground on the other side.

"One of the British ladies waved a muffin by
the gate," I told Flori. "Mr. Peppers might have
stopped there, but then he spotted fry bread
across the street."

"*Buñuelos*. I told you that," the little girl corrected. "And I'm telling Daddy that your donkey
scared us and ate our food. You owe us resiter . . .
resto . . . restitution!" Her small face pinched into
a frown.

She was about eight, I estimated, and going on
law school graduate. Her brother was probably
around four and more understanding, especially
since Flori was suggesting a replacement treat.

"Restitution, you say?" Flori asked. "Well, I suppose we could make you some fresh *buñuelos*.

Why don't you come into the café and we'll make them right up and call your parents."

"No, we're busy," the girl said.

"Oh really?" Flori said, in exaggerated seriousness. "Too busy for my special chocolate *buñuelos*?"

The boy seemed ready to go with the nice grandmotherly stranger offering chocolate.

"No!" Little Miss Litigious declared, stomping her foot for emphasis. "Daddy's a lawyer. He'll sue for more."

No wonder people didn't like lawyers, I thought, and then caught myself. I knew one lawyer I sure liked a lot. Loved? I didn't dare think that. Still, watching Jake in action sure was—as Flori said—a fine sight.

Flori frowned down at the girl "What is this talk of suing? Children shouldn't say such things. How about another sweet? We have gingerbread muffins straight from Santa's workshop."

"Santa's not real and a bad influence," the girl said haughtily. "My mother says so. And I'm not a child."

I didn't know her parents. If they were suehappy Santa haters, I feared I might not like them. All the same, I pitied them. They had their hands full, and just wait until this kid reached her teens. I shuddered for their sakes. Sidekick did too, either that or he was loosening up for more headbutting.

"Well," Flori said, turning up her chin. "Then I guess you won't want any of Santa's special hot cocoa."

The little boy timidly admitted that he liked hot cocoa. And presents.

Flori added to the temptation. "Hot cocoa with whipped cream and chocolate sauce on top. I suppose we'd have to ask your mother or father first. We wouldn't want to get sued for giving you something so sweet and delicious. What's a number for your parents so we can call and ask?"

The girl crossed her arms stubbornly. She was a tough one. At her age, I would have caved for hot chocolate. I'd cave now, except for the small problem of livestock on the lam. Jake and Juan were near Jake's office and holding out their arms to herd Mr. Peppers down Jake's driveway. I pictured his brick-paved drive, bordered by wall on one side and leading to a walled courtyard in the back. The viewing crowd had moved down the street, keeping a cautious distance.

"I wonder if our British friends will want a full English breakfast after all this excitement?" Flori said. "Didn't Addie say that includes beans? We have frijoles and chorizo and eggs and what else? Fried tomatoes, is that part of it? We could substitute salsa, couldn't we? And some chiles. Everyone loves chiles." A full New Mexican fry-up was taking form.

"Yeah," I said, my mind wandering. I wished Mom were here to see this. Not the part about me nearly being run over. That would only reinforce her idea that I suffered from altitude-induced poor judgment. Not our visitor donkey terrorizing kids either, although I could forgive Mr. Peppers for cuteness alone, and he had been goaded. No, I wished she'd been here to see Jake in heroic action. She wouldn't ooh and ahh. Mom didn't express that kind of emotion, but surely she'd be impressed. *Wouldn't she?*

Applause burst out down the street. Jake and Juan emerged from the driveway. Mr. Peppers walked placidly between them with Juan's apron serving as a makeshift halter and cape. When they reached the entrance to the temporary paddock, they paused so that the British visitors could shower Mr. Peppers in pats and praise. Mr. Peppers raised his lips in a grin and rolled his eyes in bliss when Jake rubbed his long ears. The ladies looked equally blissful. Sidekick pranced over to his friend and led the way back to the patio, as if it had never been their intention to make a break at all.

Flori easily sold the ladies on "full Santa Fe" breakfasts. A few asked for photos with the Western wranglers, and I was recruited to take a group shot of the ladies, Jake, and a highly reluctant Juan. Jake tipped his hat to them as they left.

"You're going to show up on vacation slideshows in Britain," I joked to Jake.

He grinned in that bashful way that made me like—love?—him all the more. Then he kissed me. Beside us, the girl groaned.

"Ugh," she said. "Gross."

"And who is this?" Jake asked. He gave her his best smile.

She was unmoved. "None of your business."

There was something about her that looked familiar. "You two look like someone I know," I said.

"No we don't." The little girl turned away. The little guy offered Jake his hand. Cute. Another picture-perfect moment, the cowboy and the adoring kid. Geez, all this Christmas sentiment was getting to me. Maybe I needed to take some cues from the surly girl, who was turning up her nose at me.

"That's it! The Crundall nose," I declared. It wasn't only the nose. Now that I put the pieces together, I'd heard kids playing across the street the other night. Plus, Dalia had told me that her grandkids were going to stay with her while their parents went skiing. "I'll bet your grandmother Dalia is looking for you. We're neighbors."

"We aren't supposed to say grandmother. It sounds old," the little boy said earnestly, earning a jab from his sister's elbow.

"Jig's up," Jake said. "Might as well tell us your names."

The girl shrugged, an implied *whatever*. "Emilie," she said. "Spelled with an 'ie.' It's French. This is Edison. You can call him Eddie, also with an 'ie.'"

"Eddie, Emilie with an 'ie.' Pleased to meet you," Jake said seriously.

"What are you two doing?" I asked. "You're a long way from home. Is your grandmother—I mean, Dalia—nearby?"

Eddie said, "We're lost."

"We are not, Eddie," Emilie snapped. "We're walking on purpose. Dalia says we are free-range young people."

I caught Jake glancing at his watch. "Sorry," he said, looking sheepish for getting caught. "Guess I shouldn't have wished for work. I'm supposed to meet with Wyatt Cortez."

I drew him aside, keeping a watchful eye on the

kids. "I know you can't tell me, but if you think Wyatt's guilty, could you give me a sign? Tug on your ear if he did it."

Jake pushed back his Stetson and rubbed his forehead, a confusing sign. "Rita," he said. "I know you found the dead devil, but you don't owe that unfortunate man anything. Didn't you say you wanted a quiet Christmas?"

I quickly laid out my worries for Jake. "Lorena Cortez came to see us this morning. She said someone has been sending threatening notes about *Las Posadas* devils. If Wyatt's innocent, then someone might be still targeting devils. *Is* he innocent?"

Usually Jake would joke that all his clients were innocent, some more than others. His seriousness worried me more than ever. "Honestly," he said. "I don't know. I've barely had a chance to speak with him. His prints were on the murder weapon, the devil's pitchfork, but that's easily explained since he says he found the body and tried to help. I managed to get him out on bail, with an ankle monitor and his hotel as collateral. If I find any evidence, either way, I'll tell you, as long as I don't have to break client confidentiality." He kissed my forehead to a chorus of giggles and ewww sounds. "You'll be okay with these two fugitives?"

"No worries," I said. "I'll call Dalia and get them back to the right place."

"Auntie Judith's!" Eddie exclaimed happily over Emilie's sputtering protests. *Perfect!* I could drop in at Judith's and casually bring up death threats and devil killers. Now all I had to do was tell Flori that I needed to skip out of work.

As I'd guessed, Flori was delighted. So was Lorena, who offered to drive us, since Mom had taken my car. She even had a booster seat in the back that she used for her grandkids. Flori thanked Lorena for the pie and cooking help and welcomed her to the kitchen anytime. "Bring us more information," Flori said. "Any little thing you think of could help."

"So you're taking the case?" Lorena said. She began gushing thanks and offered to pay us in cash and pie.

"We're preliminarily looking into the case," I said, pointedly, aiming my words more at Flori than Lorena. "Not a word to anyone, though, especially the police or my . . ." I felt silly adding, ". . . my mother."

Flori said it for me. "Rita's mother is visiting. We wouldn't want her worrying. Best to keep it a secret." She held a finger to her lips, winking at the kids.

"Secret," Eddie said solemnly.

"A secret," Lorena agreed. "Except, can I tell Wyatt? He needs to know that I support him and don't think he's a killer."

She might not think it, but I could. Lorena dropped the kids and me off in front of Judith Crundall's mansion. We walked across the gravel and stone expanse of Judith's front drive and garden. Eddie kicked at pebbles.

"So, are you having fun with your grandmother?" I asked the kids.

Emilie said sourly, "Dalia won't let us watch TV or use the computer. She says electromagnetic waves will fry our brains."

More cheerfully, Eddie reported that they'd made paper snowflakes and stayed up really late to say hello to the moon. He stopped talking abruptly when we reached the door. "Shhh," he said. "Auntie Judith doesn't like noise."

"She doesn't like kids," Emilie clarified.

I hesitated to knock. When I tapped, the door swung open immediately. Barton's assistant, Shasta, stood in the foyer, a phone to her ear, her thick-framed glasses tipped at an off angle. She put up a finger in a one-minute gesture. "Yes," she said, "Yes, I'll check into that. I don't know what you heard, but I haven't seen that item. Yes. Yes, I'll look again." She rolled her eyes dramatically.

The kids and I waited, some of us more patiently than others. Emilie heaved herself on a wooden bench and groaned in boredom. I resisted the urge to peek down the magnificent hallways with their tempting features of beamed ceilings and inset cubbyholes. Eddie entertained himself by removing his shoelaces.

A few more terse "yes" and "no" answers later, Shasta stuffed her phone into the back pocket of tight jeans. "Dalia's been looking all over for you kids," she said. "That's one mystery solved. Where have you two been?"

"We got far away and got lost and saw a donkey and a goat," Eddie said, his laceless shoes now in his hand. One of his socks featured Spider-Man, the other turtles. "And the donkey ran at us and stole our—"

"We weren't lost," Emilie snapped. "Come on, Ed, let's go to the artifacts room and say hi to Mr. Barton."

"Oh, the artifacts room," I said, seeing an opportunity to ask Barton Hunter if anyone might want to stab him with a pitchfork. "I'd love to see that. Can I have a peek too?"

Shasta's drawn-out "Well . . ." followed by "we're really busy" was an obvious prelude to a put-off. I refused to acknowledge it. I grabbed Eddie's hand. "Sure seems like a fun place. Will you show me, Eddie?"

Shasta retied her long red hair into a bun, which promptly fell to one side like her glasses. "Oh, why not?" she said with an exasperated sigh. "It's chaos in there, but you won't get chewed out for losing things that are already lost. Maybe *you* can find our missing friends. I think we have someone of yours too."

Missing friends? Someone of mine? I held back questions and my midwestern urge to apologize for barging in. Emilie led the way down a hallway lined with windows and a brick floor, suggesting that this part of the house was once a covered patio. She swung open a red vermillion door and Eddie skipped ahead, pulling me with him. My apprehension grew. Who was this friend and why was he or she missing? Maybe I wasn't the right person to help look, given my penchant for finding dead people. I steeled myself, prepared for anything.

I stepped inside and stopped short. My mother raised her eyes from a magnifying glass, straightened, and shot me a perplexed frown. "Rita, what are you doing here?"

I could ask her the very same thing.

Chapter 8

W ell!" Mom said indignantly, when I did ask
her that very question. "I couldn't sit idly
around the house. Celia's still asleep and
I already organized your spice rack and I will
say, your sock drawer is a mess, but I left it alone
and started on your front porch. Lots of dust and
pollen out there. In the spring, you should give it
a good scrubbing, Rita."

I pushed aside worries of the "organized" spices
I'd have to disorganize when Mom left. "I meant,
this is great, Mom. I'm glad you got out. I was just
surprised to see you. Pleasantly surprised. How
did you get here?"

I regularly drive, walk, and jog by Judith
Crundall's mansion. She's never once invited me
in for tea, let alone to inspect her private collection. Mom stood at a light table, a magnifying
glass hovering over what looked like old negatives. Nearby, masks adorned in tiny colorful

beads and dyed feathers rested on a massive oak table.

Before Mom could speak again, Dalia entered in a swirl of natural fabrics and a cloud of incense perfume. My neighbor greeted me with "Namaste" and a hug before swooping in to give the kids kisses that made Emilie squirm and Eddie giggle.

"I kidnapped your lovely mother, Rita," Dalia said, releasing the kids in a wave of patchouli and sandalwood. "I spotted her out freshening the aura on your porch—"

"Sweeping," Mom specified.

Dalia continued unabashed, "Brushing away all those old dusty spirits. I told her she must walk with me on this lovely bright day and tour my sister's house and gardens. I love to show the place off. The old family home. Of course, it was never my home. Judith and I lived such different lives. Sometimes, I feel like a museum docent in here."

She reeled off historic features, including bullet holes from an early governor's assassination, cocktail glasses once sipped from by D. H. Lawrence, and a wagon wheel that rolled across the Santa Fe Trail. All I could think was *Mom got a house tour?* I was happy for Mom, and pretty darned envious. Cass and I had recently bought benefit tickets for an architecture tour. I doubted our fifty dollars would get us beyond foyers and gardens. I was tempted to invite myself on a Crundall mansion tour right that minute. That, however, wasn't why I was here.

I introduced the kids to Mom and explained

that I'd found them downtown. "We had quite an exciting morning ourselves. There was a donkey on the lam."

"We were fine!" Emilie said again.

Dalia's brow wrinkled. "All the way to Tres Amigas, dears? You really did free range. Let's not tell your mother." Dalia smiled at Mom and me. "My daughter and I have a few differences of opinions about raising children," she said. "I'm sure you understand that."

I laughed politely. Mom muttered something about devils.

Shasta, who'd been flipping through stacks of paper at the oak table, interrupted. "Dalia, you helped with that 1980s inventory. We need to rectify that and find those . . . oh, whatever Barton insists we call them. Those 'friends.'" She snapped long nails coated in chipped red polish. "I *need* organization."

Mom's head snapped up from the negatives. There's nothing my librarian mother loved more than finger-snapping organization. I sidled closer to Mom, ready to drag her away if necessary. I hadn't goaded her into a Santa Fe vacation so she could rectify spreadsheets and dusty files.

Dalia brought her hands together in what could be the preamble to meditation or a yoga pose. She tilted her chin toward the high plaster ceiling and smiled serenely. "With calm and peace, we will locate our 'friends.' They can't have gone far. They're elderly and ready to return to their families."

Shasta grumbled that they wouldn't be returning anywhere unless we found them. "And where is Barton?"

Dalia lifted a knee in a balancing yogi pose. "Barton went to the collections storage room. Perhaps he's already located them. I don't sense their spirits here."

Shasta rubbed her forehead as if in pain. I sensed that this was not a good time to quiz her about Francisco and devil threats. I could understand her apparent frustration with Dalia. My neighbor is kind and well meaning, but all that calm can set the noncalm on edge. Plus, there are only so many sage smudgings and purifying saunas, séances, and sweat lodges one can—and wants to—accept. Dalia paced slowly around the room, palms outstretched.

"Who are we looking for?" I asked. The room was large, with big paned windows, brick floors, and an array of tables and file cabinets. Boxes, files, and a few laptops cluttered the tables, but there couldn't be that many places to hide, unless some of the doors led to closets. I supposed that someone had thought to check the closet.

"Friends!" Eddie exclaimed happily. He launched into a story about how his best friend back home was allergic to peanuts and strawberries. As the allergy list continued, Mom piped in, again surprising me with her in-the-know information.

"They've lost some of those what-do-you-call-them dolls," Mom said. She stuttered a "ka" sound before throwing up her hands and saying, "Oh, those southwestern dancing dolls you see in all the gift shops around here."

"*Katsina*," Shasta supplied, tapping a pencil on a spreadsheet. "More commonly written as kachina with a 'ch.' And, yes, they're all over in tourist traps and art galleries, but the ones we're looking for are valuable and sacred to the Hopi people." She continued in a tone of rote memorization. "They are representations of spirit beings, so sacred we should not call them by name, so alive that if we must refer to them at all, we should call them 'friends.'"

"Must make them harder to find if you can't describe them," Mom pointed out, and I had to agree.

Shasta sighed. "Yes, well, my boss Barton insists that we be sensitive. Since he's not here, though, I'll say. The ones I need are about ten inches tall. Hopi. Carved in the 1860s." She opened a folder and produced a faded color photograph. "Here they are, listed with the exact archival location and storage container. I found the box, but nothing inside except this." She frowned and picked up a figure that looked straight from the Five and Dime.

"Kokopelli," a deep male voice said.

We all looked up and saw the tall, blond, sensitive expert himself.

"Barton!" Eddie cried, and rushed like Sidekick, crashing into the consultant's knees.

"My favorite junior archeologist," Barton said, swooping Eddie up onto his shoulders. "Kokopelli, the hump-backed flute player," Barton continued in a voice suitable for melting chocolate. I found myself thinking that if my college professors had sounded like that, maybe I would have finished the liberal arts degree I started. However, then I never would have discovered my true love,

culinary school and cooking. Or New Mexico. Or
Jake.

Barton drew rapt attention from everyone
except Emilie, who spun in a swivel chair, eyes
glued to a book. "Kokopelli has been sacred to
southwestern peoples across cultures for thousands of years," Barton intoned. "You'll find
him in petroglyph art and he's prominent in
Hopi and Zuni mythology, symbolizing fertil-
ity, replenishment, dance, and mischief." Barton's expression contained a dash of mischief,
set off by two adorable dimples. He reached up
and covered Edison's ears, sending the kid into
a fit of delighted giggles. "Kokopelli is a several-
thousand-year-old sex symbol."

Mom murmured an "Oh my."

Barton flashed us a smile to rival Manny's
toothpaste-commercial whites and picked up the
object. "Now, this particular piece, I'd estimate as
Chinese manufacture, circa 2000."

Shasta groaned. "I thought so." She tapped a
spreadsheet and said, "Dalia, when you invento-
ried the collection, were so many things missing
and misplaced?"

I sensed Dalia harden under her floaty layers.
"You should have seen the mess the collection was
in when I started. I left it all in the original boxes
and renumbered everything so it could be found.
I purified it the best I could, with sage and bless-
ings. I got a shaman to come in too, over Judith's
objections."

"You did a fine job, Dalia," Barton said, smoothing the sparks between her and Shasta. "Your

sister has interacted with the collections more. We can ask her some questions when she's feeling better." He turned his smile to me. "Now, I'm being rude. We have lovely guests."

I reintroduced myself to Barton. "We met at Tres Amigas," I said. "You and Dalia had breakfast there the other day, and my daughter's in *Las Posadas*."

I was about to ramble on, assuming he wouldn't remember me. "Of course," he said. "I never forget a pretty face." He smiled at Mom. "And this must be your sister."

I swear, Mom giggled. Giggled! I was so shocked my mouth hung open. I clamped it shut before Mom could chide me on my manners.

"This is my mother," I said primly. "Visiting for the holidays. It's so nice of you all to show her around."

Barton strolled over to look at the materials Mom had been examining. "Ah, negatives of old man Crundall's Acoma expedition. Fascinating. That's Sky City, if I'm not mistaken. It's been occupied for over two thousand years, the legends say. And, I adore having guests. I like to show off what Ms. Crundall's doing to everyone I can. She's a fine person, returning the collection to its rightful owners. I hope that more private collectors will follow her example."

Dalia took the knockoff Kokopelli, raised the object high, and turned in a circle. "Judith will feel better too. The spirits, returned to their people, will heal her."

Shasta pinched her temples and declared she

needed more coffee. Her boss frowned at her departing backside, but quickly returned to smooth charm. "Let us hope you're right, Dalia," he said. "May the spirits cure dear Judith."

Mom and I shared a skeptical eye roll, which was cut short by Dalia addressing us. "I know Mr. Hunter is a scientist and probably thinks I'm silly," she said. "So do all the doctors and specialists. Judith did too and is probably still merely humoring me. I kept telling her, though. There is darkness in keeping this collection, bad energy, the evil eyes of many cultures. Not the objects themselves, mind you. They're victims of my grandfather. They're sad. Weeping. Having them here, in this house, it's what's making Judith ill. She'll feel better when it's all gone."

Barton again excelled at diplomacy. "We mustn't judge your grandfather, Dalia. He was a man of his era and he did compile an extraordinary and extensive collection, unlike any I've ever seen."

Dalia, however, was ready to judge. "I don't know if Rita told you, Helen," she said to my mother. "But we have boxes full of bones. Human bones. My grandfather was an archeological grave robber."

Mom gasped.

Ick, I thought. No wonder architectural tours didn't let visitors peek in the closets or under the beds. You never could tell what these seemingly fine old mansions contained.

Barton smoothed over the horror. "Museums all over the world have similar items. Think of the mummies from Egypt or the Andes. Prehistoric hunters pulled fully preserved from peat bogs. Here in the U.S., the law compels federally funded museums to return sacred objects and human remains to their peoples. It's called the Native American Graves Protection and Repatriation Act. NAGPRA for short. It's a slow process and contentious too."

"Contentious," I repeated, my mind working. "Is anyone really upset about Judith repatriating her . . . ah . . ." What should I call them? Her bones? The unmentionable friends?

Barton set Eddie down and the boy ran over to jump on his grumpy sister's lap. "I suppose you could say that," Barton said slowly. "It's not the same as a museum, say, giving up one of its best-known pieces. Then the public might get up in arms. The Crundall collection is privately held, meaning that the federal law doesn't apply. Now, museums might secretly yearn for some pieces, but they'd know they couldn't ethically or legally acquire or keep them."

I nodded. I knew a little about this topic from the news. Local tribes had reclaimed various objects—and relatives—from universities and museums around the country.

Mom asked my next question for me. "Well then, who would care? It sounds like no one could object to Judith Crundall doing the right thing."

Barton agreed. "Private collectors could still legally buy her items. Believe me, many would kill for the chance. There's a lucrative market for Native American items, particularly sacred objects. Not only are they one of a kind, they're divine."

"Surely there's no market for the old bones," I murmured.

Barton shook his head, his face handsome puppy-dog sad. "Ah, that's where you're wrong. There's a market, a black one involving a lot of money. Speaking of bones, care to see some?"

Chapter 9

B ones, bones, bones," Eddie sang merrily.
"We're off to see the bones, bones, bones."
The situation was disturbing for several reasons. First, there was the bone ditty, which would
be creepy in any context. Coming from an adorable kindergartener, it sounded like a horror film
in the making. Second, there was Barton and me,
strolling down a cool, art-lined hallway like the
happy couple of the estate. We held Eddie between us, swinging his hands so he could kick up
his feet and "fly." Celia loved this game as a kid,
although Manny and I rarely got our swing co-
ordination right. Barton, Eddie, and I were eerily
in tune. Third, there was Mom, who'd practically
shoved me off with Barton, insisting that she'd
"just be in the way of you two young people."
Like that wasn't a blatant matchmaker line. Plus,
who could miss her pointed stare at the man's
well-manicured, ringless hand.

I wasn't worried about swooning over Barton

Hunter's smooth cuticles or charming dimples. Barton was too prettily handsome for my taste, although I could see his male-model appeal. If I ran into the British ladies again, I'd ask for some of their digital photos of Jake in hero cowboy mode to show Mom. Now that was a man I wanted to be alone with. Whenever that might be.

I refocused on positives. I was about to get a private tour of Judith Crundall's collection room. Plus, Mom had unknowingly helped my secret noninvestigation. Alone with Barton, I could ask him about Francisco and threats to devils.

"So Judith inherited this collection," I said as a way of breaking the spell of domestic bliss.

"Yes, and it truly is amazing. Her grandfather collected pottery, baskets, hide paintings, amulets . . . It's certainly not all bones, although that's what we're starting with, as well as the sacred and ceremonial objects." He smiled conspiratorially at me. "For Ms. Crundall's health, you understand."

I smiled back. "Dalia's my neighbor. I know about her spiritual healings. She sage smudged my former landlord's house so much I thought we'd need to have a smoke restoration company come in afterward."

"They're two very different sisters," Barton said diplomatically. "Different mothers from what I understand, but the same headstrong father. I think they both must have some of him in them. They're each stubborn idealists in their own way."

We stopped in front of a key-padded door. Barton punched numbers, and I thought about my sister and me. We had our differences. Kathy never found bodies, for one. She'd also stayed in our hometown and enjoyed a seemingly perfect marriage. Last I'd heard, her kids had played nice, nonsatanic pilgrims in their school's Thanksgiving performance. Maybe Celia and I had some of my father's genes. I wouldn't know. In the past, when I'd asked Mom about my father, she'd been uncharacteristically vague. Maybe I'd quiz her if she started pressing me about Jake again, which she surely would.

"Here we are," Barton said. Eddie ran in first. The windowless room had a dusty chill and was filled with rows of metal shelves packed with brown, archival boxes.

I looked around in awe. "Wow. The collection must be huge. You said there are baskets and nicer stuff? Why keep it hidden away? Doesn't Judith want to display some?" I felt bad that my Bundt pans were in a storage room at my landlord's house. If I had a real collection, I'd want to see it.

"It's better preserved this way," Barton said. "Stuff this valuable, you don't want the maid knocking it over with her feather duster."

I laughed. "That's one of my big worries!"

Barton chuckled. "Yeah, I hear you. More importantly, though, most of the collection isn't 'art' or items you'd display. The value is in its archeological and anthropological significance. Colleges or museums would be particularly interested in old man Crundall's notebooks and the material objects."

Barton led us down a few rows, his fingers grazing the boxes. "Ah, here. I was going to start working on this beauty today." He took a box down, opened the lid, and removed a black velvet cloth, revealing the suture marks of a pale, bare skull.

"A head!" Eddie exclaimed with wide-eyed awe. The kid was either a budding archeologist or future creepy skull collector.

Barton carefully reached inside and picked up the skull. "Yes, a cranium, actually, of a young woman. Probably in her late teens or early twenties. It's an interesting specimen. You can see here, from this indention, that she suffered a blow."

"Cranium," Eddie repeated reaching out his hand.

I drew back, repulsed. Poor woman. Bet she never counted on being hit on the head, let alone stuffed in a storeroom. "Who was she?" I asked.

Barton carefully replaced the black cloth. "Impossible to say. The bones were excavated in the late 1800s out in the Four Corners region. Some arrowheads Mr. Crundall collected in the same dig suggest this young lady lived in the 1200s or possibly earlier."

I forgot my revulsion and marveled. *So long ago.* What had this girl's life been like? Cass, Sky, Celia, and I had driven out to southwest Colorado a few years ago and hiked around the amazing cliff dwellings at Mesa Verde. I could barely comprehend the time spans or remember the names and eras of all the peoples who'd called the region home. I asked Barton how he kept it all in his head. "Are you from around here?"

"Me? No, I'm from all over. I go where my work takes me. I've been in this part of the world before, but I still have to keep on my toes. People can get awfully touchy about history in these parts, even thousand-year-old history."

I knew all about that. Cookie spellings and minor chile sauce modifications could get locals up in arms. "I've been living here full-time for a little over three years now," I said, gazing at the lost girl. "I still feel like an outsider sometimes, and there's a ton to learn."

Barton's eyes twinkled. "That's the fun part."

He was right. It was fun and I wished I could know more about the long-deceased woman in the box and how he planned to find her rightful home. However, I wasn't here for archeology or bone repatriation.

"You're feeling better?" I asked. "I heard you had to miss the play the other night."

He gently put the cranium back in the box. "Yeah, thank goodness! At the time, I was feeling awfully sorry for myself. Then I heard what happened. I could have ended up like this unfortunate woman." He gave me a wry smile. "That sounded terrible, didn't it? I feel truly terrible about what happened to Francisco."

"Did you know him?" I asked.

The handsome consultant shook his head slowly. "Just to say hello. He worked outside mostly, in the garden and fixing up the patio and walls. I'm holed up in here or the main archives room. I feel responsible. I should have been on that roof, not him."

Eddie, oblivious, grabbed Barton's hand and expanded on his bones song, adding in "cranium" and the even more disturbing refrain of, "Miss Rita has a secret. Secret, secret, secret."

Conscious of Edison's impressionable little

mind, not to mention his parroting repetition, I said, "You can't blame yourself. Migraines don't make appointments."

"Still," Barton said. "I keep thinking if only I'd done something differently. I rushed to a pharmacy to get my prescription medication, but it takes time to work and makes me dizzy immediately. I knew I couldn't get up on that roof."

"Absolutely not," I said, hoping he'd forgive himself. "Who else knew you couldn't make it?"

"Ms. Crundall and poor Francisco. It came on fast. I was working and planned to get into costume here and drive Ms. Crundall down. I felt like an ungrateful wimp begging off. It's not like a migraine is something other people can see, like a broken leg, you know? Francisco was here fixing a table in the archives room for me. Ms. Crundall recruited him as my replacement."

I gave what I hoped was a comforting smile. "Did you tell anyone else about the devil switch? Shasta? Someone at the pharmacy?"

Barton shook his head no. "No, I didn't think the pharmacist would care, and Shasta had left with Dalia to help with the donkey and goat. I think I owe Shasta a bonus. I hear that she thought I was dead and was actually worried. I must not be the world's worst boss."

I pondered who could have found out about the devil switch. Francisco had called Lorena Cortez. Maybe he'd called someone else too. Or maybe Lorena had told Wyatt and now didn't want to admit it. Or Wyatt could have recognized Francisco, the presumed romantic rival he'd banned from his hotel. I made a mental note to ask Manny these questions, not that I expected many answers from him.

Another idea occurred to me. What if murder hadn't been part of the plan? Perhaps someone simply wanted to scare Barton off and set Judith on a different path, and things got out of hand. "You said that some collectors would kill for the Crundall collection. Is there anyone particularly upset that Judith is giving it back rather than selling it?"

Barton didn't answer. He tucked the skull box under his arm and wandered down the row of shelving, tapping numbered labels as he went, Eddie skipping behind. I followed too, not skipping, and wondering how many of the neat cardboard boxes were coffins in disguise. Near the end of the row, Barton pulled out a small, slender box. "This goes off to the cataloging room, Edison," he said, handing the box to the child. "Can you carry it very carefully for me? Whatever you do, don't open it."

Eddie gripped the box and took off toward the door.

"No running," Barton called out. He and I followed. I wondered if he'd heard my question.

Barton shut and locked the door behind us. "You asked if anyone is upset," he said. "The police assured us that they have a suspect, someone with a beef against Francisco. Do you know otherwise? Why do you ask?"

Because I can't keep my nose out of crimes? Because I can't refuse nice people bearing pies? "I'm worried about my daughter being in the play," I said truthfully. "And about the other devils.

There are some . . ." I searched for the right word. "There are some questions still about whether Wyatt Cortez is the killer." Then I added, pointedly, "And if Francisco was the intended victim."

Frown lines creased his otherwise perfect forehead. For such a clever guy with millennia of historical facts stuffed in his head, he was taking a long time to catch on. "But if Francisco wasn't the target?" He paused. "You mean me?"

"You did say people would kill for some of the stuff in there," I reminded him. "With you gone or scared off, Judith might change her mind about the collection. Do you know someone who might think that way?"

Barton sighed. "*Someone,*" he said with a sarcastic edge. "But I doubt that someone's going to come after me with a pitchfork during a Christmas performance. A bit melodramatic, don't you think?"

"You don't know what people are capable of."

He gave me a smile that has probably melted weaker hearts. "And you do?"

"I do. I was married to a cop, and I've been involved in . . . well . . . incidents around town. You shouldn't brush off the possible danger."

His dimples really were cute. I wasn't about to take the handsome glow personally, though. Barton Hunter was probably the type who flirted with everyone. I used to think Jake was a serial flirter, until I realized he was aiming his charm primarily at me.

Barton thanked me for my concern and added, "Are you watching out for me? I'd like a pretty personal bodyguard."

Saying I had a boyfriend sounded way too presumptuous. I smiled and deflected. "So who is upset with Judith?"

The dimples dimmed. Barton hesitated, as if debating whether to tell me. "It's no one. I shouldn't have mentioned it."

"But if you or another devil might get hurt, and the next performance is Saturday night—"

My anxious speech was interrupted by the door to the main archives room swinging open. I cringed for the sake of Judith Crundall's perfect plastered walls. Shasta held a precarious stack of papers.

"More calls!" she announced, thrusting slips of pink paper at Barton. "That man from the Rosebud Reservation called again about some eagle feathers. And an elder from Ohkay Owingeh called. They're a Pueblo just to the north of here, you know? Anyway, he thinks we have some kind of ceremonial cloth of theirs. If we do, he demands it back, like last century, and also some turtle shells that he says would be theirs, definitely not Acoma's. If the turtles are here, he wants them back in time for the turtle dance on Christmas Eve. And that lady from Tesuque, she wants a timeline on some dress for their dance . . ." She paused to take a breath. "Long morning," she said by way of apology to me.

Tell me about it. I'd help spark a miniature livestock stampede and pretty much agreed to look into a Satan slaying. At least I didn't have to take Barton Hunter's messages or work for him. The charm he'd practically oozed at Mom and me had dried up. He ticked off orders to Shasta, telling her to call the eagle feather guy back pronto. "I don't know of those feathers right off, and we don't have time to look for them. The turtle-shell guy's called before, asking about other objects. He's grasping at straws. Everybody thinks we can send their stuff back yesterday. There's a process. Deflect, Shasta. That's what I'm paying you to do."

Her face went as red as her hair. For a moment, I thought she was about to snap back. I might have, but then Barton was her boss, and archeology grad students can't have tons of job opportunities in their field.

"Fine. I'll call them all back," she said, pushing her glasses into a new state of askew. Then she added, with admirably low sarcasm, "Anything else? Coffee? Lunch?"

"Cappuccino," Barton said briskly, before listing other tasks they—as in Shasta—needed to get done.

Time for me to get going too. I had my own lists to make and Mom to entertain and a teenage devil to check on. I told Barton and Shasta I'd get out of their way. "Thanks for showing me the collection. I've taken up too much of your time."

Shasta opened the door to the main archives room right at the moment Barton took me by the shoulders and kissed both my cheeks. Out of the corner of my eye, I spotted Mom, beaming. So much for my plans to issue a firm, professional handshake. "It has been my pleasure," he said.

"Thanks," I said stiffly, trying not to lean back too obviously. "I mean, thanks again for the tour. It was great." Except for the skull and Eddie's bone ditty and the awkward kisses.

Barton escorted me to my glowing mother. "I'd be happy to show you lovely ladies around anytime," he said. "We're never too busy."

Shasta's harried look said otherwise.

I waved to the kids. Eddie waved back. Emilie continued reading. At least she'd given up on her campaign to sue Mr. Peppers and me for *buñuelos* losses. I took Mom's arm and guided her toward the door. She was gushing about how we'd both "absolutely love" to come by again, especially me. She was right. I did want to return, although not for the reason she hoped.

We stepped outside, accompanied by Shasta, Barton, and Dalia.

"Thanks again. I have to get back to work," I said, hoping to ditch him and get Mom headed toward home. We had just stepped off the porch when a bright yellow SUV skidded into the driveway. Brakes squealed, gravel peppered my face, and I yanked Mom—hard—out of the way. She gasped, yet recovered quickly to grumble about reckless drivers. The vehicle was sporty and laden with roof and trunk racks. Thumpy bass beats vibrated the tinted windows until the driver shut off the engine and stepped out. He wore the too-big, childlike clothes of a ski dude. Baby blue nylon pants slipped below his hips and neon orange ski goggles held back a tussle of sun-bleached hair. He was probably in his late twenties and had a long, tanned nose with a characteristic dip. He raised the imperious nose, gave an offhanded "hey" greeting, and strode toward the house.

On his way, he patted Shasta on the butt. She stifled a yelp and a smile.

"You can't park there, Trey," Dalia said, jogging after him. "Your mother's physical therapist is coming this afternoon. She wants to take Judith out in her wheelchair for some lung cleansing."

"She can manage," the man said. "I live here too, you know."

He slammed the front door in Dalia's face, ending their conversation.

Barton leaned close to me. "You asked who's upset about the repatriation, Ms. Lafitte? I give you Judith's only son, the third William Harold, better known as Trey."

"Only son," I murmured.

"The heir apparent," Barton went on. "And in case it wasn't apparent, he changed his surname to Crundall following his father's death. The way he acts, he's already the lord of the manor. It's no secret what he'd do with the family collection."

"Keep it?" I asked, already guessing I was wrong.

Barton snorted. "Only long enough to find the highest bidder."

Chapter 10

Your sister touched stingrays," Mom announced later that evening. "She said they felt like wet velvet." We were hanging out in my tiny kitchen after dinner. Mom had insisted on washing and drying the dishes. I was seated at the table, staring at my laptop. Instead of checking e-mail like I told Mom, I was Googling men. Namely, Trey Crundall, Barton Hunter, and Francisco Ferrara. If Mom took the time to polish the glasses, I'd add Wyatt Cortez.

"That's nice," I said, distracted. Thanks to online newspapers and Trey's laxness about social media privacy, I'd learned that the Crundall heir was a low-ranking amateur snowboarder and ran a ski shop downtown. He'd studied at the University of New Mexico, where he'd majored in sports administration with a minor in anthropology. His extracurricular interest in marijuana legalization aligned with his police record. He'd been cited for transporting a backpack full of pot gummy bears and brownies out of Colorado. He also had over a dozen traffic citations, from speeding to driving off with a gas nozzle attached to his vehicle. In the dozens of online photos I found, he was either blissfully skiing and raising beers with buddies or zoning out in slack-jawed boredom at Crundall Foundation events. Nothing pointed to him working up the ambition to kill a fake devil.

I'd also skimmed through various news clips about Barton Hunter. He was mentioned in stories about wealthy collectors like Judith Crundall, who were doing the right thing with questionable collections. He'd served on some boards and penned opinion pieces, as well as academic articles. I only glanced at the academic pieces. His dry summary of pot shards from central Oklahoma wouldn't drive anyone to kill, I figured. The few photos of Barton I found included him looking good in suits at posh gatherings and supervising an archeological dig as a blonder, prettier Indiana Jones.

"The kids went swimming in the ocean," Mom said, shaking her head unhappily. "Did you know that shark attacks are quite common in central Florida? I looked it up." She pulled open my silverware drawer with a clatter. "You need a different drawer divider, Rita. Your dinner and salad forks are mixing."

I peeled my eyes from the computer screen, feeling guilty. I should be paying full attention to Mom. Just one more search . . .

"You're right," I said as I typed. "I would separate the forks, but there's no space."

Mom's voice brightened. "What if we moved those bowls you have over there into the cabinet here? Then you could clear out this drawer to the left and move all your spoons there, and I'm sure you must have items we could thin out."

My eyes drifted back to the screen, where search results for Francisco Ferrara + deadly accident awaited me. "Sure," I said, vaguely aware that I was sentencing my kitchen to total reorganization chaos. I noticed an article far down the screen. Francisco Ferrara, a professor of history and archeology, involved in a deadly accident on Christmas Eve, fifteen years ago.

"That's it," I murmured to myself.

"I knew you'd approve," Mom said, gathering up an armful of spoons and forks and dumping them on the table. "I'll just move the silverware and the can openers and other clutter to the right, and do you really need *all* these corkscrews, Rita? My goodness, *three* corkscrews?"

I let her have her way. She hummed happily as she worked. I skimmed a flurry of news stories. All said that there was no indication the perpetrator had been drunk. All discussed the victim, a hardworking single mother named Juanita Ortiz. She was my age at the time, walking home from work along a dark road, treacherous with ice. One article mentioned her young son, Angel, who would be taken in by relatives. The family, as expected, was devastated.

I gave silent thanks that my loved ones were inside and safe tonight and shut the computer. The accident had happened around this time of year but years ago. If a family member of the deceased woman wanted vengeance, why wait?

"Ta da!" Mom declared, waving a hand.

I dutifully got up and admired Mom's first emptied drawer, fearing I'd never find my vegetable peeler, let alone a corkscrew, again.

"I'll tuck away all the things you probably don't use very often," Mom said. "Like those wine and margarita glasses. Really, they shouldn't take up a whole cabinet, should they? You have such limited space."

"Sure, Mom," I said, resigned.

"You'll wonder why you didn't do this sooner," Mom said, patting me on the arm.

I thought about her words after she retired to the living room to watch *Jeopardy*. Had someone craving vengeance decided they'd waited long enough?

Mom went to bed by nine to keep on her "normal" Central Time zone schedule. I called Flori. I knew she'd still be up. I hoped she wasn't gearing up for another night of knit tagging.

"I need some information on Francisco, our dead devil," I said after polite greetings and apologies for disturbing her and Bernard. "I know it's late, but—"

"Perfect timing!" Flori said. "Come on over, I'm throwing a Knit and Snitch. Oops, Hazel's spiking the punch. Gotta go." She hung up.

I left Mom and Celia a note saying I'd run over to Flori's. I didn't describe the Knit and Snitch because I didn't know what it was.

Flori ushered me in out of the cold. "The gang's all here," she said.

The gang, crowded around Flori's long dining

table, consisted of seven elderly women and Bill Hoffman, the kingpin of Flori's elderly informant network. Bill, now in his nineties, had suffered insomnia for decades. To while away long nights, he kept track of international gossip over a ham radio and local happenings with a police scanner.

I wondered which he was listening to tonight. Headphones suitable for a nightclub DJ covered his ears and he was writing on a yellow notepad. The rest of the group brandished knitting needles, some in shapes and sizes I'd never seen before. One lady worked yarn around a hoop the size of a basketball net. Another wielded four needles and several balls of yarn. The lady sitting at the far end of the table brandished needles the length of my arm and yarn the thickness of my finger.

"Those needles are massive," I said to Flori, nodding toward the jumbo knitter. "What's she making? Socks for a brontosaurus?"

"How did you guess?" Flori said.

I decided I didn't need—or want—to know any more about Flori's rogue knitting pals and their nocturnal activities. I told Flori it was nice that her friends were visiting.

"I summoned them," she said. "It's like those quilting groups where they stitch and . . ." She hesitated. "It isn't a nice word." Flori, who has no qualms about pinching hunks and breaking and entering, is chaste as an angel when it comes to swearing.

"Stitch and bitch," said a sweet-looking grand-motherly type with fluffy white hair and a massive margarita in her hand.

"Hi, Miriam," I said to Flori's rogue knitting partner.

Miriam raised the margarita. "After sunset, I'm the Silver Purl."

Flori explained the knitting group. "Unlike those foul-tongued quilters, we're getting stuff done. We're sleuthing while we work."

I held in a groan. When I left with the kids this morning, hadn't Flori promised to keep our investigation both preliminary and a secret? Now all these knitting snitchers knew, and worse, so did Bill. He raised a milky blue eye, took me in, checked his watch, and made a note.

"Come sit and knit," Flori said. "Would you like a drink?"

Would I ever! However, I couldn't sneak back home with margarita on my breath. Mom would catch me for sure. I settled on hot apple cider and squeezed in at a far corner of the table beside Flori, who handed me needles and a ball of black yarn so I could "blend in." She knew full well I couldn't knit. She'd tried to teach me and had finally given up, telling me I was "good at other things."

I rewound the ball of yarn for something to do. The ladies on my other side were discussing knit targets, including the statue of the dancer in front of the Pájarito. The lady with the basketball hoop called dibs on making the dancer a warmer loin cloth. Snickering laughter erupted. This was definitely Flori's kind of group.

"Ah, the Indian brave. He's right under the scene of the crime," Flori said, loud enough to cut across the giggles.

A hush fell over the group, save the clicking of needles and Bill's radio squawking.

Flori continued. "Remember, the first person who provides evidence to solve the devil killing gets free meals at Tres Amigas for a whole year."

Margarita glasses clinked.

I groaned. Flori chronically gave away free meals in exchange for information. The meals were redeemable with secret code words that I could never keep straight, and Flori refused to keep a written list. The codes were secret, she said. Plus, there was informant confidentiality to consider.

Across the table, a woman with a thick silver bob drew out a flask and doused her coffee cup. She took a slug, breathed out like a seasoned shot drinker, and declared that she'd solved the crime.

"That's nice, Hazel," Flori said. "But you only get the free meals if you provide real, solid evidence."

Hazel pursed her lips. "Well, it's obvious who did it, isn't it?"

A few people murmured Santa and Wyatt Cortez.

"No, no," Hazel said. "Come on, we have better memories than the young people give us credit for." She looked challengingly around the group. Everybody but me, Flori, and note-scribbling Bill had their eyes fixed on their knitting.

"The Ortiz family, of course," Hazel said. She raised her cup in the direction of Flori and me.

I'd reached the end of my ball of string. I picked up my needles and wrapped some yarn around one. "You mean the relatives of the woman Francisco Ferrara accidentally killed?" I said, trying to sound casual as I cocooned the needle in yarn.

Miriam coughed pointedly at the word *accidentally*.

"So you don't think it was an accident?" I asked.

Miriam admitted that it was "technically" ruled an accident. "But my niece's friend was at that party," she added. "She was one of the servers. She said that everyone had at least one drink. Who knows if Mr. Ferrara didn't have more? He wouldn't let the police give him a Breathalyzer test. That's suspicious, isn't it? The Ortiz family must think so."

"Exactly," said Hazel, in a "case-closed" tone.

I was wondering how many tipsy ladies I could stuff in my car. They were all pretty petite. Probably four, and I could do a couple runs. None of them should be driving either.

Flori, showing off her mind-reading talent, said, "It's a good thing our group dues pay for taxi rides home, isn't it, ladies?"

Hazel grumbled that her last taxi driver wouldn't wait when she jumped out to tie a lovely knit hat on a statue. "Just because it was in Cathedral Park, he claimed it was sacrilegious and drove off and left me." She shrugged. "I got more done without him."

I was thinking more about the dead woman's son and other relatives. "I wonder what happened to the son. Angel? Was that his name? Didn't he go to live with his grandmother?" I silently thanked the Internet for allowing me to sound in the know. Now if YouTube could teach me how to knit.

No one answered right away. Several sets of eyes flicked nervously to Flori.

Flori put down the piece she was working on, which I feared was another ski mask. "I'll say it. I'm not afraid of her. Josephina Ortiz was my school chum back in the day. She's a witch, and her grandson Angel's a killer."

I gaped at Flori.

"See!" Hazel crowed.

Needles clicked. Everyone else kept quiet, except Miriam, who politely asked me what I was knitting. "Such a lovely yarn choice," she said.

I put my hands over the embarrassing yarn lump and asked the obvious questions. "A witch and a killer?" Hazel might actually have solved the case. "Who did he kill? When?"

"Angel was a juvenile at the time," Flori said. "So his name wasn't in the papers."

"But people heard," Miriam said, nodding at Bill. "It's rather sad. Angel had a difficult childhood and I don't think he meant to kill. It was a schoolyard brawl. He punched someone, hard, and the young man fell and hit his head and died. Tragic all around. Angel's actually turned into quite a nice young man. I heard he's a wonderful baker and he takes care of his grandmother."

His grandmother the witch. I waited for someone to bring up that topic. Hazel obliged.

"She's not really a witch," Hazel said belligerently. "That's only something superstitious villagers up in the mountains believe."

"She might be a witch," the lady closest to me said. "If she wants to be. She is rather frightening and, besides, we mustn't judge."

Flori agreed. "To each her own. I will say, Josie has always had a way with casting the evil eye and issuing curses. All the women in her family do. Her mother was legendary." To me, she said.

"Rita, you'll be interested to know that Josie worked at the Inn of the Pajarito for many years. I hear she still shows up there a lot. Wyatt Cortez lets her walk about and rest in the housekeepers' lounge. She gets a bit muddled about times and decades."

Sympathetic murmurs for the forgetful witch went around the table, and the conversation turned to the logistics of knitting giant socks for the green dinosaur mascot of the Sinclair gas station.

"What does Josephina Ortiz look like?" I asked Flori.

Flori smiled, sending her wrinkles fanning across her round, rosy cheeks. "Josie hasn't aged well. She was about your height. A trouble with her back makes her my height nowadays. She likes to wear black and shawls. No pointy hat. She's not a Halloween witch. She's a *bruja*, more mischievous than mean."

I was beginning to picture her perfectly. "She speaks Spanish?"

"Oh yes, that's what she spoke at home as a girl."

I left soon after, but not before setting the Knit and Snitchers on the task of locating Josephina and Angel Ortiz. As Flori pointed out, Josephina wasn't the type to list her number and address in the phone book. Stepping out into the cool air, I dodged an incoming taxi. I was feeling pretty good. I'd gotten what I came for, a new motive and a lead on either a witness or a killer. The trouble would be explaining to Manny that I'd actually seen a witch.

Chapter 11

"Manny always loved my thumbprints," Mom said. I knew she meant a favorite holiday cookie, though my mind flashed to an absurd image of Manny collecting cookie-dough fingerprints. I imagined my ex in his supercop mode, dusting cookies and cordoning off baking sheets with crime scene tape.

"Everyone loves your thumbprints, Mom," I said.

She waved off the praise modestly and pressed her thumb into another ball of vanilla-flavored dough. It was Friday evening, and we'd eaten our comforting baked ziti early to clear space for cookie production. Christmas carols played on the radio, Celia sat at the kitchen table beside me, and Hugo purred at my feet.

Celia dug out a last spoonful of lemon curd and filled a thumbprint. Back home, Mom used her own homemade strawberry jam. Here, we were using up some of the half-empty jelly jars that mobbed the back of my fridge. Blueberry, strawberry, lemon marmalade, and prickly pear thumbprints already cooled on the counter.

The prickly pear jelly was pale apricot in color and impressively homemade by Dalia using fruits harvested from our yards. I'll admit, I was a little skeptical, having had a painful run-in with local cactuses. But Dalia had a hot method for removing the spines. She burned them off using a small kitchen torch. For good measure, she strained the pulp three times. The remaining juice was slightly tangy with elusive hints of strawberry, watermelon, and bubblegum. I loved it. Mom had deemed it "interesting."

I helped myself to a barely cooled cactus thumbprint. Celia polished off a raspberry jam version. My sometimes sullen teen had cracked over a week's allotment of smiles during cookie making.

"These are great, Gran," she said. "Have you tried Flori's *bizcochitos*? They're award-winning, like your thumbprints."

Mom beamed at the mention of her county fair win and vowed to try a *bizcochito*. "They're not spicy, are they?"

"Only when Flori rolls them in cinnamon sugar with hot pepper in it," Celia said, devilishly. I decided not to mention Flori's other additions of lard and wine.

Mom took out the final tray of thumbprints. "What flavor do you think your father would like best, Celia?" she asked.

"I don't think we have to worry about—" I started.

Mom interrupted. "Really, Rita, be nice. It's the holidays, and Manny worked so hard capturing that awful Santa. Now if your lawyer friend hadn't gotten him out of jail . . ."

Celia wisely kept her head down and focused on nibbling cookie crumbs.

"Jake's simply providing a basic right," I said, glossing over the fact that he charged hefty fees for this right. "Presumption of innocence," I continued grandly. "And Santa could actually be innocent. We can't have an innocent Santa go to jail on Christmas, can we?"

Mom looked up. She'd moved on to her wonderful, soft gingerbread cookie recipe. Molasses globbed in slow motion into her measuring cup. "Oh?" she said, raising her eyebrows. "Why would you think he's innocent? We both saw him. He certainly *looked* like a killer, Rita. You're not getting involved, are you? Not after we talked . . ."

We hadn't really talked. Mom had issued a warning and I'd evaded the issue. I knew I had no chance of coming out ahead in this conversation. I'd either have to outright lie or upset my mother.

"Jake's a good and honest man," I said, sticking to the truth. "With a sweet tooth too."

Celia joined in Jake's defense. "Yeah, we can make Jake a plate of cookies. He'll love these cactus thumbprints and your gingerbread cookies, Gran. Maybe we can make dog biscuits for his bulldog, Winston. We'll say they're a gift from Hugo."

I smiled gratefully at Celia.

"He *would* like cactus cookies," my mother said, as if she expected such questionable behavior from a man she was still calling an ambulance chaser.

I offered up another lovable characteristic. "Jake

makes his grandmother's recipe for sweet mince-meat empanadas every year," I said. "They're little hand pies, with dried fruits, spices, and brown sugar. You'd love them, Mom. They remind me of Grandma's apple mince pie. Jake said he was going to bake a batch this weekend and give us some."

"Does he make his own crust?" Mom demanded.

I had to reveal that he used pre-made tortilla dough if frying the pies, or store-bought pie crusts if he was baking. I laughed it off. "Men, right? It's impressive he's making pies, though. He makes fabulous biscuits too, with lots of butter and a maple syrup glaze." I stopped myself before pointing out that Manny's culinary aptitude began and ended at microwave dinners, and even then he'd managed to mess up his Hungry-Man meals.

Mom acknowledged that biscuit making was nice. She wiped her hands on her apron and said, "So, have you met his mother and father?"

"Not yet," I said, feeling like I was failing a test. Mom launched into a storm of questions about his parents' ages, why and when Jake divorced, and what other relatives I may—or may not—have met. I told her what little I knew, most of which came from Flori. According to her, Jake's ex-wife was a filmmaker and had left Jake for the greener pastures of Hollywood. I didn't mention that Jake had been brokenhearted and waited as wistfully as Winston for a couple years, hoping she'd return. That worried me a little. Did he still have a spark for his ex? I'd seen her photo on a film Web site and like everyone said, she was tall, blond, and beautiful.

"I met a cousin," I added, with more enthusiasm than the event warranted. The cousin was a bland accountant named Bob who worked in Albuquerque and seemed nice enough. Jake and I had run into Bob at a coffee shop. The meeting hadn't been planned. Doubt crept around the edges of my brain. *Why hadn't I met his parents?* They lived near Taos, only an hour's drive away up the Rio Grande. Jake and I had taken a day trip up that way in the fall. We'd stopped to gaze at golden aspen leaves and eat at a humble café known for its green chile cheeseburgers and bulldog mascots. Winston had been delighted. I had a photo on my phone of him drooling over his new bulldog girlfriends.

Maybe Jake was feeling protective of our relationship, like me. I reached for another cookie, thinking I should have kept the secret longer.

Thankfully, Mom turned her attention to Celia and her friends. "So, this boy Sky you hang out with . . ." Mom said.

Celia coolly informed Mom that Sky had a boyfriend. "A supercute guy from the prep school," she said, landing hefty disdain on "prep."

Mom, to her credit, said that was very nice for Sky. "Sky's good-looking and polite. A nice boy. No young gentlemen for you, dear? Did your school have a Christmas dance?" When Celia scrunched her face in disgust, Mom supplied tales of my dancing woes. "I remember when Rita and Albert Ridgeland—he has a lovely dental practice now—went off to junior prom. I had to put my yardstick between them, they were dancing so close."

"Albert was a clutcher, Mom, and sweaty," I said. That night marked the launch of my disastrous, foot-stomping dance moves. I munched on a cactus cookie, hoping to wipe away the memory.

Celia grinned. "I don't dance," she told her grandmother. "I don't have time for boys either, other than friends."

"You're a smart girl," my mother said. "I'm sure you'll know the right boy when you meet him. Take your time. But not too long."

I got anxious just thinking of that advice.

Celia took it in stride. "How did you know, Gran?" Celia asked. "How did you and . . . ah . . . Granddad meet?"

I could understand her terminology trouble. Celia had never known her grandfather, and I only had a five-year-old's foggy memory of him. I saw my chance to quiz Mom. "Yeah, Mom. Tell us some stories about you and Dad," I said. "Was there dancing? Smooching on Great-Gran's porch?"

Mom stared at the gingerbread recipe printed on a faded, smudged card I'd carried around since college. She waved a hand. "Oh, I don't know. That was so long ago. I don't recall. Are you sure you wrote out the spice measurements correctly in this recipe, Rita? This looks like an awful lot of ground cloves."

Was Mom employing my time-honored deflection technique? Mom, who'd been fussing that I didn't share enough? Celia raised an eyebrow over her milk glass. Mom continued muttering about the spice proportions and stuck her head in the fridge, presumably looking for cold butter, though I knew the recipe called for good old-fashioned Crisco. It was Christmas, I decided. We should all be allowed some deflection.

I changed the subject. "I think we should all go

get a Christmas tree for outside. Jake's secretary is making birdseed ornaments and popcorn strings that would be perfect. He could help us haul the tree and decorate."

"That would be nice, dear," Mom said, and I swear she breathed a sigh of relief. "I do miss my Christmas tree."

"We can get some white lights," I said, feeling bad that we hadn't re-created more of Mom's holiday traditions. "We'll decorate the porch in lights," I said, "And I can get electric candles for the window. It'll be just like home."

Mom looked dubious, especially when Celia announced that it was time for devil practice.

"You don't have to drive me, Mom," my teenager said as we sat in the driveway waiting for the car to warm above frigid sputtering. The night was cloudless and a nearly full moon glowed behind the cottonwood towering over my landlord's house.

"You won't even know I'm there," I said, which was always a lie in teenager's ears.

"Yeah, right," Celia said. Sounding more cheery, she said, "If you're hoping to hear the play's canceled, don't waste your time. We all got a message today from Ms. Crundall herself. She says the play must go on! Francisco would want us to and we can't let bully creeps scare us. Anyway, Dad says they have their man. They just need more evidence."

I tactfully kept quiet. Manny hadn't exactly embraced my tip about Angel and Josephina Ortiz as potential suspects/witnesses. He'd been predictably snarky when I told him that the elderly Ortiz was a real live witch and not a figment of my imagination, as he'd suggested the night of the murder. He'd then recounted the futile afternoon he'd spent interviewing Wyatt Cortez's staff of un-jolly elves. None of the elves would say anything bad about their boss, although Manny gleaned that they hadn't been pleased with their costumes.

"I'll hover in a dark corner with Cass," I said. "She's going with Sky. I won't be the only concerned mother there."

Celia gave a skeptical sniff. "I'm going to have to make Sky an extra-tall imp costume. He says he won't let me go up on the roof alone. Dad says the same thing, but he can wear his cop costume."

"Think of us all as your biggest fans," I said.

Celia said suspiciously. "*All* of you?"

"Jake and I will be there too," I said, in a tone that invited no debate.

"Whatever," my daughter said. "If you're going to be visible from the street, wear something red and jump around like you're meant to be there. That could be cool. An entourage of imps."

I'm an invisible mother," Cass said, when I found her hovering in a dimly lit spot near the "hombres" restroom.

"Then we're a club," I laughed. "I promised to hide in a dark corner."

My friend tucked a stray length of long blond hair back into a loose bun held up by a turquoise knitting needle.

I nodded toward to the needle. "Where'd you get that?"

Cass reported finding it by downtown art. "You know that wonderful grouping of stone fish heads on Marcy Street? The fish are suddenly wearing stocking caps and scarves. The work of someone we know, I'd guess? I found calling cards for Night Knitter and Silver Purl and thought I could negotiate some free muffins in exchange for the needle."

"I'm sure that could be arranged," I said.

We were in the "Grande Banquet Hall" of a restaurant on the Plaza. The place had changed hands recently and the new owners had gone all in for taxidermy décor. I looked over my shoulder at a moth-bitten buffalo beside us. I couldn't imagine why anyone would think banquets and deceased buffalo went together. Or banquets and all the other unfortunate creatures hanging from the walls. I avoided the glass eyes of a bodiless antelope and a roadrunner frozen mid-stride on a sideboard.

"Yuck," I said.

Cass agreed. "They're supposed to make fabulous margaritas here, but who wants to drink them if you're surrounded by dead wildlife? The bar area downstairs is worse, floor to ceiling stuffed fish and other aquatic beings."

As we made small talk about all the taxidermy

we'd never decorate with, I kept my eye on Celia.
She and Sky stood by a snacks table, chatting with
some of the other younger cast members. Sky,
taller by at least half a foot, hovered next to Celia,
the perfect best friend, protector, and backup imp.
I thanked Cass for her son's diligence.

She shifted farther from the buffalo. "Sky's kind
of shaken by that devil's murder. He was down
by the singers that night and looked up and saw
you miming death," Cass said. "He said he knew
right away what you meant, so he ran to check on
Celia." She smiled. "You do manage to find . . .
excitement."

You could call it that. Or trouble.

"Ooo . . ." Cass said, nudging me. "Look at what
someone added to the snacks table. Tamales. I
bet they're the sweet kind. I spent the whole day
working on holiday necklace orders and didn't
have time to eat. I don't suppose our kids would
deny their own mothers food."

I was happy for the excuse to join the performers, as well as Dalia and Judith. Judith sat in her
wheelchair, pale and hunched. Cass grabbed a
plate and started down the food table. I snagged
a Mexican wedding cookie as weighty as a snow-
ball and went to join Judith.

With a veined hand, she waved away my reintro-
ductions. "Yes, yes, I remember you. I'm not that
dotty yet. You're Celia's mother. I can see the re-
semblance. She's a fine young devil. I'm proud to
finally have a young lady playing that role." Her
smile cracked to a cough. When she'd recovered
her composure, she said. "We girls couldn't play
such parts when I was young. Foolish convention."

"I'm proud of her," I said, wondering how I could politely bring up her dead devil.

Judith did it for me. "She's brave too, after what happened with our first devil. A girl after my own heart. I don't want anyone to worry, though. I've hired extra security. You see those big men by the buffet?"

I had noticed the beefcakes in tight black shirts hungrily eyeing the cookie platters.

Judith coughed again. Dalia fussed over her sister, urging her to hold a kachina. The wooden figure was clothed in hide and decorated in fur and ragged feathers. "The eagle spirit will make you stronger, Judith. Say the prayers we worked on."

Judith stuffed the figure into the cup holder of her wheelchair. "Honestly, Dalia, if a dozen medical specialists can't cure me, I don't see how old dolls will." For good measure, she reached up and batted at the feathered dream catcher dangling like a child's mobile above her. "I look like a fool."

Dalia's Zen training was paying off. She smiled serenely and fluffed Judith's afghan. "Now, now, what's the harm?" she asked. "Better than those doctors irradiating you with their scanners."

I changed the subject back to the bodyguards and thanked Judith for providing them. "I'm the one who found Mr. Ferrara's body," I added. "I'm sorry. I know he worked for you."

Judith, who'd just given the dream catcher another firm whap, put her arm down and looked truly sad. "I do feel bad about Francisco. I volunteered him for the devil job after pretty Mr. Hunter could barely hold his head up. I thought it would be good for Francisco. The man punished himself too much. Then look what happens, some nut goes and kills him." She shook her head slowly and let Dalia put the kachina in her hand.

"Some nut?" I asked. "Then you don't think the killer targeted Francisco?"

Judith shrugged. "Wyatt Cortez is a fool. Silly man thinks that playing jolly in a Santa costume will fix his marriage. I can't see him stabbing Francisco. You ask me, the police have the wrong man. They don't ask old women, though, do they?"

They didn't ask me either, or listen to my tips. "So who do you think did it?" I asked, taking a shot.

The hacking cough kept Judith from answering. "Not a clue. If you'd told me last week that someone in *Las Posadas* was going to die, I'd have bet on me." She reached up and sent the dream catcher spinning. "And my dear son wouldn't mind one bit."

Chapter 12

I met Cass back at the buffalo. She slipped me a sheath of waxed paper, like a spy passing off illicit documents. Dalia stood at the podium, trying to dislodge the microphone to give to Judith.

"Try this," Cass whispered as Dalia tapped the microphone and said, "Testing, testing, namaste, greetings."

My mind was still on Judith. Did she think that Trey wanted to kill her? But why would he kill Francisco? I opened the wax paper triangle and thoughts of murder vanished. "Oh my gosh, piñon brittle!"

My friend nodded. "Yep, pure gold. Misty Crowe brought it. The pine nuts are harvested from her family ranch, all by hand. Must have taken forever, and then to shell these tiny things?" She nibbled her own bit of brittle appreciatively.

Local piñon brittle truly was a rare treat. I savored a bite, trying to detect if Misty Crowe had added anything special to the melted sugar and nut mix. A dash of smoked red chile powder, I thought, likely from her home village of Chimayo. The little village attracted thousands of pilgrims, drawn to a chapel that boasts miraculous, curative dirt. Culinary pilgrims also flocked there, seeking out the heirloom chiles.

Having failed to get the microphone to her sister, Dalia was giving a combination pep talk/obituary. "We all mourn the loss of our fellow performer, Francisco," she said, to light applause and a few amens. "He performed in *Las Posadas* over two decades ago and had returned this year to help. Let us take a moment to remember him."

Cass and I bowed our heads. I sneaked a peek, curious what the rest of the performers were doing. Some seemed to be praying. Others were scavenging the buffet table. Could one of them have recognized Francisco behind his devil mask? It seemed like a long shot. I recognized many of the performers. They were nice people who sang in the choir at Flori's church and came to the café. Some were elderly, others closer to Celia's age. Would one of them really strike down a fellow cast member? The dark side of my brain told me they might. On the other hand, why interrupt their own play? And why then and on the rooftop of the Pajarito?

My thoughts shifted to Wyatt in crazed Santa mode. Maybe I was overthinking the crime. How much easier if the murder had been spontaneous, fueled by anger and jealousy and the stress of playing a jolly hotel Santa.

Dalia called for another round of applause, this

time for the *Las Posadas* bodyguards. "Gentlemen,"
she said theatrically. "Take a bow." The three men
gave rather bashful waves. The tallest one, bald
with a tattoo necklace, wiped powdered sugar
from his black outfit. The shortest and pudgiest
hid a cookie behind his back.

"They're trained in all sorts of defensive tech-
niques," Dalia said. Then she quickly added,
"We don't expect that these fine gentlemen will
have to employ their skills. The police have a suspect, whom I won't name but some of you surely
know. That person is out on bail but being closely
monitored with an ankle bracelet. During our
performances, he will be under constant police
surveillance. There is no need to worry."

She then smoothly transitioned into the planned
changes to the route and the devil lineup. Barton
Hunter, she said, would bravely play the first
devil. Young Celia Martin would go next, newly
stationed at a taproom with a second-story patio
overlooking the Plaza.

I didn't hear about the third devil. I was too busy
mentally weighing the pluses and minuses of Celia's venue. On the positive side, I'd been in the
taproom and knew it would be easy to guard the
balcony entrance. Jake and I and the rest of Celia's
guardian entourage could also stay out of sight.
On the other hand, the bar was often crowded
and might be hard to fully monitor. Then there
was Mom. First Celia was a devil. Now she was a
devil performing at a beer joint.

Cass spotted one of her jewelry clients and went
to say hi. I headed for the buffet table as an excuse
to check on Celia. On the way, I stopped to intro-

duce myself to one of the guards. His name tag
said "Gary" and he had powdered sugar on his
chin.

"That's my daughter," I said, pointing toward
Celia. She was laughing as she and a cute dark-
haired boy stood on tiptoes to place devil horns
on Sky's head. His imp headpiece reminded me of
Sidekick's nubby goat horns. "You and the other
guys take good care of her," I told Gary.

He mumbled that he would and blushed.

Geez, where had Dalia hired these guys? Bashful Security Company? I, however, wasn't one to
talk.

A hand, firm and warm, gripped my shoulder.
I smelled masculine aftershave and felt the presence of a cheek near mine. Instinctively, I leaned
back, feeling the scruff of a male chin. Then,
with a jolt, I realized it wasn't the scruff I was
expecting.

"Oh my gosh, I'm so, so sorry!" I said to the
smiling face of Barton Hunter. "I thought you
were someone else."

"My bad," he said. "Or my good luck." His tone
matched his devilish attire, trim black jeans and
a black T-shirt printed with a red outline of a
devil head. "I apologize. I'll admit, I was spying
over your shoulder, hoping to find more of that
fabulous brittle. I'll settle for this." He selected a
caramel-topped brownie, brushing my arm as he
did.

"Want to introduce me to your daughter?" he
said. "I'm really behind compared to the other
performers now and I hear Celia's the best devil
around."

Celia scowled when she saw me approaching. "I can't go yet, Mom. Dalia got a voice coach from the Santa Fe Opera to come in. She's going to help us project."

The woman in question was as petite as Flori. She raised her head, touched her breastbone, and, in a voice so powerful and dark it seemed to come from the depths of Hades, pronounced "*Váyanse de aquí!* Be gone!"

"Awesome, right?" Celia said.

Awesome enough to give me chills. I explained that I was just introducing Barton Hunter, fellow devil. "He's working on Judith Crundall's collection," I said. "Remember? Gran and I were down there the other day?"

Celia said, "Hey," the teenage version of salutations.

Sky thrust out his hand. "I know about your work," he said, voice filled with awe. "I read about you in the paper. My father is from Tesuque Pueblo. He's part of the ceremonial dancers, and he says you're getting a drum back to us and costumes for the Eagle and Bear dances. Oh, I'm Sky Clearwater, in case, you know, you need to know."

Barton shook his hand vigorously. "Pleased to meet you, Sky. I believe I met your father when I visited Tesuque. A fine artist and exceptional community supporter. You tell him, my assistant and I are busy working through the collection and as soon as we document the items properly, we'll be delivering them personally."

"When will that be?" Sky asked. "In time for the Christmas dances? We're doing the Eagle Dance this year. I'm participating."

I hoped to take Mom to one of the Pueblo dances.

Celia, Cass, and I had gone to a performance at Tesuque over the summer. We'd stood on the sidelines with members of Sky's family and watched hundreds of dancers fill the dirt plaza. I'd seen dances before, but I was always entranced by the rhythmic drumming and chants, the dancers disappearing into the sacred underground kiva, and the mingling of native and Catholic spiritualties. I was equally amazed by the feast afterward, when families opened their homes to friends, relatives, and total strangers. I'd tried to imagine strangers squished onto Mom's sofa, waiting for space to open up at a rotating table of guests. Mom would be in a panic. Heck, I would be too! On the other hand, Mom and Aunt Sue would love some of the popular feast foods, like macaroni salads and fancy Jell-O dishes.

Barton and Sky were talking about a hide cape that Barton had sent out for cleaning. "Private collections can be a challenge," Barton said. "Let's just say the record keeping isn't what it is in museum collections."

With Celia booming her lines in the background, I half listened as Sky described an internship he'd done at the Native American arts museum downtown. He added, with a frown, "I've heard things about the Crundall collection."

Barton shook his head, his expression wry. "It's going to good places now." He waved the remaining half of his brownie. "You seem like an enthusiastic young man. If you want a holiday job, you're welcome to help."

Sky nodded eagerly.

Barton continued. "There's one caveat. We're dealing with a lot of bones at present."

Sky drew back, as if the words were a rattle-snake. "No, sorry," he said, a blush rising to his cheeks. "My dad. My people, we don't . . . we don't talk about or touch those things."

"A lot of people don't," Barton said kindly, soothing Sky's clear anxiety. "It's best that way."

Barton was up next for vocal practice. I drifted back to the taxidermied buffalo and Cass, who was checking her phone. "Ugh. The holidays," she said, sounding like Manny. "I'm so behind on custom jewelry orders! What were you, Sky, and Mr. Handsome chatting about?"

I reported that Sky had almost gotten a job. "Handling the Crundall collection bones," I said. "He turned it down."

Cass shuddered. "I should hope so. His father and I were never a couple per se, but I learned a bit about Pueblo philosophies. Even speaking of the dead by name is taboo. Handling bones would be a big no-no. Sky's a pretty modern, mixed-culture kid. Taboo or not, though, I wouldn't want him spending his holiday messing with bones."

In the center of the room, the singers had assembled and were warming up with "Feliz Navidad." Celia, Barton, and Devil Number Three flexed their jumping muscles. I hummed along, enjoying the fun Christmas moment and thinking I wouldn't be seeing this in Bucks Grove, Illinois.

Out of the corner of my eye, I thought I saw movement by a stuffed black bear, posed in claws-out mauling mode. The bear, like the buffalo, looked slightly mangy and wouldn't be coming back to life. I nudged Cass. "I thought I saw something over by the bear."

Cass squinted. "I don't see anything except Smokey's stuffed mama."

Neither, apparently, did the security guards. Gary was gazing longingly toward the desserts, and the next nearest guy could have been napping behind his dark glasses.

"There," I said. "Look! The witch!"

"What?" Cass said, but I was already moving around the buffalo, gesturing for her to follow. I whispered. "From the rooftop, the night of the murder. Her name's Josephina. Flori says she's an old schoolmate and into cursing people. Flori didn't know where she was living. Manny thought she was a figment of my imagination." She was certainly no figment. She wore layers of gray tonight, a coat, shawl, and hood draped over her crooked back.

Cass reached for her phone and pressed the video button. "He won't think that now. What are we going to do?"

"Stay back and watch," I said. How embarrassing to be afraid of a little old lady. Just then the lady in question turned and looked me straight in the eye. "*El diablo!*" she hissed, pointing to Celia and friends. She clutched what looked like rags of tattered fabric covered with feathers.

"Hey!" Gary finally perked up. "Ma'am? Are you in the play?"

Josephina spun and muttered something that made Gary shrivel back. Then she scuttled from the room.

Before I could say anything, Cass said it for me. "Follow that witch!"

Chapter 13

'd never dare say so, but Josephina reminded me of Flori, if only in her ability to evade. By the time I'd caught Celia's frowning attention with my gestures of "be right back," pointing, and miming spy glasses, Josephina was scooting down the stairs and headed for the exit.

"Fast little thing, isn't she," Cass said as we jogged down the stairs.

"Let's hang back," I said, only partially out of fright.

We smiled at the hostess stationed near the front door. "Waiting for a friend," I said, in lieu of "Tailing a witch."

The hostess returned to studying her seating chart. Cass peeked out the door. "She's going around the corner."

We followed, keeping several yards and strolling tourists between us and Josephina. A kid on a skateboard zoomed past us. People scattered and I momentarily lost sight of our witchy target.

"Where'd she go?" I asked. Josephina was gone. I sniffed the air and thought I caught a whiff of sulfur, the devilish stench I'd smelled the night of the murder. Just as quickly, the smell was gone, replaced by sweet piñon smoke and the delicious perfume of a nearby bakery. *Don't be silly*, I chided myself. She's an old lady with a bad back. The witching could be a rumor, or a hobby, or a perfectly acceptable belief system.

"There!" Cass said. She pointed down the street, where the passenger door to a low-slung truck was closing. "Shoot! I think she got in that truck."

We jogged down the street. Cass held out her cell phone with the video function on. *Here was something for Mom's Christmas memories*, I thought. I imagined the jiggly footage of dark sidewalks, our feet, and a blurry witch getting away.

The truck pulled out, revved its motor in a throaty, sputtering roar, and then inched forward at a snail's pace.

"Dang," Cass said, fiddling with her phone. "I can't get the zoom to work. I wanted to get the license plate."

So much for our tailing. The truck had picked up speed. The best we could do was see which way it turned, not that it would tell us much. I hoped that Manny—or the Knit and Snitchers—could track down Josephina and her grandson. If one of them was the murderer, though, I didn't have to worry. They'd have killed for revenge. They wouldn't be going after my daughter and the other devils. *Unless Josephina was really off her rocker.* She'd certainly scared Gary the guard and she'd pointed to the devil actors.

A horn blasted behind us. I jumped. Cass cursed.

Miriam wrenched down the passenger window of Flori's white whale of a Cadillac. "Get in!" Miriam said cheerfully. "We're going tailing."

Cass jumped in the back before I could warn her off. Flori's driving was scarier than any witch, especially at night.

"Come on," Flori said impatiently from the driver's seat. She used a throw pillow to boost her height. Even with the pillow, her bifocals barely rose above the steering wheel.

"Celia's waiting . . ." I started to say. But that reminded me I was doing this for my daughter. I jumped in and buckled up. Flori stomped on the gas, belatedly released the hand brake, and accidentally slammed on the horn.

"Woo-hoo!" Miriam yelled, without dropping a stitch.

"Silver Purl, keep a sharp eye," Flori instructed her friend. "If you see that truck turning, let me know. It's awfully dark out tonight. I'm having trouble seeing far ahead."

I decided not to point out that nighttime was always dark and Flori probably shouldn't be driving, regardless what her great-nephew the optometrist and the DMV told her.

"Up there," Cass said, after a few miles. "The truck's turning off the main road. I bet I know where they're going. I have an artist friend lives out here. The sign says dead end, but there's a dirt track across private land and an arroyo that leads to some houses."

"Hang on!" Flori said. We bumped off road. Miriam cheered and held up her knitting like a roller-coaster rider. I clutched my seat and tried not to scream.

Flori was unperturbed. "Good thing this arroyo's dry or we'd be ice skating."

The track turned to even less of a road after we crossed the dry creek bed. In the beam of Flori's headlights, rough tracks headed out to the left and right. Josephina's ride had turned right, the taillights disappearing over a small hill. Flori swung the bouncing sedan in the same direction. At the top of the hill, a sign speckled with pot shots marked the track as Camino Sin Nombre, the "Lane with No Name." A row of mailboxes, most dented or missing their fronts, clung to a rail fence, their numbers ranging from 201 to 207.

"Good," I said. "We know where they went now. We can look up the owners of properties out here in the morning."

Flori, however, had a different idea. "We should stop by for a little chat," she said.

"We came prepared," Miriam said. "We have cookies. *Bizcochitos.*"

Cass and I reached for our phones simultaneously. "I'm texting Sky," Cass said. "If we're late, he can drive Celia home. That is, unless she has your keys, Rita, and can drive herself."

The car keys were in my pocket, jabbing at my thigh. I thanked Cass and hovered my index finger over the tiny phone screen. What to say? Out on a drive with Flori? That didn't sound like a good reason to desert one's child at devil practice. Celia might find my sleuthing embarrassing, but she was used to it. I went with honesty. *Following lead on devil killer. With Flori and Cass,* I wrote. Then

I gave the street name and mailbox numbers. Just in case.

An emoticon shot back in return. A devil's face frowning. Then, after a minute, another text flashed up. *BE CAREFUL!*

From the front seat, Miriam held up a tiny knitted onesie, cute for any newborn wanting sophisticated all-black evening attire or aspiring to a career in spying.

Cass complimented her stitches. I kept my eye on the gravel track, which had turned into a rutted path leading to a squat adobe cottage. A massive cottonwood towered over the little house, and two pillars of rain-melted adobe bricks flanked the entranceway to the driveway and dirt yard. I'd expected ominous. I was wrong. The cottage actually seemed quite homey. Real candles flickered in the front windows, and white lights, just like Mom used, decorated a scraggly juniper by the door.

"Should we beep?" Miriam asked. "My mother grew up out in the lonely country, and she always said to beep to let folks get ready for company."

"We're tailing and interrogating, Miriam dear, not social visiting," Flori said to her friend. She unbuckled her seat belt, which promptly became stuck in the fluffy folds of her goose-down coat. I reached over the seat to help her out. In the process, Flori's elbow leaned on the horn.

"That'll alert them," Miriam said.

The lace curtain across the front door twitched open, then fell. The candle lighting the front window went black. *Great.* We'd just alerted the witch. As we approached the front door, with its

peeling red paint and misshapen plastic wreath,
I rethought my feelings of homey. In a fairy tale,
we'd be lured in, plied with food, and . . . well, I
didn't want to think what happened next.

We stood on the porch of sagging planks raised
a few inches off the ground.

"Who dares knock?" Cass whispered.

"We could draw straws," Miriam suggested. "If
we had any."

Flori settled the matter by raising her fist and
rapping. The door creaked open on its own. The
scene inside was straight out of a fairy tale, all
right, but not the Grimm stories I'd been conjuring. No, this little cottage could have modeled for
greeting cards. The front room combined a small
kitchen and sitting area around a pretty kiva fireplace. Bite-sized empanadas rested on a rack set
on an antique stove, and delicate lace doilies covered the headrests of the sparse but fine furniture.
A slender young man with dark hair was lighting
a log in the fireplace. The match caught a tower
of twigs, sending smoke curling up the chimney
and flames licking at the kiva's plaster face.

"Hi," he said pleasantly enough, looking over
his shoulder. "You're here to see Nana? She said
we'd be getting visitors."

I sipped warm, spiced tea and discreetly checked
my watch. For the last half hour, Flori and Josephina had been reminiscing about their school-
days. Josephina had appeared after the young

man introduced himself as her grandson, Angel.
He didn't seem like a killer, but I could have been
swayed by his wonderful baking. I savored an
empanadita, a bite-sized empanada filled with
pumpkin.

"These are wonderful, Angel," I said, reaching
for another. "What spices do you use?"

He made a zipping motion across his lips,
brushing the top of a scraggly goatee that needed
another decade or so to fill in. He nodded toward
his grandmother. "Family secret."

A secret I'd love to get my hands on. I nibbled
some more and tried to detect the spice mixture.
Josephina and Flori sat in armchairs by the fire.
Angel, Cass, Miriam, and I were at the small
round dining room table. Miriam had come prepared with yarn and needles in her coat pocket
and was humming along to the carols on the
Spanish language radio station playing softly in
the background. Cass had kept her coat buttoned,
ready to go, and was studying a glass cabinet. The
cabinet was filled with dusty medicine bottles
and oddities suitable for a witch, or someone with
extreme food tastes: pickled chicken feet, dried
amphibians, and some unrecognizable bottled
blobs.

A few feet away, Josephina cackled that Flori
had stolen her middle school beau. Flori countered that Josephina had put a curse on him.

"That boy got a skin rash and would never leave
the house," Flori said. "Said he was allergic to sun,
of all things. Did you know, he moved to Minnesota?" Flori shivered.

Josephina cackled happily. "My *abuela*'s special curse."

My *abuela*, namely my grandmother Pat, had never cursed anyone. She also wouldn't consider Minnesota one of the frozen circles of purgatory, and the closest she came to swearing was "oh me" and "sugar." I leaned across the table and said to Angel, "I kind of met your grandmother the night a man was killed at the Inn of the Pajarito. Did she say anything about what she saw?"

He glanced over his shoulder at the octogenarian schoolgirls. "*Sí*, she saw a devil. A dead devil." He crossed himself and I noticed a skull tattoo the size of a quarter between his thumb and index finger. Some things are best homemade, like pies and cookies. Tattoos, not so much. The skull ink bled into his skin, blurring the lines. The same was true of blotted X marks below his knuckles and a wavering barbed wire band near his collarbone. However, the image on his forearm, I couldn't fault. There, ink outlines showed two spoons in cross formation. Angel had told us how he worked in various restaurants in town and hoped to make his way up from fry cook to chef. He certainly had a talent for baking.

"Did she recognize the devil?" I asked carefully.

Angel's voice fell to a whisper. "Nana has some troubles, 'specially at night. She remembers old times really well. New stuff?" He shrugged and shook his hand, palm down, suggesting that recent events were hit or miss.

Cass dropped her voice to a whisper as well. "But why was your grandmother at the hotel?

Why not stay down with the crowd watching the performance?"

Angel tugged nervously on his spindly goatee and said he didn't know. "Nana used to work at that hotel. Sometimes she gets confused, you know, about the year and how old she is. All she said, when she called to ask me for a ride, was that her curse finally worked. She was really happy."

Logs snapped in the fireplace, sending embers floating upward into the darkness of the chimney. I realized that Josephina and Flori had stopped talking. A smile stretched across Josephina's wrinkled face, revealing a toothless gap. Her laugh came out with a whistle. "It worked," she said.

"Josephina," Flori said calmly. "How did your curse work?"

Our elderly hostess got up and bustled to the kitchen. "*El diablo*. I gave him the *maleficio*. I killed him."

"Nana, no!" Angel said sharply. "You did *not* kill that man or curse him. Please, stop saying that."

His grandmother chuckled and turned her hunched back to us to root through the cabinet of disturbing curiosities. When she turned, she held a small ceramic owl.

"*Tecolote*," she declared.

"Oh dear," said Miriam, crossing herself with her knitting needles.

One of my favorite breakfast places was a café called Tecolote. I knew it meant owl, a bird I'm quite fond of.

"Cute," I said, since no one else was acknowledging Josephina's treasure. "Nice owl."

Josephina waved the figurine across the table. Miriam and Cass recoiled. Angel tried to snatch the object from his grandmother but she was too quick.

"An owl is a symbol of witches," Cass whispered to me. "Like foxes."

"Josie," Flori said gently. "You're not cursing any of us, are you?"

"I'm cursing the devil," her school friend replied. "All the devils."

Now that wasn't cute. "The devils in *Las Posadas* are only actors," I said. To Angel, I said, "She knows that, right?"

"Yeah, sure, sometimes," he said, getting up from the table. "Nana's tired. It's way past dark." He put a hand on his grandmother's shoulder. "Time for sleep, Nana. No wandering tonight."

I didn't need more hints to leave. Neither did Cass. She was already adjusting her scarf and thanking Angel for the empanadas. Flori approached her old friend, who was murmuring in Spanish I couldn't understand. Flori spoke in Spanish first, then English. "Did you hear me, Josephina? We know your curse worked, but who acted it out? Who stabbed Francisco?"

Josephina looked confused. "Florita?" she said. "Ah, Florita, we're late for class."

Flori patted her old friend. "Yes, Josie. Let's take our nap now. Lay our heads down. You go ahead with this nice young man."

Angel guided his grandmother to her bedroom. The rest of us stepped outside. The air was cold and dry. Overhead, constellations twinkled across the vast sky. I identified the North Star and the Seven Sisters. Those were the easy ones to recognize. So was another light coming across the horizon, this one not so festive.

"Uh oh, the fuzz!" Miriam said, pointing to the blue and red lights of a police car barreling over the hill.

Chapter 14

Manny stepped out of the patrol car and stood with his hands on his weapons belt. I squinted into the flashing lights. The siren whirled on, then immediately groaned to a halt. Manny turned to glare at the driver. I recognized her as Deputy Davis, who'd tipped Mom off to my sleuthing and lost the bet about my body finding. She gave a "sorry" shrug to Manny and waved cheerfully to me.

Manny opened the rear door of the cruiser, but instead of a criminal, a girl devil stepped out.

"Hey, Mom!" Celia said, looking a tad chagrined. As they approached, she explained. "Dad came by practice and I told him we had cookies and that you . . . ah . . . had a lead."

Manny, to his credit, didn't say something snarky about amateur sleuths. He let his glower do it for him.

"We're visiting a school friend of mine," said Flori.

Miriam added, rather belligerently, "That's what we old women do around the holidays. It's no business of the police."

Manny's glower morphed into a skeptical smirk. "Now? Out here in the middle of nowhere?" In the distance, the lights of Santa Fe glowed.

I weighed my options and decided to tell Manny the truth. "We found Josephina Ortiz," I said. "You shouldn't bother her tonight. She has some memory problems after dusk, but she could be an important witness. Perhaps she'll be able to say more in the morning." Or she'd wake up refreshed for more cursing.

Manny's elderly aunt suffered dementia and the mental shadows that set in at dusk. I knew he understood. He frowned, but nodded. "Did she witness the killing?"

We on the porch shrugged. "Unclear," I said. "But she was there. She thinks she cursed the devil to death."

"She's a practicing witch," Flori explained. "So were her mother and her grandmother before her. They cursed my first boyfriend and gave him skin problems. I forgave them. It freed me up to marry my old fool, Bernard."

Deputy Davis said that was a good curse, then. Manny turned to her. "Did you run the address, Davis?"

"Oh yeah," she said. "The office just sent the info. The property belongs to Josephina Ortiz. There's no record of problems, 'cept her grandson who has a rap sheet. Manslaughter as a juvenile." She held up a cell phone, presumably containing the information.

"Let me see that," Manny said, stepping back to take her phone.

I felt bad. Angel had given us snacks. He seemed to take good care of his grandmother, and he'd barely known his deceased mother. Could revenge overcome the kind parts of his nature? "Angel's here too," I said wearily. "But he has his hands full with his grandmother. He was putting her to bed."

Manny announced that Angel would be talking to him, bedtime or not. He ordered Deputy Davis to follow him, and told the rest of us, including Celia, to wait by the patrol car.

"My, my, how thrilling," Miriam said, not moving from the porch.

Flori put up her feather hood, but otherwise didn't budge. Cass nodded to the patrol car. I followed her. We climbed in the backseat with Celia, leaving the doors open so we could listen.

"How was practice?" I asked Celia, who was sandwiched in the middle.

"Fine," she answered. "The vocal coach was cool. That guard Gary called the police when the old lady started acting odd. When Dad showed up, I told him about your text. I thought you might have followed her. Hope you don't mind I told him."

I didn't mind. Manny could be a pain, but I wanted the devil slayer nabbed, whoever he—or she—was.

"Knock louder," Manny ordered Davis, who was already pounding. "Here," he said, pushing her aside. He thumped his fist on the wood and yelled, "Police! Open up!"

"Try the knob," Flori suggested.

Manny twisted the knob and the door cracked open. He reached for his holster.

"Hello?" Deputy Davis called out, peeking in the opening. "Hello? Anyone home?"

Flori motioned for me to join them on the porch.

"Go on," Cass said. "Celia and I will hang out here."

I joined the crowd just outside the door and looked inside to an empty living room. "They were right in there," I said to Manny. "Angel could be tucking his granny into bed."

"Go check," Manny snapped.

"What? Me?" Manny was usually pushing me out of investigations. He'd wanted me to wait at the car, for heaven's sake.

"Well, Davis and I can't go bursting in without a warrant," he said. "Aren't you, the witch, and the manslaughter guy chums?"

Ah, so I was to do his work for him. Part of me wanted to refuse out of principle. The other part of me was curious and kind of worried. I stepped inside.

"Angel?" I called out. "Sorry to bother you—you have some more guests." When no answer came, I crossed the cozy living room and cautiously opened a door I assumed led to the bedrooms. A short hallway, with a floor of old-fashioned packed clay, led to three doors. I went down the hall, peeking inside each. Two revealed beds tidily made and empty. The third door opened to a back porch and darkness.

"They're gone," I said to Deputy Davis, who'd come up behind me. We looked out into cold emptiness disappearing into pitch black. There was no sound except Manny banging around in the living room and, in the distance, a soft hooting. "*Tecolote*," I whispered.

"Weird . . ." Deputy Davis said, stretching out the word. "Maybe the old lady really is a witch."

S he can't really be a witch," I said to Cass the next afternoon at her jewelry studio. It was Saturday, and this evening the show would go on for *Las Posadas*. I prayed for no incidents. No bewitching or threatening letters and especially no murders. "I mean, not some magic witch who shape-shifts into an owl." I rolled a smooth silver ring around my palm. Instead of her usual torches, Cass held a large sewing needle and was stitching "imp" horns on a red hoodie for Sky. I'd stopped by to chat while Mom and Celia toured art galleries.

"She could be a witch that doesn't transform," Cass said. "I know some authentic witches. One owns a nice little jewelry studio out in Abiquiú. She's more of a good witch, though. No cursing that I've heard of. She'll do healing spells and find lost objects and stuff like that."

I thought of Dalia, earnestly trying to cure Judith with amulets, sacred dolls, and funky teas. "I have absolutely nothing against good witches," I said, for the record. "Where do you think Josephina and Angel went? Did you hear a car drive away?"

Cass jabbed her needle through a curved fabric

horn. The horn was yellow, a good contrast to the red hoodie. She said she hadn't heard anything. "Although Celia and I were talking, and Manny was noisy with all that blustering. Maybe Angel and his granny went out the back and over to a neighbor's house we couldn't see." Cass looked up from her sewing and grinned. "Or they both turned into owls and flew away."

I recalled the hooting and shivered. Manny had vowed to look for the elusive Josephina and her grandson. As he put it, he didn't appreciate people messing with him. He'd also followed me and Celia home. He claimed he only did it to pick up a plate of Mom's thumbprint cookies. However, I wondered. He'd been curious enough about my lead to drive out to the Lane with No Name. And he planned to back up Celia's bodyguard at her performance tonight. Would he do that if he truly thought that Wyatt Cortez killed out of jealousy? Manny must have doubts. Not that he'd tell me.

"Witches are part of the folklore around here," Cass said. "Years ago, I dated a guy researching New Mexican folk traditions. We went all around, out to the remote villages and up in the mountains. He'd get people talking about water spirits and evil eyes and crows flying across their paths. Coyotes, foxes, magical clowns, you name it. If you know too much about that kind of stuff, you can see signs and omens everywhere."

A dead devil was more than a sign. "Do you think Josephina could have killed Francisco? He was a good-sized man." I cringed, thinking of the force needed to pitchfork a person. "No . . ." I said, answering my own question.

"You'd have to be pretty forceful," Cass agreed, stabbing the imp horns with her needle. "Angel's probably stronger than he looks."

I felt protective toward the aspiring cook. "I'm swayed by his fabulous baking," I admitted. "And his kindness to his grandmother."

"Blinded by empanadas," Cass said with a smile. "That's probably in some folktale. Those were fabulous. I'd kill for his recipe." She put a hand to her mouth. "Not really."

I left Cass to get on with her backlog of Christmas jewelry orders and mentally listed all the things I *should* be doing. Buying and wrapping presents. Getting that Christmas tree. Decorating the house. Cleaning the house. I sighed. Tonight's performance had me edgy and anxious. Once it was safely over, I'd get back to Christmas tasks and fun. I automatically headed down Palace Avenue. Walking would help me think and burn off nervous energy. Plus, the weather and scenery were lovely. Sunny skies pushed the temperature to the high thirties, which in the high, dry air felt like brisk autumn forties. Shop windows glittered with jewelry, antiques, and ornaments ranging from snowmen to skeletons.

I was waiting at a four-way intersection when my phone rang. My spirits soared. Jake! He'd said he had a client meeting today, and I hadn't expected to see him. Maybe he was free.

"Hey!" I said, stealing Celia's usual greeting.

"I'm walking around downtown, looking for a date. Want to grab a coffee?"

"Love to," he said. "But I have bubbly on the way." His tone was jovial but with an edge. "I'm at the Inn of the Pajarito with Wyatt Cortez. We have some news we thought you'd want to hear."

"Good news!" Wyatt's voice boomed in the background.

"News you *should* know," Jake said pointedly.

Wyatt Cortez met me in the courtyard of his hotel. Thankfully, he'd swapped out his Santa costume for a green suit coat with a red handkerchief tucked into the pocket. Better yet, he looked like his normal self. Jovial. Businesslike. And happily excited. "Two alibis!" he exclaimed.

He stepped aside to allow an oversized elf to open the door for us.

"Feliz Navidad," the elf offered in a monotone.

"And a merriest Christmas to you too, young elf!" Wyatt said, slapping the gloomy man on the back. Once inside, he enveloped me in a hug. "Yep, two alibis, and it's all thanks to you and Mr. Strong, giving those police the kick in the pants to keep digging."

"Two?" I said. I realized I should sound happier for him. "That's great!" I added. What wasn't great was my fear confirmed. An unknown devil killer, with an unknown motive, was still on the loose.

"Come on," Wyatt said, grabbing my arm. "Lorena's here and we've popped open some bubbly."

I walked with him past the tinseled tree and into his glitzy bar. Jake and Lorena stood to greet me. "Looks like your feeling was right," Jake said quietly.

"I knew it all along," Lorena said, raising her glass. "Rita, I'm happy to tell you that you're fired." She leaned in to give me a hug and whispered in my ear, "Unless you'll keep going on the sly. I desperately want justice for dear Francisco."

Under the gaze of Wyatt, I couldn't answer. I wouldn't have known what to say anyway.

"We'll talk later," Lorena said, patting my hand. "I'll be bringing you and Flori some pie. Any flavor you want. Blackberry thyme? Pumpkin with a cookie crust? Chocolate chile?"

I forced my mind from the whirlwind of delicious pie possibilities. "Who are these witnesses?" I asked. "Was one Josephina Ortiz? Was she . . . ah . . . lucid enough?"

Wyatt poured me some champagne, and I took a tiny sip, wary because bubbly makes me lightheaded.

Since Wyatt was busy imbibing, Jake answered. "The police haven't located Josephina or her grandson yet. They're not happy that those two ran off. Looks suspicious, which is also good for Wyatt's case. They found a housekeeper who saw Francisco go out to the roof. She wanted to watch the play, but she had to work. She was coming out of the supply closet when Josephina came up the stairs and, I quote, 'put the curse on her.' So she hid."

I wasn't seeing an alibi yet, for Wyatt or Josephina. I took a sip of bubbly, which went straight to my nose and nearly made me sneeze.

I was rubbing my nose as Jake continued. "The housekeeper was still in the supply room, when she heard an awful scream. She then heard loud, running footsteps and the door to the stairs slam.

She waited a few more minutes, frightened. Then the elevator came up and chimed. She dared peek out and saw Wyatt, dressed as Santa."

Wyatt paused in his bubbly celebration. "I went up to check that the roof was unlocked for the devil. My poor housekeeper didn't come forward right away because she feared evil spirits were involved. Then she was afraid I'd fuss at her for not cleaning a suite on time." Wyatt smiled at Lorena. "Of course, I assured her she was much appreciated. I wanted to give her a raise, but Mr. Strong here says I should wait until the dust settles."

Lorena, who hadn't touched her bubbly, gave a halfhearted smile.

The hotel owner shook his head. "It's like I always said, I tried to resuscitate Francisco but it was too late. Rita, you must have arrived when I was around the side of Pie in the Sky, looking for the water spigot over there. Crazy of me, to think water might revive him. We shut the water off in winter. There was all that blood . . ."

Lorena shuddered and looked near tears. Her husband took her hand, squeezed it, and told her he was sorry. "For everything," he said.

I understood acting foolish when in shock. I'd mimed murder when the killer could have been sneaking up behind me.

"Josephina's a frail older woman," I said. "Francisco could have easily fought her off. The housekeeper didn't see anyone else go up or down from the roof? What about the running footsteps and slamming door? Josephina is quick, but I wouldn't call her a runner."

Jake provided a more plausible scenario. "Could

be that the killer was already up there, waiting for Francisco or Barton or any devil."

I tried another sip of my drink. The bubbles made me cough. "So there's another witness?" I asked when I recovered.

Jake grinned. "Actually more than one, but I'm counting them as a group. Your British customers who let the donkey out. They're staying at the Pajarito. They say they spoke with Santa right before the devil was due to go on."

"Ho, ho, ho," Wyatt said. I'm sure he intended it to sound merry. Instead, it sent shivers up my arms. I caught Jake's eye and raised my eyebrow.

"In itself, not a great alibi," Jake admitted. "But the ladies also say that they were nearly knocked over by a man in black, running out the door from the stairway. Unfortunately, they didn't get any kind of look at him. They can't even say for sure that it was a man."

"Tell her the good part," Wyatt urged,

Lorena groaned softly.

"They said they smelled sulfur when the person in black knocked into them," Jake said.

Wyatt raised his glass. "I owe you all so much," he said. "Rita, Jake, you took time out of your holidays to help me. Lorena, I owe you everything. We'll get through this. Together." He clinked his glass to each of ours. "Christmas is truly looking up now."

Not for me. I had a killer to catch.

Chapter 15

"Váyanse de aquí!" Celia yelled. Her operatic bellow cut through the glass door to the tap-room's balcony and the background rumble of packed tables of Saturday night beer drinkers.

I spun my barstool from the boring view of beer tap and flat-screen football highlights, to one much more interesting. Outside, my daughter jumped up and down, legs frog-style, arms raised, one holding a plastic pitchfork spray-painted red. Sky, the gangly imp, danced behind her, squatting low and then springing up to either side. He held smoke flares and flashlights shaped like flames. They were having great fun, and so was the crowd below. Each time Celia yelled, boos and hisses erupted.

I would have been having fun too, if I weren't watching for a killer and squeezed on a barstool between my ex and Gary the bodyguard. Gary was dutifully following Manny's orders to blend in. In my opinion, he was going overboard with the act. So far, Gary had downed two beers and just as many bowls of free pretzels. Manny's idea was to look inconspicuous. Then, if anyone suspicious approached the door, we'd nab them. Or I would. Between Gary's fixation on snacks and Manny's eye roving to an attractive waitress, nabbing might be up to me. I flexed my ankles and shoulders and envisioned the perfect tackle.

I'd have backup. Deputy Davis and Jake sat at a table by the entrance. Every time I glanced their way, I found his eyes watching the door and hers fixed on him.

Gary bumped me with his elbow. "You gonna drink that?" he asked. Not taking my eyes off Celia, I reached back and pushed my untouched pint of porter his way.

"Thanks," he said and added, generously, "I'll put my empty glasses in front of you. You know, for your cover."

Lovely. My cover as the mother guzzling beer during her daughter's Christmas pageant. At least I hadn't had to justify my absence from the ground-level audience to Mom.

She'd approved. "Of course you should chaperone her, Rita," she'd said. "A young girl playing a devil at a beer hall . . . it's simply not proper. And after a man died? This Christmas play gets stranger and stranger."

Outside, Celia leaned over the balcony brandishing her staff. A bray burbled up among the boos.

Manny also had his back to the bar, watching Celia but mostly scanning the room. The stools were tight together and our shoulders occasionally bumped. Manny and I had done a lot of sitting at bars over the years, his idea of a good time. I felt a twinge of nostalgia. The twinge evaporated just as quickly when his gaze again landed on the short-skirted waitress.

"I don't think that's our guy," I said sarcastically.

Manny snorted and turned his attention back to the balcony. "You don't think anyone's our guy. First you stuck up for a bloody Santa. Now you're saying this manslaughter guy, Angel, can't be the killer because he has a nice name and you like his empanadas."

"I did not say that," I said. "His name has nothing to do with it. All I said was, you didn't see him with his grandmother. He was gentle with her. Considerate. Worried. Why would he risk going to jail and leaving her alone?"

Manny grabbed a handful of pretzels. "'Cause old granny thinks she's a witch and she asked him to?" Through a mouthful of pretzels, he opined about witches and their ways. "Ridiculous. Weird women out to make trouble and bother the police," he said. "Of course, there's always the random nutcase suspect. That's what your criminal-defender boyfriend would have us believe. I admit, that would be a tidy explanation. Covers the threatening letters and the killing all in one. You come across a nutcase, other than your friends, you let me know."

I was saved from more of Manny's proclamations by the cute waitress smiling at him. I swiveled away from my ex and focused on the performance. Sky waved sparklers behind Celia's horns. Her commanding yell morphed into an anguished cry. They both raised their hands and dramatically withered to the patio floor, hidden behind the adobe balcony. The crowd cheered, thinking the devil was vanquished. A soloist began a plaintive song. The peace wouldn't last for long. In a minute or two, Celia and her imp would reappear, scaring off the inn seekers and hopefully their donkey too.

I nibbled a pretzel. Outside, Celia and Sky were cuing each other for their next act. They counted down three, two, one on their fingers, and then Celia popped up and yelled *"Váyanse de aquí!"*

I had to stop myself from cheering. Manny, however, had pushed his stool out and was leaning on the bar, mumbling into his hand. I snapped to attention and noticed that Deputy Davis had too. What did they see?

"Two o'clock," Manny said into the radio I now noticed in his palm. "No, Davis, *my* two o'clock. By the carved bear, moving north!"

I felt for Deputy Davis. Manny's directions were always self-centered. I spotted the figure by the bear. A scruffy young guy with quarter-sized holes in his sagging earlobes was moving along the edge of the room. He wore an army surplus–type jacket, several sizes too large, and a baseball cap turned off center.

My heartbeat sped up, and I yearned to jump in front of the balcony door. Manny continued to face the bar. "Stop staring at him," he said under his breath, jabbing my elbow for good measure.

"I'm not staring," I said. If anything, we had a believable cover as a grumpy formerly married couple. I moved my elbow away from Manny's and noticed a familiar face on the other side of the room.

"Trey Crundall, my three o'clock," I said, trying not to move my lips. I added. "Don't look."

"Why tell me if I'm not supposed to look," Manny grumbled. He leaned forward on his elbows and looked out from under his arms.

Trey wore a bulky ski jacket. He clutched a beer in one hand and could simply be looking for a friend or a place to sit. Or, he could be meeting the scruffy guy. I grabbed one of Gary's empty beer glasses and pretended to drink from it as Trey shook his head slightly and turned around, taking a free table near Jake and Deputy Davis. The scruffy kid stood awkwardly for a minute or two, shuffling from foot to foot. Then he cast one more look in Trey's direction and stomped out of the room. Manny reached over and slapped a hand in front of Gary, breaking the bodyguard's perusal of the beer menu.

"Do not let anyone touch the door to the balcony," Manny ordered. He stomped off after the scruffy kid, with Deputy Davis jogging behind him.

A few minutes later, Celia and Sky burst into the room with cheeks pink from the chill and devilish enthusiasm.

"Hey!" Gary said, looking conflicted. "No one's supposed to bother that door."

I assured him it was okay. It was. The performance had gone off without a hitch. "You were awesome, honey," I said, hugging Celia. "You too, Sky. You make an amazing imp."

Sky grinned bashfully.

"Where's Dad?" Celia asked.

"He was here the whole time except the very end when he had to go." Go do what? I looked around for Trey, but he too had gone. "Police stuff," I said, and offered the teens celebratory root beers. Both said they were parched. Sky teased Celia that her voice sounded like a frog's croak. Jake sauntered over to compliment the actors and give me a sur-reptitious squeeze.

When Manny returned a few minutes later, he scowled first at Jake and then at the teens' frothy mugs.

"Root beer," I said. "What happened?" I half ex-pected him to clam up, especially in front of Jake.

"Petty drug pusher," he said. "A new client for you, counselor? Or do you only look for big-time criminal clients who can pay?"

Jake smiled serenely. "Me? I'm dreaming of a no-crime Christmas."

Me too, and after tonight's calm performance, I could almost believe that my dream would come true.

Outside, my festive mood soared higher. Col-ored lights sparkled in the Plaza, strung in pretty loops high in the treetops. Mary and Joseph had found shelter in the bandstand, dec-orated as a manger. Mary sat on a hay bale and munched a cookie. Joseph joined the singers in a borderlands version of "Deck the Halls," com-plete with mariachi-style yells and yodels. Volun-teers served up hot cider and goodies under heat lamps. Barton and the third devil hammed it up for photos with audience members. Shasta was double-tasked with managing Sidekick while also playing the role of devil portrait photographer. The goat aimed his ribbon-wrapped horns at the knees of any passerby in his reach.

When we reached Mom, she kissed Celia on both cheeks.

Celia adjusted her devil horns and said, "So? What'd you think, Gran?"

Mom told Celia that she was the very best devil in the entire performance. "The best I've ever seen, in fact," she added.

I had to hand it to Mom. She wasn't going to lie and say that she thought a Christmas devil was a great idea. However, she knew good devil acting when she saw it.

Manny went back to work, taking a reluctant Deputy Davis with him. I spotted Flori standing under a heat lamp handing out hot cider. Or, rather, she was warming her hands with a cup of cider and letting everyone else ladle their own. Sky and Cass headed for the snacks, along with Celia, Mom, and Gary the ever-hungry guard.

Jake and I were about to follow when I heard my name being called. I looked but saw only happy people enjoying cider and swaying to the Christmas music.

"Over here!" Dalia's voice sounded far away.

"There," Jake said, amusement in his voice. "Over by that garbage can by the kitchen gifts store."

"Oh dear," I said with a smile. Dalia was trying to pull Mr. Peppers away from a trash can. A boy in angel wings, chased by a girl devil, weaved in and out between the beams of the portico.

Dalia sighed in exasperation when Jake and I joined her. "This donkey is under strict instructions to avoid processed wheat and sugar, so I kept him away from the cookie table. But then he smelled something in this trash can. I think it's a donut box. No, no, Mr. Peppers. Think of your health, dear."

Eddie came to a panting stop. He held a Mexican wedding cookie as big as his fist and his nose was dusted in powdered sugar. His sister, seeing me and Jake, assumed a bored pose, leaning against the wall.

Jake patted Mr. Peppers and whispered something in his big donkey ear. I swear, Mr. Peppers grinned. Taking the lead from Dalia, Jake gently moved Mr. Peppers away from the tempting trash can. They stood a few feet away, both facing the Plaza in a charming Western silhouette.

"The teeth on that donkey," Dalia said with a shudder. "I love all creatures, but he latched on and chewed a hole in my best wool shawl." Then she smiled. "But it was a lovely evening, wasn't it? The stars are in alignment, finally. Barton did a fine job, and Celia was an angel. Well, a devil angel."

I beamed at the praise heaped on my favorite devil. "No threatening notes? Nothing amiss?" I asked.

Dalia didn't know of anything. "Thank the stars! I'm so relieved, especially for Judith's sake. Now she can concentrate on enjoying Christmas and getting better. We all can."

Everyone except Francisco. I felt sad for him, forgotten in life and death, except by Lorena.

Dalia nudged me. "Your handsome cowboy has a way with donkeys, doesn't he?" Before I could answer, she said. "I hate to ask, but I don't suppose Jake could take Mr. Peppers back to his pen? I'd like to go check on Judith, make sure she's doing okay."

"We'd be happy to," I said, a sentiment echoed by the wheezy bray of Mr. Peppers.

Jake offered to do the task alone. "You're sure you don't want to hang out with Celia and your mother?" he asked. "I think I can handle this wild minidonkey."

Mr. Peppers was walking along between us like a well-trained show dog.

I was reluctant to leave Celia. However, she was surrounded by friends, family, and Gary, and I'd love a bit of time alone with Jake. I jogged over to the cookie table and told my daughter where I'd be. While I was there, I took Sidekick off Shasta's hands. She barely had time to thank me before Barton barked at her to take more photos.

Sidekick was happy to join his donkey buddy, and Jake and I and the miniherd took a twisting route of side streets to avoid traffic and known sources of baked goods. Peppers and Sidekick sped up as we neared Tres Amigas. On the last block, the donkey and goat began to trot. Jake and I jogged along, unable to resist laughing at the donkey's excited honks and wheezes. Once back in their garden manger, Peppers and Sidekick bellied up to their hay bale. Jake leaned over to kiss me.

"I've missed you," he said, warming me from my heart to my toes. He cupped my chin and kissed me again as fluffy snowflakes fell on my cheeks.

"Snow!" I said, delighted.

He wrapped an arm around my shoulder and we both gazed up at the falling crystals.

"Beautiful," he said, looking at me. We secured the livestock and walked, arm in arm, back to the Plaza, taking our time. When we turned the corner, however, my heart leapt, and not from romance. An ambulance was screeching up to the curb, lights flashing and siren blaring.

My maternal worries kicked in full force. *What if I'd relaxed too soon? What if the ambulance was coming for Celia?* Dropping Jake's arm, I took off at a run, pushing through the crowds to find my daughter.

Chapter 16

Jake, at my heels, repeated that it would be okay. I knew he was probably right. No, surely right, I told myself, slowing a little. I spotted Sky, his imp horns rising above most other heads. He stood by the bandstand. As I got closer I saw that he was holding devil horns, limp and sagging. My stomach lurched.

"Sky!" I called out, eyes fixated on the horns. Behind the snacks table, with its festive hot cider and cookies, EMTs were working frantically.

Sky looked my way, his young face wrinkled in concern. "She passed out," he said when I reached him. "She was fine and then . . ."

"Then she fell out of her chair," Celia's voice nearly made me swoon with relief. She and Mom came around the side of the bandstand. Celia looked fine. Mom was shaking her head and screwing the top back on a water bottle.

"Rita, where have you been?" Mom demanded.

"There's been a medical emergency." Then catching sight of Jake, she shook her head some more.

Now was not the time to explain. "What happened?" I asked.

"It's Ms. Crundall," Celia said. She pointed toward the cluster of EMTs still blocking my view. "Sky and I were right there. She looked fine, and then all of a sudden, she was out of it." My daughter shuddered. "She was breathing and all, but she wouldn't wake up. We called 911."

The EMTs lifted a stretcher and hurried it to the waiting ambulance. One of the EMTs held a bag of fluids high above the pathetically small and blanket-covered figure of Judith Crundall. They hefted her into the back of the ambulance and climbed in after her. We watched as the lights flashed into the distance.

Jake put his hand on the small of my back. "I'm sorry about your friend. You're okay?"

I reached down and squeezed his hand, relieved but also worried about Judith and her family. "Where's Dalia?"

Celia tilted her head to the south. "Dalia missed it all. We think she went over to talk to the hotel that sponsored the first devil. Flori went to find her." My daughter pulled an exaggerated frown. "I volunteered to go, but Flori said I should stay here with Gary."

Gary stood guard over the cookie table, his eyes darting between plates of *bizcochitos* and the remains of pie.

"Looks like you're in good hands, then," Jake said with a hint of a smile to Celia. He kissed the top of my head and asked if there was anything he could do. When I said no, he said he'd call it a night. He tipped his hat to a still-frowning Mom, gave friendly fist bumps to Sky and Celia, and slid off through the crowd. Sky made his goodbyes too. "Mom went back to her studio," he said. "I better go tell her what happened."

"We should get going as well," my mother said, pointing to her watch. It was nearly nine, Mom's appointed bedtime.

Celia watched the ambulance turn the corner. "We tried to help," she said again.

"Ms. Crundall will be okay," I told Celia. I hoped I was telling the truth.

My daughter's mouth was firm set. "Yeah. I hope so. I like her. She comes off kinda harsh sometimes, but that's because she does and says what she wants. She's cool."

Like Flori, I thought, as we weaved through the crowd to an unpopulated spot by a park bench. The bench was covered in festively colored yarn. The knit bandit stood nearby with her white-haired husband, Bernard, and a distraught Dalia. When they saw me, Flori waved me over.

"Perfect," Flori said. "Rita, Dalia here needs a ride to the hospital and Bernard can't find our car keys." She leaned in and lowered her voice. "The old fool."

Said fool winked at me and patted his front jacket pocket. Bernard went to great measures to discourage Flori from driving at night. "I'm gonna flag a cab," Bernard said.

Finding a cab seemed as likely as flagging down a flying reindeer. Streets were still blocked off for

Las Posadas and crowds clogged those that were open. My car wasn't far away.

"Mom?" I said. "Do you mind if we—"

She read my mind and answered before I could finish asking. "Of course we'll take you, Dalia," Mom said.

S he doesn't have her protectors." Dalia held up a small kachina to a nurse, whose unsmiling face contrasted with the happy dancing pandas on her pastel scrubs. We'd waited a good fifteen minutes for the crabby nurse to appear. Dalia had spent the time giving a tarot card reading to an ashen-faced woman with an obviously broken wrist.

"The protectors are her spiritual medicine," Dalia added, enunciating as if the nurse might not understand English.

"She's got medicine," the nurse replied. "We're a hospital. You can see her soon."

Dalia thrust the kachina into the nurse's hands. "Take this to her. Please. She'll want it." The nurse looked rightfully dubious. With a put-upon sigh, she stuffed the figure in her pocket and disappeared through the swinging doors marked STAFF ONLY.

When the broken-wrist lady left for treatment, Dalia paced the room. Mom and Celia worked on a crossword, and I turned my thoughts to the puzzle of the dead devil. We'd all thought that the play went off without a hitch. Perhaps it had. Judith was elderly and ill, and by her own admission, she might be nearing death's door. Or was someone trying to help her get there? Francisco had worked at her estate. *If he'd discovered a plot to kill her . . .* I grasped at possibilities, but couldn't get a firm grip on any.

When Dalia paced my way again, I asked if she'd been with her half sister before her collapse.

"Yes," she said, her voice wavering. "I was with her most of the night. Most days lately too. My husband's joking I left him." She gave a nervous laugh and said it was good that Phillip's online spiritual consultation business was keeping him busy.

"It's not your fault, Dalia," I said. "What was Judith doing before she passed out? Had she eaten or drunk anything?"

"Only half a cookie," Dalia said, shaking her head. "It's so hard to get her to eat and drink enough since her stomach's been feeling off. I forced her to have some warm cider. I shouldn't have let her come out, but she insisted. She always gets her way, just like our father."

"So you got her the cider," I said, hoping to steer Dalia back to the timeline of events.

Dalia rubbed a purple crystal hanging from her neck. "No, I asked Trey to. He was walking by, not even going to stop and say hello. I insisted he do something nice for his mother. He heaved and sighed like a big child. I swear, that man will never grow up." Her hand flew to her mouth. "Oh my stars, Saturn protect us!"

I knew exactly what she was thinking. Or at least, I thought I did. "Trey got that drink—" I started to say.

"Trey! No one's told him yet! Oh, how could I be so scatterbrained? Here I was badmouthing him and he doesn't even know his mother's in the hospital." Dalia patted the layers of her flowing skirts, searching for her phone.

I kept my thoughts to myself. Maybe Trey already knew. He would, if he'd dumped poison in his mother's cider.

An hour later, I was being the dutiful child, politely nodding as my mother repeated the word, "See?"

The "see" was uttered with such triumph that Mom didn't need to add "I told you so." But, of course, she had told me so and would continue to do so for as long as I lived seven thousand feet above sea level. I took a swig of water to show I'd learned my lesson.

"Water, Rita. Hydration. I've been telling you, you need to drink more. Dehydration can have very dangerous consequences. I told your sister too. Don't think because you're at an ocean that you're getting enough water."

Mom turned to Celia, who wisely held up her bottle of water, acquired at ridiculous cost from the hospital's vending machine. "Yum," Celia added, further shielding herself from the hydration lecture.

A few minutes earlier, the nurse had returned with Judith's doctor and his diagnosis of her condition. Simple dehydration. Just like Mom had been warning about. Mom was downright smug. We were all relieved.

"The body's electrolytes can go haywire," the doctor had said, to Mom's chorus of "See" and "I knew it."

"You have to be careful," the doctor then preached to the Mom choir. "Especially this time of year. People think about water in the summer when it's hot. In the winter, folks tend to forget."

"It's just as well I couldn't get Trey on the phone," Dalia said as Mom, Celia, and I prepared to leave. Judith was going to stay with her sister. "I hope he listens to the messages all the way through," she said. "Oh, what if he doesn't and thinks his mother is dying?"

Maybe it'll shock some proper fear into him. I kept this thought to myself and said he'd probably listen to all the messages. "I would," I said. "If I saw a bunch of messages."

Dalia twisted her crystal necklaces. "I wouldn't! I'd hear that first one and rush right up here in a panic. An utter panic." She seemed to have forgotten the part about forcing Trey to get his sick mother hot cider. Pulling me aside, Dalia said, "Rita, I hate to ask after you've already done so much, but could you maybe possibly, if you have time, stop by Judith's house and see if Trey is there?"

Frankly, I didn't want to. I was beat and yearned to get home to my comforting cat and uncomfortable sofa bed. But Dalia rarely asked favors, and I knew she was worried. "Okay," I said. "I'll drop off Mom and Celia first and then run down there."

Dalia promised me baskets of brownies and cakes. Between her and Lorena, I'd have a bounty of holiday sweets. Maybe the real Santa would bring me a gym membership.

Back at the casita, I told Mom to lock the door. "I'll be back soon," I promised.

"You're sure you don't want me to come along with you?" she asked through a yawn.

I declined with thanks. "Go on to bed," I urged Mom. "We'll have a full, fun day tomorrow. Let's go get the Christmas tree and decorate and make some more cookies."

I drove the few blocks down to Judith's house feeling tired but relieved that Judith was going to be okay. No one was poisoning her, and no one had targeted *Las Posadas*. My quest for a happy holiday was back on track.

I pulled into Judith's drive. As I expected, the main house was dark, including Trey's wing in the back. I couldn't help a snarky thought. This full-grown man child had his own mansion wing. If he'd grown up with my family, he'd be lucky to get the corner of Mom's basement not devoted to canning supplies and the laundry machine. I bet Trey didn't even appreciate the advantages he had. *Like having someone go out on a cold winter's night to protect his nonexistent feelings.*

With a resigned sigh, I parked, stepped out into a biting December wind, and rang Judith's doorbell. I wasn't going to wait long, not in this cold. When no one answered, I tugged my scarf tighter and started to turn back to my car. A sound caught my attention. A thump, followed by a snapping of branches. *Just the wind*, I told myself, though peering across Judith's xeriscape garden, I saw a flickering light in the archives room.

Was Barton still working? He'd surely want to know about Judith, if he hadn't heard.

I walked across the gravel, the wind sweeping up the crunching noise of my feet. The air held the faint sweetness of moisture, a scent I'd become attuned to since living in the desert. Something made me tiptoe and bypass the door to the archives room. I sneaked around the corner to a window where the candlelight was brighter. Through a filmy curtain I saw two forms locked in an embrace. One was thick and shaggy-haired. The frivolous heir, Trey. The other had long, loose hair and a voluptuous figure. Shasta. I guessed Barton's assistant wasn't getting overtime hours for *this* activity.

I looked away quickly. Trey clearly wasn't overwrought about his mother. Time for me to call it a night.

My steps sounded extra loud now that I feared discovery as a peeping Tom. There was another sound too, though. The sound of footsteps that were not mine. I froze, trying to hear above the wind and rustle of dried grasses. The sound seemed to be getting fainter. I rounded the corner and glimpsed a figure slipping into the darkness beyond my car.

I followed, hopscotching to flagstones to lessen the sounds of my steps. I was nearing my car when my cell phone rang at full volume. Heart racing, I fumbled through my purse. The phone made it through three loud, tinny strains of my new "Jingle Bells" ringtone. In between rings, I heard the footsteps, turned to pounding feet running away.

I listened until I could hear them no more. Then I said, "Hello?" letting exasperation creep into my voice.

The apologetic voice of Barton Hunter greeted me. "Rita. Ms. Lafitte. This is Barton Hunter. I'm so sorry. It's too late to call. I apologize if I you were already asleep."

"No, no," I said, trying to sound more pleasant. "You didn't wake me." That was for sure. I doubted I'd ever get to sleep tonight. I backtracked, got in my car, and locked the doors, just in case the prowler had hung around. "What's up, Barton?"

He explained that he'd gotten an earlier message from Dalia about Judith's trip to the emergency room. "I called back but couldn't reach her," he said. "Is Judith okay? Dalia mentioned that you were driving her to the hospital, or I wouldn't have bothered you."

Well, at least I was calming someone's nerves over Dalia's rampant message leaving. I told Barton that Judith was fine. "Dehydration, that's all."

He breathed a sigh of relief. "Thank goodness. If you see Judith, tell her I'm thinking of her and want her back in that collections room as soon as possible."

I told him I'd relay the message and we hung up. The romantic candlelight was still flickering in the window when I backed out of Judith's driveway, my headlights off. Back on the road, I saw no sign of anyone. Still, my heart raced as I hurried to my front door. Who had I seen? A prowler? The killer? I locked my door against the cold winter wind wailing down the creek valley and lay awake a long time, ears tuned to the branches scratching like witchy fingernails against the windows.

Chapter 17

Mom greeted me the next morning with hot coffee and an update from the sub-tropics. "I'm afraid the heat is getting to your sister," Mom said direly. "Kathy, Dwayne, and the kids are going zip-lining over an alligator farm this afternoon. Zip-lining! Over alligators! Can you believe it?"

I poured myself coffee before trying to work out the how and whys of zip-lining in flat Florida over toothy reptiles. Even after caffeine intake, I couldn't imagine the logistics or the attraction. "Why?" I asked.

"My question exactly," Mom said. We shared a moment of shaking our heads in wonder. Mom poured herself more coffee and joined me at the table. "It sounds dangerous to me. Remember how Kathy loved swinging out over the lake on that rope when she was little? Kathy has always had a rebel streak."

Those words brightened my morning as much

as the coffee. Kathy, the rebel? Good, dependable Kathy who shared every detail of her life with Mom and showed up routinely for family dinners? I basked in being the daughter taking her mother on a nice Sunday Christmas tree hunt. "There are all sorts of ways to celebrate Christmas," I said generously. I couldn't get too smug. I was, after all, still the daughter exposing Mom to devils and a dead body.

Mom looked dubious. "There's other bad news. A burglar." She shoved the *Santa Fe New Mexican* under my nose. "I went outside to get the newspaper, little knowing how dangerous it is around here. Right here!"

I took the paper with trepidation. "Surely not *right* here . . ."

"Oh yes," Mom said. "Your street, Rita. A few houses down, from what I can tell. You should consider moving closer to town. These wild yards and adobe walls offer criminals all sorts of places to hide undetected."

I had considered moving once, when two killings took place pretty much in my own backyard. A little cat burglar wasn't going to scare me.

"This kind of stuff happens everywhere," I said. "Even in places without walls. We have good locks, and I bet the burglar is looking for bigger prey than our casita."

Mom again needlessly reminded me that I was a single mother. "I made some hard decisions based on you girls when you were young. I hope someday you'll understand that. In fact . . ." She paused, then got up suddenly and ducked her head into the refrigerator. When she turned, empty-handed, she grabbed the coffeepot and refilled my cup. "You're doing a lovely job with Celia, don't get me wrong. I'm only concerned for you both."

"We're fine, Mom," I said, distracted by the article. I was actually feeling safer by the minute. A common burglar. Is that who I'd encountered last night? If so, I felt good on two counts. One, my presence had scared him off. Two, and more importantly, a run-of-the-mill burglar had nothing to do with devil threats. My fears of yesterday had been unfounded. I could relax and let Manny handle the case.

According to the paper, a black-suited burglar was striking houses on the east side of town. Some of the affected addresses were on my street. However, the burglar favored high-end electronics. My fanciest electronic device was a new toaster oven that boasted the ability to bake entire pies and pizzas. Burglars, I assumed, weren't the nice sorts to make pies. I pointed out the electronics angle to Mom.

"See, it's fine," I said, unable to repress the smile that brought a scowl to Mom's face.

"How can a thief be fine, Rita?" she said. "First a murder. Now a burglar."

"At least we don't have alligators," I said. "And something smells wonderful."

Mom surely recognized my unsubtle change of subject. She kindly obliged. "I mixed up some spiced pumpkin bread this morning. It's cooled enough that I can cut us some."

I quickly estimated the time needed to mix up, bake, and properly cool a quick bread. "You were up early, Mom. Did you sleep okay?"

She cited the time zone difference and "some things on my mind."

I could guess several things that might cause Mom to lose sleep. Murder? More questions about Jake? Albert the dentist and how to fix me up with him? Our lack of fruitcakes? I was relieved when Mom abruptly turned the conversation to the baking spices she'd added to the bread.

"I discovered cardamom from a Swedish lady at the Lutheran church," she said. "I made braided cardamom bread last month. Your sister thought it was lovely, although your brother-in-law didn't care for it. Dwayne said the taste was odd."

Kathy and I shared at least one similarity. We'd both married men with the taste buds of fussy toddlers. Manny refused all ethnic foods that didn't have "Mexican" in their title. Tex-Mex, New-Mex, and Arizona-Mex were okay with him. Some actual Mexican foods, he wouldn't touch. And French or Asian? No way. He also shunned most green vegetables other than chiles. My brother-in-law, Dwayne, on the other hand, considered Taco Bell too exotic. He favored noodle casseroles and comforting Midwest hot dishes.

Mom and I chatted about baked goods until she declared it time to "get on with the day."

I decided that meant it was also a decent hour to call Dalia and check on Judith.

"Be sure to warn her about the burglars," Mom said darkly.

Dalia answered before the second ring. "Oh, Rita, I'm so glad you called. Did you find Trey last night? We haven't heard from him."

"Sorry. I went over there last night but . . . ah . . . no one answered the main door," I said, truthfully though evasively. "I'm sure he'll call today." I wasn't sure of that at all.

Nor, from her snort, was Dalia. "We'll be getting Judith home soon anyway," she said. "The doctors say she's fine. As fine as she can be. I pestered the emergency room doctor to run some more tests. He said that's for Judith's specialists to do. I swear, Rita, I'm about to call in every natural healer I know."

I thought of Cass's friend, the healing witch, which reminded me of Josephina. Had Manny managed to track down her and Angel? I'd call Manny today, under the guise of finalizing plans for Celia's Christmas Day schedule. Last I'd heard, Manny had volunteered to work Christmas Eve and Christmas Day. He liked the overtime pay and avoiding holiday gatherings, which worked out great for me. I told Dalia I'd stop by later.

My neighbor thanked me and again promised me sweets in return. We were about to hang up when I remembered the burglar. I described seeing someone in Judith's driveway.

"Could it have been Trey?" Dalia asked. "Since he was in middle school, Judith's had problems with that boy sneaking in and out of the house."

"I'm sure it wasn't Trey," I said. "Be careful. Tell Judith to lock her doors. The paper says the thief is after electronics, not . . ." I struggled to find a less icky way to describe Judith's collection.

"Grave goods?" my usually positive-thinking

neighbor said. "The sooner that awful collection is out of the house, the better. I wouldn't care if a robber took them, except that wouldn't help Judith's karma or the spirits, would it? It's bad enough that some pieces are lost or misplaced. Shasta's been working overtime trying to work out the archival mess."

Shasta was working overtime, all right, but that wasn't my concern. I had enough trouble disclosing my own love life. That, however, was about to change. When Dalia hung up, I called Jake. Time to get him and Mom together for a fun activity, no bodies or criminal defending involved.

This isn't quite as manly as chopping down a towering pine with an ax," Jake said. We trailed a few feet behind Mom and Celia, leaders of the potted Christmas tree hunt. Celia was pulling a wide red wagon, supplied by the nursery owner and claimed by Winston as his bulldog chariot. The expedition wasn't exactly meeting my Midwest image of horse-drawn sleighs down snowy forest paths either. But I loved it. The Southwest sky was a brilliant, cloudless turquoise. The gravel paths were lined with metal roadrunner figurines, brightly colored Mexican pottery, and a few prairie dog holes. The tree offerings included potted Colorado blue spruce, dark green firs, and native piñon, as well as chubby barrel cactus and spiraling agaves.

"You look like a woodsman," I told Jake, patting his oilskin jacket. A bit of red and green flannel shirt poked out at the collar. Winston wore a co-ordinating red flannel doggy coat.

Jake smiled. "I could wrangle that cactus into the truck for you." He pointed to a tall cactus covered in stubby arms, raised as if cheering. "Bet it would look fine with some lights."

I grinned. "No thanks. I don't want a Christmas tree that attacks."

With some effort, Celia pulled Winston and the wagon over a small hill. "How about that one?" She pointed toward a blue spruce with a wide bottom and incongruently spindly top. It sat to one side, separated from the perfectly shaped trees nearby.

When Mom pointed out a more conical candidate, Celia stood up for the lopsided pine. "It has character," she insisted.

"Well, then that's what we want," I said. "Woodsman . . ."

Jake was already pulling on leather work gloves and evicting Winston from his ride. With Celia's laughing help, Jake hefted the tree onto the wagon and we took turns pulling it back to his beat-up Ford. "My father hauled a lot of logs in this truck," he said. "He used to heat the ranch buildings with wood. This is a lucky little tree, safe in its pot."

I felt lucky too. Mom seemed to be warming to Jake. He'd patiently answered more questions than a census survey. We now knew his parents' ages and former occupations. The schools he attended. The kinds and names of pets he'd owned since childhood. The type of pie he preferred for Christmas dinner. The answer to the last was good-old fashioned pumpkin.

Mom had approved of pumpkin. "I'm glad to hear you don't eat cactus like Rita said," she'd said. I'd let the jab at cactus cookies go uncontested so that pie harmony could reign.

"He's quite polite for a lawyer," Mom admitted back at the house. We were watching out the living room window as Jake and Celia positioned the tree "just right." According to Celia, it should be visible from the sofa and far enough off the porch that birds could safely fly to it. She planned popcorn strings, orange slice ornaments, and tiny solar lights.

"He's very polite," I agreed. "A nice man. Probably just as nice as Albert the dentist."

Mom wasn't ready to go that far. "His profession, though, Rita. What if he becomes influenced by criminal types?" Before I could protest, she added, "I know, some of his clients must be perfectly innocent and in need of help. Your father . . ." She paused, looking out the window to the holiday scene of Jake and Celia hanging pine cone ornaments. Winston was rolling joyously on a patch of warm, rust-colored sandstone.

"What about Dad?" I said, after Mom remained silent for a few beats.

Finally, she said, "He was swayed, I suppose is the word, by one of his clients. It hardly matters now, does it? I'm only mentioning it because I want you to be careful, Rita. I worry about you and Celia, living in such a different place, all alone."

We were hardly alone or Wild West pioneers. I was more interested in the tidbit about my father. "Mom, you never told me that about Dad. What do you mean, swayed?"

Mom waved a hand. "That was long ago, and I made the decision that you and your sister wouldn't have to worry about your father's mistakes." She waved to Celia, who was gesturing for us to come outside. "Let's go join the fun."

I followed, my thoughts jangling as much as the jingle bell Winston had just swiped off the tree.

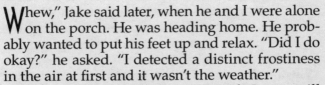

"Whew," Jake said later, when he and I were alone on the porch. He was heading home. He probably wanted to put his feet up and relax. "Did I do okay?" he asked. "I detected a distinct frostiness in the air at first and it wasn't the weather."

"Sorry for the inquisition," I said. I was still trying to work out Mom's words. Swayed? Had Dad done something unethical? Criminal? Mom sure wouldn't abide that, and it might explain her frostiness toward Jake. I'd have to find a quiet time to sit down and talk with her alone. Until I knew for sure, I wouldn't worry Jake with Mom's lawyer bias. "You won a lot of points with my mother today. Good answer about pumpkin pie."

His eyes twinkled. "I thought it best not to mention my affinity for avocado cream pie."

"Smart man," I said.

He looked over his shoulder and then took me in his arms. "Since I have some points built up, how about I gamble some? Can I lure you over to my place for a nightcap? It is still the weekend. What if I promise to get you back before curfew?"

"Promise?" I said with a grin.

"Maybe. Maybe not."

That evening, it was me disregarding my promise to be home by ten.

"It's my casita," I said, defiantly snuggling closer to Jake. "I can go home whenever I please."

"Exactly," he replied, kissing the top of my head.

Two wineglasses sat on the coffee table. We were lounging on a fluffy sheepskin rug, watching the embers crackle and glow in his stone fireplace. I tugged the blanket closer, reluctant to get up. Winston, lying at our feet, got up and rearranged himself with a thump.

"Plus, it's snowing," I said, glancing out the window.

"Right again," Jake said. "Doesn't that mean you have to stay?"

I let myself believe that for a while. Then I sighed. "Or it means I should get going before the roads turn treacherous. If Mom's still up, she'll scold me for staying out too late, risking bad roads and burglars."

He grinned. "We're always kids to our parents. Want me to drive you back? I don't like the idea of you fighting off snowdrifts and robbers either."

Although reluctant to leave his company, I declined. I had all-wheel drive. Plus, I knew where to park to make the least noise in the driveway. Hopefully Mom would already be in bed and I'd sneak to my sofa bed.

My cold, lonely, rib-jabbing sofa bed, I thought, shivering until the car's heater worked up a tepid breeze. I drove slowly through the snow-coated streets, admiring the indigo blue of the night sky and the soft silence that comes with snowfall. At my address, I turned into the driveway that should have been quiet as a mouse. Except it wasn't, and I had no chance of sneaking in undetected.

Mom and Manny stood under the glare of Manny's headlights and the porch light. Our little Christmas tree blinked weakly, its multicolored solar lights cloaked in glowing snow.

"Rita!" Mom said when I got out, trepidation growing. "Where have you been? Do you know it's nearly eleven? I tried to call."

Uh oh. I'd muted my phone's volume at dinner and forgotten to turn it up again. "Mom," I said, forcing my tone to remain calm. "Please tell me what's going on."

Manny stepped forward and drew me aside, over to the blinking tree. "What have you been up to?" he asked.

"Me? I went out after dinner to see Jake. So I'm a bit late getting home. It doesn't require the police."

My ex was staring out into the darkness. "I'm not here because of your love life, Rita," he said, his voice hard. "I'm here because some creep threatened our daughter. When I find him, he's going to wish he's the one who's dead."

Chapter 18

I stared at the note, typed in the kind of faux-handwritten cursive used for wedding invitations. The floweriness of the letters somehow made it creepier. So did the primitive line drawing of a devil stabbed by a pitchfork. Snowflakes fluttered onto the plastic evidence bag containing the note. I let them pile up and obscure the vile message.

"Notice how it's addressed to you," Manny said.

I had noticed that, along with the threat to Celia's life if I didn't stop investigating.

"But I'm *not* investigating," I protested, garnering a skeptical "Right" from my ex. "Okay," I clarified. "I was before, but not now, after nothing happened at *Las Posadas* yesterday. I spent the day with Mom and Celia. We got a tree." I gestured toward the dimly lit spruce in case Manny hadn't noticed that festive touch.

Manny said, "I guess our letter writer didn't get the memo about your holiday vacation." A crime scene van pulled up and white-suited guys jumped out. Manny directed them to look for footprints and fingerprints. He then cursed the fluffy snow, which was picking up and coating everything— including footprints and evidence—in cottony clumps.

Celia opened the door a crack. She was dressed in flannel pajamas and fluffy slippers, both with smiling skull images on them. "It's no big deal!" she said with an exaggerated sigh. "Mom, Dad, I *told* Gran that I didn't want to bug you."

"Your grandmother did the right thing, honey," Manny said. "I don't want you to worry. Go back inside and keep warm."

"I'm not worried," Celia grumbled. "I'm not scared either. The jerk can't even draw."

At her feet, Hugo poked his head and a tentative paw outside. The paw touched snow, jerked back, and Hugo retreated. I brushed snow from my shoulders and stomped my caked shoes. "Let's get inside and talk, all of us. I'll make tea or hot cider."

I expected Manny to say he was too busy for tea-time. "Good idea," he said, following me inside. "Celia, your mother and I have to talk while you get a bag together. I'd like you to stay at my place tonight."

Celia scooped up Hugo, who nuzzled into her choppy black hair. I'm grateful that Manny and Celia have a good relationship. She likes to hang out at his house, especially when she wants more leeway with her curfew. They go to movies to-gether too, action and vampire films that I'd never want to see. Now, however, her face registered her confliction.

"Gran's here . . ." she said. A few feet away, my mother sat in an armchair, "staying out of the way." She flipped pages of an upscale real estate magazine. I knew she had no interest in multimillion-dollar adobe mansions.

I filled in where Celia left off. "Yes, Manny, we talked about this. Celia should be here while her grandmother's in town. It's a special visit."

Manny drew me aside, "What about the special visit you got from some psycho tonight? The letter's not all. Since you weren't here, you don't know. The creep tapped on Celia's window and plastered the note up there. That's how she found it."

I gasped. "Did she see him?" I asked.

Manny shook his head. "She thought she saw a red hat with white trim." Manny's voice fell an octave lower. "Like Santa."

My stay-calm voice failed me. "Celia, you should go stay at your father's tonight, honey."

She started to protest, but Mom chimed in. "We'll all sleep better knowing that you're safe and sound in a policeman's house, honey. We'll meet up tomorrow, like we planned, and go to the Native American arts museum with Sky. Maybe we can take our nice friend Gary the bodyguard too. I'm sure Gary would love a trip to the museum."

I imagined Gary in his dark glasses fidgeting through a museum tour. An inappropriate stress giggle bubbled. I covered it with a cough.

"We'll have to pack Gary a lot of snacks," Celia said dryly. "You guys, I don't need a guard. It was just some weirdo." Still, she stomped down the hall to pack a bag and her favorite pillow.

Mom thanked Manny for coming and plied him with thumbprint cookies and half a loaf of pumpkin bread. "For breakfast tomorrow," she said, handing him the bag of goodies.

Manny politely thanked her and turned on his charm. He smiled, told her how he'd missed her cooking, and reminisced about her holiday feasts.

Mom soaked up the praise. "You should come for Christmas dinner, then!" she said, either ignoring or somehow missing my obvious cringe.

"We have a small place . . ." I said.

"Didn't you say your landlord's big house will be empty?" Mom persisted. "Or we can set up a long table in this living room. Manny, I know you have family here and will want to be with them, but if you have time, we'd love for you to stop by. A true family meal for Celia. We'll be dining promptly at—"

"At noon, if I remember right?" Manny said with a beaming smile to Mom. By the time the smile reached me, it had faded to a one-sided smirk. "I'll try to make it," he said. "If I'm not busy catching the criminals you stir up. I'm warning you Rita, you need to—"

"I know!" I said. "I'm off the case. No investigating."

The crime techs tromped around from the side of the house, shaking their heads and reporting that there was nothing to find. Celia gave me a quick hug good night. "Hey, you can use my bed," she said. "That's a good thing, right?"

Not really, I thought later, lying under her heavy quilt with an even heavier cat kneading my stomach. I'd sleep on the sofa bed any day if it meant my daughter was safe and sound down the hall.

"What should I do, Hugo?" I asked. He purred unhelpfully in response. The letter, though threatening Celia, was aimed at me. Had the writer struck out because I'd gotten too close to the truth? But I hadn't come close. I hadn't accomplished anything that I could tell. Wyatt had alibis, and Lorena had "fired" me from the investigation. Did one of them know something I didn't? Then there was Trey. Had he seen me outside the archives room last night? He could have thought I was spying when really I was innocently delivering a message. Angel and his witchy granny were also still unaccounted for. She'd likely cast a spell instead of writing up a note, and Angel didn't seem like a flowery font type of guy. I sighed and flipped over. Hugo curled up at my side, purring and lulling me to sleep. I knew one thing. I couldn't let the investigation rest.

Flori greeted me at Tres Amigas the next morning with a cleaver in her hands. A pork roast lay on the counter, awaiting dismemberment. It wasn't the roast that had the most to worry about, though.

"If I get my hands on that horrible person," Flori said, waving the knife. "Well, I don't care if it is Christmas. Anyone who would threaten Celia has it coming."

"So you heard?" I asked, rubbing my eyes and yawning. I should have slept better in Celia's bed, with the cozy feather topper and cuddly cat. Instead, I'd tossed and turned the length of a marathon.

Flori said she'd heard from her gossip network last night. Bill Hoffman, monitoring his police scanner, had sounded the alarm, hearing Manny bark orders over the police channel. "I've called another Knit and Snitch for the afternoon," Flori said. "I'm combining it with a *bizcochitos*-making lesson for Addie's British friends if you'd like to join us."

Addie came in, her face a scowling contrast to her bright British tea-towel apron. "I'm with Miss Flori. What balderdash and poppycock and hogwashery and—" She stopped, running out of British and/or Harry Potter words.

I told them I appreciated their concern. "Someone sneaking around at night picking on a teenager can't be that brave," I said, with more confidence than I felt. "And any poison pen writer's a bully and a coward. It won't work. If anyone asks, though, I'm *not* investigating. I'm a busy cook, showing my mother around town with no time for anything else."

Addie nodded seriously. "Got it."

Flori held up her cleaver, "If anyone asks if you're investigating, we'll put them on our suspect list."

After calling to check on Celia, I threw myself into work and kept to my plan. Whenever anyone asked me about my holiday plans, I elaborated on my busy schedule in a loud voice and in

great detail. I told customers I barely knew about
our Christmas tree and my mother visiting and
all the things we had planned.

I kept up my act with Flori's knitting group,
who came in at the tail end of lunch and took over
three tables.

"Of course. You're very, very busy," Flori's
graffiti knitting co-conspirator, Miriam, said
knowingly when I mentioned a choral concert.
"You have a lot going on." She looked up over
a silver mitten the size of a football helmet and
winked.

"Yes," said Hazel, the flask wielder I'd met at
Flori's last Knit and Snitch. "Way too busy for investigating a murder and threats and whatnot."

Twittering ensued and a lady with blue-tipped
curls said, "Too busy to know that my great-niece,
who works at the pharmacy, confirmed filling a
migraine prescription for a handsome blond man
the night of the devil murder. She was worried he
couldn't get home, he was in such pain and nau-
seous and dizzy to boot. She got her assistant to
take over and she drove him the few blocks to his
apartment. She said he was so polite, even in his
agony. Quite a looker too."

The ladies tittered about Barton Hunter's masculine beauty and polite charms and complimented
the great-niece, who was finishing her pharmacy
internship with honors.

Hazel broke in with more information. "Bet
you're too busy for a rumor about witchy Josephina
Ortiz too. Hear tell, she's staying out at her former
sister-in-law's condo by the Japanese hot spring.
Talk about the last place anyone would look for her!

Those two hate each other, and Josephina's not the type to abide by condo regulations."

"Maybe they worked out their differences in the hot spring," Miriam said generously. "It's quite a lovely place. Oh, and Rita, you won't want to know that Angel Ortiz was washing pots and pans at that fancy steak place that all those businessmen in snappy suits go to. I sometimes sit at the bench outside their patio and knit and watch the view. Of nice tushes!" She snickered and started incorporating a new color into her knit.

I thanked them and confirmed that I wasn't interested in the least. Then I went to the kitchen. "I see that you told them again," I said to Flori.

Flori was putting the fixing touches on a towering platter of nachos. "Well, I had to clue them in," she said. "They're the Knit and Snitchers. They'd never believe that we *weren't* investigating, and they'd find out anyway. They'll be discreet. Anyway, I bet we've already learned more than that stubborn ex of yours."

In the dining room, Hazel was dousing the teapot with clear liquid from her flask. Discretion was exactly what I worried about.

"Hazel gets a bit rowdy around the holidays," Flori said, when I pointed out the teapot tampering. "She's a pastor's wife, though. They know how to keep their lips zipped."

Addie, emerging from the pantry with an armload of cookie supplies, giggled. "That lot? Discreet? The darling with the flask told me the rowdiest stories about her grandson, who she says is a right looker. If he's anything like her, he sounds like a handful." She giggled and released her cookie ingredients onto the table. Flour puffed, causing her to sneeze and laugh some more.

"Sorry, Rita," she said, recovering her composure. "I shouldn't be laughing, not with what's going on."

"Of course you should," I told her. "It's the holidays and everything's okay. Celia's safe. The police are investigating. That note was all bluster."

My everything-is-okay theory was soon broken by Hazel. I heard knitting needles clanging on a flask first, followed by a sharp voice. "Incoming!" Hazel yelled above the chatting. "Message from Bill."

The room went silent. Addie, Flori, and I went out in the main dining room and watched as Hazel poked at her cell phone until Bill's creaky voice came on the speaker.

"Just in," he said. "Police en route to Judith Crundall's place. Got a call about more devil letters. This is Hoffman, over and out."

All eyes turned to me.

Miriam spoke first. "You need a cover, Rita, if you're planning to pop by the Crundall mansion. Say you're bringing them some baked goods. Or some knitwear. I'm making a mitten you could take. Does Judith have a big one-handed statue that could use something warm and festive?"

"Take the nachos," boozy Hazel ordered.

I couldn't very well take a half-eaten plate of nachos or a mitten fit for a giant.

"You can have my fourth trial run of *bizcochitos*," Addie said, clapping her hands in excitement. "They're fresh from the oven."

Addie's culinary endeavors are usual best uneaten. Even squirrels and other woodland creatures shun them. If she doesn't burn her recipes to a crusty char, she manages a questionable substitution. I've choked down pies in which she mistook salt for sugar, and cinnamon rolls she decided would be more "surprising" with chipotle chile. Before I could find the words for a polite refusal, she ran back to the kitchen and returned with a plate of *bizcochitos.* They actually looked pretty good. No obvious burning. No saline residue that I could tell.

"They're lush," Addie said, clasping her hands. "Truly luscious."

"What's wrong with them?" I whispered to Flori as I got in my coat. "Salt? No sugar? Cumin in the sugar coating?"

Flori furtively glanced over her shoulder. Leaning in, she whispered, "She followed my recipe quite well this time except . . ." Flori paused then said, "She didn't use lard!"

"Butter?" I asked.

Flori's expression was grim. "Shortening! She left out the egg too. They're vegan!"

Chapter 19

I arrived at Judith Crundall's bearing the plate of vegan *bizcochitos* at the same time Manny was stomping out the front door.

He stopped at the threshold, leaving the door open. Behind him, I caught a glimpse of Judith Crundall in her wheelchair.

"You're letting a draft in," I pointed out.

"You're meddling," my ex retorted. "Wasn't it just last night that a psycho threatened our daughter to stop you from messing around in a murder case? What does it take to get you to stop, Rita?"

I held up the platter of cookies. "I'm not meddling. I'm delivering a plate of Christmas cookies to Ms. Crundall. She just got out of the hospital, you know, where they frown on drafts." I was glad that Flori had decorated the cookie plate with a big red bow. I patted the bow for emphasis.

His eyes were on the cookies encased in plastic wrap. "Are those Flori's *bizcochitos*?" he said, his tone betraying interest.

I could have been mean and let Manny believe he was about to taste the tender, spicy joy of Flori's cookies. However, it was Christmas, and I was done being petty with Manny. "Addie made them," I said, and his hand whipped back. "They're actually quite good." I'd tried one in the car. They weren't quite as tender as Flori's, but the spices were right and the cookies weren't burned or overly salted—nearly a first for Addie. "Addie followed Flori's recipe," I told Manny, "except she substituted shortening for the lard. They're vegan." Even Manny—who's never baked a cookie that someone else didn't mix or remove from a pop-open can—raised an eyebrow. "Addie's sweet on a vegan," I explained.

Manny rolled his eyes. "I suppose they can be hot too. Like that redheaded assistant bone sorter, Shasta. You know, the one with the sexy-librarian glasses? I was hoping she'd be here."

I shook my head at my ex, marveling that he could maintain such consistent boorishness. "And how do you know she's vegan?" I said.

"I asked if she wanted to go grab a burger the other day," he said with a shrug. "She turned me down saying she's vegetarian or vegan or something weird like that."

And maybe because she sensed Manny's true character. I held in my sarcastic retort, since I wanted information. "Why are you here, anyway?" I asked in what I hoped was an innocent, totally naïve tone. "Is something wrong?"

I'm a horrible actor, and Manny knows me too well. "Like you don't already know," he said. Still, he reached into his open jacket and pulled a clear evidence bag from the inside pocket. "Another *Las Posadas* devil also got a note last night. Barton Hunter. He said he arrived here for work this morning and came in the front doors. It wasn't until he went through the archive entrance later that he found the threat. He almost didn't call. Said he thought it was a prank. When Judith heard, she called us."

I yearned to read the note. I tilted my chin, trying to catch a glimpse. All I could make out was the same flowery font.

"Want to know what it says?" Manny asked, dangling the evidence bag closer.

I sensed a test or a trap. "No." I busied myself by tucking the festive red plastic wrap around the cookie plate. "I have no interest. I'm not involved, remember?" Besides, I could ask Judith or Barton. Heck, probably Bill Hoffman had heard what the note said over his gossip airwaves.

Manny snorted, tucked the letter back in his jacket, and headed to his car. On the way, his radio buzzed on and I recognized the voice of Deputy Davis. "Checked on the third devil, sir," she said through static crackles. "No note that he knows of. We couldn't find anything around his perimeter. He lives in a condo. Upper floor. Coded lock on the front entry. Maybe the perp couldn't get in. He says he's worried. Says he wants to quit the play."

"Good for him," Manny grumbled. "He won't have to quit. I ordered Crundall to shut it down." He got in his car and slammed the door.

Judith Crundall looked in no mood for orders from Manny Martin or anyone else. When I peeked in the front door, she was still sitting in the foyer. "Well, come in and shut the door," she said, her eyes narrowing at me. The "what do you want" was left implied. She shoved one of Dalia's curative dolls into a tote bag hanging from the side of her wheelchair. The colorful throw blanket on her lap met a similar fate.

"Cookies!" I said in my chipper voice that comes out under stress. "I just wanted to pop by and see how you were feeling."

"Like death," Judith croaked. Seeing what must have been my horrified expression, she said. "I'm drowning in hydration and back to my usual aches, pains, and shakes. What is it they say? Getting old isn't for sissies? I was never a wilting violet, but I feel like one these days."

Footsteps sounded in the hall. A waft of patchouli announced Dalia before she rounded the corner. "Thank you!" she gushed, when I again presented my cookie cover. "We needed some fresh baked goods around here, didn't we, Judith? We were just about to have some tea. Rita, won't you join us?"

Judith waved a dismissive hand, sending a feathery dream catcher attached to the back of her chair spinning. She swatted it again and said that she couldn't think of eating. "No offense," she said to me. "I can't stomach cookies. All that butter."

"Likely lard," Dalia said, making her half sister wince.

"They're vegan!" I announced proudly. "Yep,

no butter or lard or even eggs in these beauties. They're our special health-food *bizcochitos*."

The corner of Judith's mouth twitched into the hint of a smile. "You all are determined to make me live, aren't you? All right. Let's go to the kitchen and try a vegan *bizcochito*. There's something for my bucket list."

Dalia fussed about staying positive and kept up a peppy chatter about cookies and energy-enhancing vibes as she rolled Judith's wheelchair down the hall. I tried to keep up with Dalia's conversation and her speed. However, I was distracted by taking in the many rooms of Judith's mansion.

"This is an amazing place," I said. "I had no idea it had so many corridors and separate wings."

"Lots of additions over the decades," Judith said as we whizzed around a corner. "The oldest room's back to the left. You step down into it. My father did an archeological dig right here in his own house. Said the foundation and a few walls are from the 1700s. We think it was built by my relatives." She reached up and patted her half sister's hand. "*Our* relatives."

Dalia said something grand and New Agey about how we're all brothers and sisters. "The old home has seen a lot," she said, coming back to earth. "It needs a fresh start. When the collection is cleared out, Judith is going to make the space into a library."

"If I live that long," Judith said.

Dalia lovingly chastised Judith and eased her chair into the kitchen. Unlike the other rooms I'd glimpsed, the kitchen was surprisingly humble.

The stove and refrigerator had the rounded curves of the forties, a retro look that was back in style. The floor was soft orange Saltillo tiles, similar to those at Tres Amigas and my casita. The cabinets were covered in tin punched in decorative outlines of birds and flowers. Through the lace curtains covering the windows, I could see well-pruned shrubs waiting out the winter, and a small adobe cottage.

"Is that where Francisco lived?" I asked.

Dalia said a prayer to the stars. Judith gave a succinct yes and wheeled herself out of her sister's grasp to a glass door overlooking the garden. With effort, she hefted herself out of the chair.

"Judith!" Dalia said, before being waved off.

"I can stand, Dalia," Judith said. "It's good for me." She allowed me to lend her an arm for balance. I was afraid she'd want to go out to the patio, where last night's snow lingered. Instead, she gazed out at the little house. "I could say that I felt sorry for Francisco, that that's why I hired him and put him up in the casita."

I waited, sensing that she'd go on.

She did. "The real reason? When I heard he was an archeologist and historian, applying for my gardening job, I thought I could get him to work on that blasted collection. It's always been a mess. I should have given it to a museum years ago, before all those laws about repatriation got passed. Let someone else deal with it!"

She wobbled, and I helped her back into her chair. Dalia plopped a furred and feathered doll on her lap.

"You're making peace with it now, Judith,"

Dalia said. She handed her half sister a porcelain plate with some of Addie's *bizcochitos* on it. Judith nibbled one and declared it "Not bad."

"Not bad" was a high compliment for Addie's cooking. I'd have to tell her.

"But Francisco didn't want to work on the collection?" I asked.

Judith, still gazing outside, said that he'd focused on the garden. "Always so much to do out there in the yard. He kept saying he'd get to the collection when he had time. I knew he was politely putting me off. I was telling Dalia about it once and she volunteered to make the inventory."

"I cleansed it too," Dalia said. "With thyme and sage essences and the help of a lovely shaman."

"Very helpful," her serious half sister said dryly. "I rather hoped that Francisco would take pity on you, Dalia. But he didn't. He was good at that and fixing things and kept to himself. I appreciated that. I don't like people bothering me."

I scratched my theory that Francisco might have discovered something particularly valuable or scandalous in the collection. "Francisco hadn't mentioned anyone bothering him or any worries?" I asked. I realized that I could be breaking my cover of this being a simple cookie-delivery stop. However, Judith had brought him up.

Neither she nor Dalia reported noticing any changes in Francisco's demeanor. "He tried to hide it, but he was excited to play the devil," Judith said, a crack of sorrow appearing in her hard outer shell.

She pointed out into the garden toward the left.

"He was working on the patio, keeping himself busy in winter. He reset some stones heaved by that cottonwood and dug out aspen suckers by Trey's rooms. Those trees are so tenacious. They'll shoot into the house if you let them. Trey said that the sound of Francisco's trowel bothered him. I told him, he was a grown man who could get his own place if my gardener bothered him. I suspect he's waiting me out."

This time, Dalia didn't fuss that her sister was wrong. She frowned deeply before passing around the *bizcochitos* again.

I wanted to know more about Trey Crundall, but not as much as I wanted to know more about the threatening note. "The policeman who was just here, he's my former husband," I said. "Did he find anything useful?"

"He tramped all over outside," Judith said. "He wanted to search Francisco's casita again. I told him he could. It was his time to waste. He came up with nothing."

Dalia said, "He asked about some library books Francisco had out on Pueblo history, but the subject was hardly surprising. Francisco was a historian by training."

"Silly man," Judith said.

I would have wondered if she meant Francisco or Manny except she added, "He tried to order me around. Told me to cancel my play. Did he do that with you when you were married? I didn't like it one bit." She gazed outside. "You know what I like even less? He was right, although I'd already made the decision. I'll send out the carolers and that devilish donkey. The human devils are grounded for now. You'll be happy about that, won't you?"

"Not happy," I said, truthfully. "Relieved. Best to be safe."

Judith muttered something about the threatening note writer should be worried about his safety.

"What did your note say?" I asked.

"Nothing but foolishness," Judith said dismissively.

"A death threat," Dalia said with a shudder. "I can tell you exactly what it said, 'Death to all devils! Death to the disturber of the bones!' Then there was a drawing . . ." She clamped her lips shut and gripped the turquoise bear hanging from her neck.

Judith made a scoffing sound. "The fool tried to draw Mr. Barton. At least, that's who we think it was meant to be. It was a very amateurish drawing. I'd expect better from Edison. And the text, so melodramatic."

And creepy. "We got a threat too," I said. "Did Officer Martin tell you?"

Judith said that he had. "I'll keep Gary on as Celia's bodyguard for as long as she needs or wants. So rude to threaten a young woman! People are terrible." She had Dalia write out Gary's contact information and told me to call on him anytime.

I pondered the letters. One threatened Celia, aimed at me. The other threatened Barton Hunter, a devil but also the "disturber of the bones." The third devil hadn't been contacted. I wondered again if there was a connection between the collection and the killing.

A soft knock at the kitchen doorway caused me to jump.

Judith reacted calmly. "Ah, Barton, I thought you might want to take the rest of the afternoon off."

The consultant politely thanked Judith for her concern. "I'm not scared of a little note. Plus, I'm afraid I have more work than ever. Remember when I told the police that the archives looked fine?"

During his pause, I prepared for bad news.

He continued. "Well, everything seemed okay, until I checked some of the boxes that were already packed for shipping. Judith, there's no easy way to say this. We've been robbed. Right under our noses."

Judith was no longer calm. She spun her wheelchair toward the kitchen door.

Dalia rushed after her. "A break-in?" she asked.

Barton shook his head. "That's the odd thing, the door to storage was locked. Shasta isn't in yet, but I'll get her to cross-check more of the inventory. Should I call the police or do you want to see first?"

Judith was already wheeling out the door. "No police," she said curtly.

No police? "An inside job?" I whispered to Barton as we followed the sisters down the hall.

"Afraid it could be," he said, shaking his head sadly. "I was pretty shocked when I lifted one of those boxes and it was as light as empty. Well, it was empty."

I was about to be shocked too, for a different reason. When I entered the archives room, I saw

Celia holding one end of a stationary red jump rope. Sky held the other end and little Eddie jumped over the string, laughing giddily. Gary stood a few feet away, his dark glasses pushed up to his forehead so he could manhandle a burrito into his mouth. Emilie was reading a book.

"Celia? What are you doing?" I asked.

My daughter flashed a beaming—and surely fake—smile. "Babysitting, Mom! Gran's resting. She says the altitude's getting to her. Dalia called to tell Sky and me that our devil and imp acts are canceled, and she mentioned that she needed a babysitter and Gary would be here. You know how much I love kids! And Gary makes us feel *so* protected."

Gary blushed and took an extra-large bite of burrito.

Warning bells clanged in my head. First, the Celia I knew wouldn't cheerfully accept the cancellation of her devil diva act. Second, Celia did like kids, to a point. She likes to encourage them in kid versions of defiant art, like washable finger paintings on sidewalks and chalk graffiti on tree trunks. She likes to have them do her bidding. However, she has never, ever expressed an interest in babysitting. In fact, the last time someone offered Celia a babysitting job, she declared sexism and stomped off. And that bit about Gary making her feel safe? She'd taken the lie too far there.

I turned to Cass's tall son. He, like me, was a bad liar. "Sky, what are you two up to?"

Sky twitched the end of the rope, causing Edison to leap out of the way. "Ah . . . earning Christmas money and having fun. We're going to play hide-and-seek, right Eddie?"

The little boy agreed happily. I figured Eddie wouldn't be too hard to fool. Neither would Gary.

I went over to Gary and put a hand out to halt his work of burrito lifting. "Gary, this is very important," I said, slowly and enunciating each word. "Do not leave Celia's side. Do not let her out of your sight." I lowered my voice and snitched on my own daughter. "She may try to trick you. Be very careful."

Gary switched his burrito to the other hand, took a big bite, and informed me through a mouthful of beans, cheese, and chiles that he would watch them "like a raptor." He swallowed and added, "I'm real good at hide-and-seek too."

I kissed my daughter's cheek and she smiled back benignly. "Have fun detecting, Mom." Before I could protest, she said, "Oops, no, I remember, you're not doing that. You're too busy."

"Exactly," I said. "Have fun babysitting. Do not evade Gary, do you understand me? He's guarding you. Judith generously hired him, and we don't want to make him feel bad, okay?"

Gary muttered that no girl could evade him.

I eyed Celia. "Do not take that as a challenge," I said.

"Okay, I promise," she said, holding up both sets of black-painted fingernails to show me she wasn't crossing her fingers through a fib. "I'll keep Gary with me the whole time. We're fine and just having fun playing games with the kids."

My skeptical stare failed to get her to open up. I wasn't thrilled about her hanging around the scene of another threatening note. However, the casita faced the same problem, and there, the only protectors were my altitude-afflicted mother and an overly affectionate cat.

"Okay," I said. "I have a few things to . . . er . . . look into," I said, as evasively as my teenager. "I'll pick you up on my way back home. Say an hour or two?"

Celia patted Edison's silky head, flat palmed like bouncing a basketball. "Sure, that should give us enough time," she said.

Chapter 20

Barton Hunter followed me out the door. He gripped his cell phone in one hand and a Ziploc bag filled with some of Addie's cookies in the other. "Impossible to get decent help," he grumbled, striding past me toward his car.

I realized that I'd parked him in. "I'm leaving too," I said, jogging to beat him to our vehicles. "I'll get out of your way."

He slowed and gave me a strained smile. "Sorry. I don't mean to be rude. It's been a frustrating day already. That note, the missing objects, an assistant who's hours late for work." He rolled his eyes and held up a paper bag, "At least I have some of those cookies you brought. I noticed your daughter and her Native American pal are hanging around too. My job offer still stands, for both of them. I need to get boxes cross-checked and headed in the right direction. Won't do Judith's karma any good if we send stuff to the wrong place."

"Too bad Celia's busy babysitting," I said. Whatever Celia was up to, if it kept her out of the creepy collections that was a good thing. Besides, babysitting was a job Mom could tell her friends back home about. Bone sorting and shipping? Not so much.

"A pity," Barton said. "Babysitting seems a waste of sharp minds."

Exactly what Celia might say. I got into my car quickly, before he could press the matter. Glancing in my rearview mirror, I saw that Barton was heading the same direction. That wasn't surprising, since there were only a few routes leading downtown. I doubted we were going to the same place. I planned to scope out Trey Crundall's ski shop.

The narrow streets of Santa Fe can be challenging at any time of year. This season, they were especially packed. Navigating through art lovers strolling along Canyon Road and weaving through side streets, I kept my eyes scanning the sidewalks and road ahead until I reached a small dead-end street a few blocks from the Plaza. When I'd first moved to Santa Fe, a building at the end of the street had sold fabric and crafts supplies. Sadly, the shop had gone under. I hadn't been down the lane since.

When I pulled up, I almost turned around. "Bums?" I said out loud. *Who names their shop Bums?* A ski bum, I supposed. Especially a man/boy who still lives with his mother.

To my surprise, a car pulled in next to me, and Barton Hunter stepped out and smoothed his fashionable wool peacoat. "Ms. Lafitte, we meet again. If you hadn't arrived before me, I'd say you're following me."

I laughed and said I was curious about Trey's shop.

"This classy establishment? I'm sure you'll find many lovely items for your Christmas list," Barton said, jokingly. He headed toward Bums.

"What are you doing here?" I blurted out. "Stocking stuffers?"

Barton stepped onto the front porch of the building, a nondescript structure with cracked adobe and a sagging portico. Ski boards and a mannequin, nude except for opalescent goggles and mittens, decorated the porch.

He said, "Then you aren't following me after all. A pity. This building is also my temporary home, compliments of Ms. Crundall. Shasta has a studio apartment in the back too, easier for her than taking the train back and forth to Albuquerque, though she still can't manage to be on time. Care to see my place? It's much nicer than this, thank heaven." He scowled at the saggy porch and the mannequin, which, at closer inspection, was missing a foot.

I'm never one to turn down a Santa Fe architectural tour. I also saw a benefit. I could check out two people close to Judith Crundall and get Barton's take on Trey.

As we walked by Bums, I spotted Trey through the window. He slouched in front of a computer, black headphones over his ears, laughing to himself.

Barton glanced in and sniffed. "I'm grateful for those headphones. Before he got them, I was subjected to action movie soundtracks during my lunch breaks."

"I thought adobes had thick walls," I said.

He unlocked an ornately trimmed wood door painted in chipped turquoise. "The walls are thick. Trouble is, this building used to be all one place. Trey's office is the old living and dining room, separated from my side by flimsy doors and panel walls." He opened his door and swung his arms out. "I'm not complaining, though. The apartment's a gem."

An amazing mix of colorful Mexican tiles and brick covered the floor. The front room featured a huge kiva fireplace and dark log ceiling beams. The beams were connected by concave plaster, like rolling waves. "Gorgeous," I agreed. "So, when you're here, do you hear Trey doing a lot of business?"

Barton's scornful snort answered that question. "I'm mostly working at Judith's during Trey's 'work' hours. When I am here, though? Pretty much all quiet except for him watching videos. Mostly he's gone, playing with his inventory on the slopes. You want my opinion, he's a big spoiled kid who's mad that his mommy doesn't give him an endless allowance."

Mad enough to send mean letters and steal from her? "Do you think Trey could be behind the missing objects? Or those awful notes?" I asked.

Barton apologized for possibly giving me the wrong impression. "I shouldn't talk of my employer's kid that way. I can't speak to the recent theft or crazy notes either. I'm hired to repatriate the collection, that's all."

He sounded like Jake, refusing to speculate about his clients. "Hypothetically?" I prompted.

"Hypothetically? I'd speculate that Trey Crundall has been skimming off parts of that collection for years."

He turned the conversation to architecture, showing me a glorious tiled bathroom and art deco light fixtures. "You know a lot about local architecture," I said, impressed.

"I dabble in all sorts of history," he said with a flare of his dimples. "We archeologists are always digging up the past."

I peeked down a hallway decorated in carved wooden beams. "The master suite is at the end of the hall," Barton said. "Of interest?"

The man was like Manny, I decided. He simply couldn't turn off the flirtations. "Nice *nicho*," I said, deadpan, admiring an inset niche in the plaster wall. A wooden St. Francis figurine stood inside, gazing down adoringly at carved animals, including a donkey.

He grinned and said, "Feel free to continue the tour on your own. I need to find the shipping slips I came for."

I wandered down the hallway, looking in a small room that smelled dusty and appeared unused, except as suitcase and box storage. Touring the consultant's bedroom seemed wrong. I glanced in, though, taking in a four-poster bed frame and a view on to the back garden. The room was bachelor messy, with clothes draped on the wooden chest at the foot of the bed and towels hanging from the doorknobs. I was moving on when something registered in my brain. A flash of red silk and lace amid the jeans and button-down men's clothes. At least the handsome outsider wasn't lonely.

I was admiring the small kitchen and an adorable antique stove when a woman's raised voice startled me. "Calm down? Do you see this?"

I stood still, cocking my head but unable to make out Barton's low, masculine tones.

Feeling bad for lurking in the dark, listening in, I went to see if I could help. When I arrived in the living room, I saw Shasta in the doorway. Her red hair was coming loose from its bun, her glasses tilted at forty-five degrees, and she was dangling something at arm's length, held in two fingers. She glanced over Barton's shoulder and noticed me. "Rita! Look at this! This was stuffed in the mailbox. I touched it! Would your boss tell you to relax?"

"This" was a cloth doll shaped like a devil. It was impaled by a paring knife and coated in what I hoped was only red paint or food coloring. *What would my boss do?* Flori would probably set up a sting operation. Or take a Senior Center class in forensics or voodoo-doll revenge. Barton's stay-calm response sounded pretty reasonable in comparison, though I'd be creeped out too if I'd touched the doll.

"It's disturbing," I said sympathetically.

"Yeah," Shasta said with a shudder. "It was sticky. It freaked me out."

Barton held up his palms in a calming gesture. "Ladies, it's a prank. At worst, a childish threat. Miss Moon, if you hadn't slept in, you'd know I found a threatening note at the Crundall house too. I think *someone* is trying to scare us off." His eyes drifted in the direction of Bums. "But you'll remember that Ms. Crundall is the one paying us and paying quite well for our urgency."

Shasta, cheeks as red as her hair, mumbled, "I remember."

Barton took a card out of his jacket pocket. I glimpsed the logo of the Santa Fe police and Manny's name. He thrust the card at Shasta, along with the bag of *bizcochitos*. "Have a cookie. They're that New Mexican kind you like. Then call the police. Tell them what you found and if you can manage it, get to work. We had a break-in at the archives too. Judith wants an inventory of what's been taken and so do I."

"Break-in?" Shasta said, rubbing her brow. She glanced at the doll and shuddered. Then she snatched the card and the bag of cookies and stomped outside to call. "Yeah, I want to report a stupid childish prank," she said, through a mouthful of *bizcochito*.

Barton turned back to a file box on the small kitchen table. With a strained laugh, he said to me, "No wonder I have trouble finding good help. I apologize, Rita, but we really must get back to work. There have been way too many distractions lately."

I'd say! As I was leaving, I made sure to step around the cloth devil. *A childish threat*, Barton had said. I'd caught his thinly veiled hint. Even if I hadn't, I knew an angry guy who hadn't grown up. Had Trey planted the devil doll to make it look like he was a target too? I headed next door to chat with him.

Stepping into Trey's shop, my suspicion waned. The man simply didn't seem sufficiently ambitious or creative to craft vile threats. He acknowledged my presence with a languid tip of his chin and didn't appear to recognize that we'd met before, if you could call him nearly running over my mother a meeting.

"Board wax is half off," he said. "We have some wicked-sick lady boots on sale."

I pretended to show interest in two hundred-dollar "wicked-sick lady boots," while formulating a plan of approach. I decided I might as well go with the truth, in a way.

"Hey," I said. "You probably don't remember me. I'm friends with your aunt."

Trey's eyes narrowed. "Daffy Dalia? Wait, you're her neighbor, aren't you? Did she send you? What does she want me to do now? Send flowers for my mother?"

What an overgrown brat. Still, I smiled. "Moms always love flowers. No, I'm here to, ah, look for Christmas gifts." No one on my gift list skied. My family came from country where gentle bumps were considered hills. Celia viewed skiing as a jock activity and thus a waste of her time. For my part, I'd much rather sit in a warm lodge with a cup of hot cocoa than careen down a slippery slope.

I drifted toward a table with better gift possibilities. There were water bottles large and small, sunblock concocted from alpine minerals, and hats blaring logos. Mom wouldn't like the words BIG AIR embroidered across her headgear. She would, however, like actual air. I picked up a canister of compressed oxygen complete with a small face mask.

"That's awesome air," Trey said, becoming more alert. Perhaps he did have a sales streak in him. "It's portable, like for your purse. You can take a hit whenever you want. I keep some behind the desk for a boost."

Despite my initial doubts, I'd actually found a good gift. And I wouldn't wait for Christmas to let Mom open it. "It's perfect," I said. I surveyed the shelves some more and casually added, "So, I saw that the police were at your place again."

His face snapped up from the computer screen. "What'd they want?"

I pretended to study the hats. "Don't worry about your mother. She's okay. It was something else." I tried on a knit cap with floppy ear flaps complete with tassels. Definitely not my look.

"What kind of something?" Trey said after a few moments of hat styling on my part. "What'd the cops want?"

I took my time putting back the hat and formulating my fib. "I'm not sure. I was only delivering cookies to your mother, but the officer in charge, he says they're close to nabbing the person writing those nasty threat letters. When they do, they'll throw the book at him. Murder, menacing, mail fraud, you name it."

"Mail fraud?" Trey said, frowning. He scraped a hand through his already messy hair.

"Yeah, some notes came in the mail," I said. "And just now Barton and Shasta found a stabbed devil doll in the mailbox outside. The police should be here soon, but if someone's messing with the mail

system, that's a federal crime." I wasn't entirely
sure that stuffing creepy dolls in mailboxes was
a federal offense, but Trey seemed to believe me.

"In the mailbox out there? Dude, I'm the victim."
He shuffled some papers into further disorder and
muttered that he bet his mother didn't even care.

I pushed on. "It looks like items have been stolen
from your mother's collection too. The feds will
get involved in that as well, since there are Native
American artifacts. Big-time jail time."

His cheeks burned red, although I couldn't say
it was from guilt. He sounded more angry than
scared when he spoke again. He also dropped his
ski bum lingo and adopted the tone of an entitled
heir. "The Crundall collection has already been
stolen, by my own dear mother. It's my heritage, to
be passed on through men of the family. Grandfather didn't leave it for *her* to give away."

What a sexist little jerk! I resisted the urge to chas-
tise him and tried another tactic. "*You* don't have a
theory about who's sending those letters, do you?"

Trey frowned. His ski bum attitude returned.
"Dude, beats me. If she had it in her, I'd say
Mother was sending them herself, trying to teach
me some kind of lesson about caring." He picked
up and dropped a stack of papers on the counter, seemingly for the sole purpose of slamming
them. "Like I care."

Chapter 21

I stopped by Tres Amigas to report on my non-spying spy expedition. Flori sat by the fireplace in the dining area. Her socked feet rested on the hearth and her hands were busy knitting something red and green. She looked cozy and grandmotherly. Looks, I knew all too well, could be deceiving.

In the center of the room, happy chaos ensued as Addie and the British visitors hooted and laughed, egged on by Hazel and whatever she kept in her flask. The other Knit and Snitchers had left for an unspecified "practice run" at the capitol building.

"What's in that flask, anyway?" I asked, pulling up a chair beside Flori. The flask was the size of Mom's water bottles and seemingly endless.

Flori peered over her bifocals and ball of fluffy green yarn. "Hazel makes homemade moonshine. She distills it from elderberries or dandelions or whatever else she finds. She tried to sell it at the Farmers' Market one year, arguing it was all homemade and home-grown, like the market rules require. The organizers kicked her out, although she was quite popular for the day she sold. Now she has an underground online network. She sells all over to, what are they called? Hippers? Hip . . . ?"

"Hipsters?" I said, unable to suppress a grin. I could imagine Hazel, doted upon from afar by trendy young bearded men in skinny jeans and tattoos.

"That's them," Flori said. "It's illegal, shipping New Mexican moonshine across state lines, and there's Hazel, a pastor's wife." Flori, a self-professed rogue knitter, had the gall to make a disapproving tsk-tsk.

I politely inquired about her knitting. "What are you making?"

Her eyes twinkled with devious glee. "Something big," she said. "You'll see soon enough."

I was afraid of that. Kicking off my shoes, I warmed my toes by the fire and told her about the theft and threat at Judith's house and the devil doll in the mailbox.

"Interesting," my elderly friend said, pausing her knitting. "Judith did always want Trey to show some get-up-and-go . . . not that kind, I'd bet." She resumed her mystery project. Still in my sock feet, I padded over to greet the British visitors. They hailed me with whoops of delight.

"What a delightful tradition," declared the woman responsible for letting Mr. Peppers escape. They wielded cookie cutters shaped like corgis— the queen's favorite dog—as well as diamonds, snowflakes, and chile peppers.

"You earned compliments on your cookies," I told Addie. "Judith Crundall ate two and she hasn't had any appetite lately."

Addie beamed. "They're coming out right nice, aren't they? I think I've finally hit my groove as a vegan chef."

Over by the fireplace, Flori coughed and fanned herself.

The ladies, fortified with spiked tea, agreed that the vegan cookies were lovely. "We've never been so merry with our baking, have we, gals?" one of them said, with a titilated emphasis on "merry." The others raised their teacups in salute and Hazel passed around the flask.

Addie buzzed among them, removing filled cookie trays and gathering up the remaining dough to roll out again. I volunteered to pop the trays in the oven.

When I returned, oven timer ticking in my hand, Addie was schooling the ladies. "The name comes from *bizcocho*, meaning a cake or cookie. The 'chito' part makes it 'little.'" Addie upped her British accent and said, "Just like digestive biscuits, only spicier."

"And better!" one of the ladies crowed. "Beats a dry old McVitie's Digestive any day."

Eight minutes of baking and five minutes of cooling later, I brought their finished product to the table, earning applause all around. While they were jolly—and tipsy—I asked them about the night of the devil's death.

"So thrilling to be witnesses," said the lady to my left, introduced as Mrs. Abbott of Leicestershire.

The inadvertent releaser of Mr. Peppers, whom I learned was Mrs. Baxter, agreed it was. "An utter delight. Like we're starring in an American police drama. That handsome lawyer says we might be officially 'deposed' before we depart. We can't wait to tell our friends. What a place they will think this is. The Wild West. Cowboys, wild broncos."

"A donkey, dear," Mrs. Abbott corrected. "It was a small, chubby burro, with an overweight goat companion." As if on cue, Mr. Peppers brayed in the back garden.

I was glad they were having a fun adventure. If only Mom felt the same way. Maybe the portable oxygen would cheer her up. Or remind her of altitude threats.

"So . . ." I said, guiding the ladies back to the crime. "You were in the hotel the night of the murder."

"Lost," Mrs. Abbott said, touching her chest, implying they barely made it out of the boutique hotel with their lives. "For such a small establishment, it's very confusing. We went down the wrong hallway and the nicest Santa helped us find our way."

I asked exactly when and where they'd encountered the helpful Santa.

Mrs. Baxter waved her teacup, sloshing the suspiciously clear liquid. "Seven-thirty sharp, wasn't it? We were remarking that the performance was right at the dinner hour, although you Americans do eat early."

"Precisely," Mrs. Abbot said. "We were trying to get outside and see the play and we took a wrong turn. That's when the kind man came to our aid."

"Santa," Mrs. Baxter said, cutting in. "I do wish we'd had some of these cookies for him. He was very chivalrous."

Addie beamed. "Santa loves *bizcochitos*," she said. "In my family, we leave a plate out by the fireplace on Noche Buena. We kids used to wonder how Santa squeezed down our chimney. He must have, though. The cookies were always gone."

Mrs. Baxter laughed. "This Santa could have gotten down your chimney, love."

Addie helped herself to a cookie and listened wistfully as the ladies described their holiday traditions back home. I feared that steamed puddings, including those steeped in whiskey and buried in the back garden to "ripen," were in our future. Addie scribbled copious notes on her order pad.

I half listened to the culinary intricacies of black bun, a Scottish fruitcake trotted around to neighbors for New Year's Eve. Hogmanay, the holiday was called, and it sounded right up Addie's alley. She asked for the spelling and recipe details.

"Wait," I said, interrupting Mrs. Baxter's timeline of black-bun creation, which included a stunning three hours in the oven, weeks of "settling," and a dram of whiskey when serving.

"Dram of whiskey . . ." Addie murmured, taking more notes. "Righto. We'll figure that one out when the time comes."

No one had reacted to my "wait." I tried again. "Mrs. Baxter, why would your Santa friend have gotten down the chimney?"

The ladies gave me quizzical looks. "He was a slight wee man," Mrs. Baxter said. "We didn't mean that Addie should actually worry about a suited bloke slipping down her stovepipes. Although strange things do happen around here, don't they?"

Mrs. Abbot chimed in. "He was on the small side for a Santa. Slender and rather short, with a lovely olive complexion. We were saying, he reminded us of a diminutive version of the Swedish Santa, Sinterklaas. He's said to winter in Spain. Lucy—Mrs. Baxter—got to use her Spanish with him."

"*Un poquito*," Mrs. Baxter said modestly.

"Your Santa spoke Spanish?" I asked.

They clarified that he did speak English but with an accent. Mrs. Baxter wanted to practice her *español*. "Mr. Baxter and I are buying a winter cottage in Andalusia," she said, and the ladies turned to the subject of future Christmases on the Mediterranean, filling Addie's head with dreams of tapas and sangria by the sea.

I thought about Wyatt Cortez. He had a Spanish surname, and most locals spoke at least a smattering of the language. He didn't have a noticeable accent, though, and no one would call him slender or short. I glanced at Flori to see if she'd heard.

She had. She'd stopped knitting and beckoned me over.

"We have to talk to that housekeeper who provided Wyatt's other alibi," she said. Scowl lines knitted across her brow. "Rita, we may have been tricked by Santa and bought off with pie."

was about to do more pie bribery. Flori fluffed my hair as I delayed at the back door. I held an extra-large piece of Lorena's luscious caramel apple pie. Lorena had brought the pie by earlier, Flori said. More grateful payment for our efforts to help Wyatt and her friend Francisco.

"I feel kind of bad," I said.

"No, no, you're fine. Your hair's a little staticky, that's all." Flori said, fussing and frowning at my hair, which was getting more electrified by the moment. "I could spritz it with water and it would freeze in place."

The temperature hovered in the upper thirties, too warm for freeze-styling hair. Anyway, I wasn't feeling bad about my style or lack of it.

"We're re-gifting questionable payoff pie," I said. "Worse, I'm presenting Jake with a moral conundrum. What if his client's alibi is a fake? Will he have to tell the police? What if Wyatt goes to trial? What if he *doesn't* go to trial?"

"Jake is a big, strong lawyer. He's used to problems like this. Best he knows now." Flori stuffed something in my coat pocket.

I looked down to see the red cap of a canister of spray-on whipped cream.

"To sweeten the news," Flori said, giving me an off-you-go pat that verged on a shove.

I shuffled down the street, wondering how to break the news and get by Jake's territorial secretary, Becky.

Luckily, one problem solved itself. Becky's desk was empty of popcorn, suet balls, and Becky herself. The light in the front room was off, and for a moment, I thought Jake must have left and forgotten to lock up. Then I heard a woof and paws thundering up the hallway. Winston skidded to a stop in front of my feet, flopped on his side, and invited me to rub his belly. Jake sauntered up the hall.

"Quite the guard dog you have here," I said.

"He likes you," he said, giving me a kiss to show that he liked me too. Would he after I delivered my news?

"I have pie," I said, holding out the plate. "And spray cream."

"Uh oh," Jake said, eyes narrowing. "What's going on?"

We settled into his office and I told him about the short, slender, Spanish-speaking Santa. He ate pie while I talked.

"Good thing you brought this pie," he said, finally. "I'd feel like a mighty sorry fool otherwise. When those ladies said they saw Santa, I just assumed it was Wyatt. They told the police the same story. No one asked them to pick St. Nick out of a lineup. Who knew there was a pack of 'em running around that hotel?" He managed a smile. "My only consolation is that the police believed them first. And I have pie."

"Want more whipped cream?" I said.

He declined. Winston aimed his toothy underbite at me, panting to indicate that he'd take me up on the offer.

"I don't like this development either," I said, "But it's not necessarily bad news for Wyatt. He still has the housekeeper alibi, right?"

Jake was already dialing the housekeeper's number. He offered me a bite of pie while we waited for her to answer.

"Dolores?" he asked, before switching to Spanish. I took a small forkful of pie and vowed once again to work on my Spanish. Maybe Addie would tutor me if I helped her make black bun and English puddings. I drew the line at haggis. No steamed innards for any occasion.

Jake held out the phone, covering the mouthpiece. "She's at Ojo Caliente, enjoying a hot-spring spa vacation compliments of Wyatt Cortez." He twisted his mouth in an upset expression. "Care to ask her anything?"

"In Spanish?" I whispered.

"English is fine." He handed me the phone.

I pictured the resort, an oasis set against a backdrop of pale, sculpted cliffs. The mineral springs had long been known for their restorative power. I could sure use that. Funny how no one ever gifted me a spa vacation after upsetting experiences, like finding bodies or receiving death threats.

Dolores greeted me in a serene voice. I explained that I was "checking up on things" for Mr. Cortez.

"What a nice man, Mr. Cortez. He gave me this gift to calm my nerves. He is very nice. Very kind."

Yeah, really kind. Or buttering up his alibi, if she truly was his alibi. I let Dolores gush about hot herbal-scented towels and lavender salt scrubs. "Later, I'll soak in my private outdoor bath," she said. "So relaxing. The bad memories are washing away. Except for seeing poor distressed and completely innocent Mr. Cortez, of course."

Of course. Before all her other memories went down the drain, I asked her about the night in question. "Can you tell me who you saw go onto the roof of the Pajarito and in what order?"

Dolores sorted her thoughts in mumbles. Then, firmly, she said. "*Claro*. First, there was the devil. The actor. I watched him, wishing I had the night off. But I was already behind with my cleaning, so I go down the hall to the supply room. I am about to enter, when I hear a sound. There is a strange old woman. She looks at me. She points and says the devil will get me. She frightens me terribly. I go into the storage room. I am taking my time there, disturbed by the woman, when I hear a horrible scream. Terrible. A death scream, if I have ever heard one, which before that moment I had not. I am ashamed to say that I continue to hide. I thought, truly, it was *el diablo*."

"And then?" I asked.

"I hear footsteps, running, and the door to the stairway slamming. A few minutes later, I hear the elevator open—the dinging noise—and Mr. Cortez's voice, like he is talking on his phone. I am relieved and dare open the door a little and look out. Mr. Cortez is dressed as Santa, very jolly. I almost call to him, but then I worry that he will find me not working, so I stay hidden. He is very kind to forgive me. Mrs. Cortez gave me pies, and Mr. Cortez gave me this time off at Ojo Caliente. I am glad that I can help them."

She was helping, all right. I couldn't get her to budge on her story. "Such a saint," she said with the Zen-like calm of the recently massaged and mineral soaked. "Mr. Cortez should come here and relax."

After I hung up, Jake nibbled pie crust and shared some with Winston. "Before you got on the line, I asked her to describe Santa," he said. "She's sure that one was Wyatt."

I snagged a bit of crust for myself. "But what if he talked her into providing an alibi? A spa vacation? Perks at work?"

Jake acknowledged that the spa looked bad. "I tell my clients all the time. No bribery until the case is closed." He waved a fork at me. "Pie bribery, on the other hand, that's okay."

Not for me, it wasn't. Was Flori right? Had I been tricked into helping a killer?

Chapter 22

On my way home, I stopped at Judith Crundall's again to check on Celia and her sudden and suspicious interest in babysitting. I spotted Sky first. He crouched behind a stone fountain. Eddie, hands plastered over his eyes, spun in a circle. The little boy wobbled to a stop, opened his eyes, and spotted the barely hidden Sky, who took off in mock terror.

I would have enjoyed the sweet scene a lot more if I knew what my daughter was up to. I peeked in the archives room, where Shasta was frowning at piles of papers. Mounds of pink packing-foam peanuts drifted at her feet.

"Hi," she said distractedly. When I asked about Celia, she waved in the vague direction of a solid plaster wall or the door outside. "I think the girls went off that way. With the big guy."

I hoped the big guy was Gary and that he was paying attention. "Discover any more thefts?" I asked brightly.

Shasta exhaled deeply. "Ugh . . . this job! Listen, I'm sorry I was upset earlier. That doll was super-creepy." She looked up and managed a smile. "I kind of wigged out on my boss, didn't I?"

"Totally reasonable to get upset," I said. "But Barton seems like an understanding guy."

She shrugged and twisted her lip. I guessed what she was thinking. The handsome consultant exuded charm, except as a boss. I thought again how lucky I was to work with Flori.

Shasta kicked up a wave of packing peanuts and announced that she was going to the storage room. "Hope I don't find something else gross," she said.

Good luck with that. I wondered about the skull of the young woman, languishing in a box. Had she been stolen? Stolen *again*?

I went back outside, where Sky was leading Eddie in a slow-speed chase. When he turned my way, I asked where Celia was.

"Bathroom!" Sky declared, skidding to a stop. Eddie careened into him, giggling. "Oh no, you got me, Eddie. Your turn to hide. Ms. Lafitte and I will count to ten."

"Close your eyes!" Eddie demanded when I didn't immediately obey. "Look away. Please!"

Sky began counting slowly and in half and quar-ter increments. "No going past the garden!" he called out in between five and a half and five and three quarters. At this rate, he'd never get to ten.

I opened my right eye a crack. Beside me, Sky was dutifully facing away from Eddie. However, his eyes were wide open and he was texting. I tried to see what he was writing without moving my head.

I spotted the words *Your mom!!* and *Bathroom. Fast!*

He hit Send and a frowny face emoticon popped on the screen, along with some blob of what looked like gold coins. Celia and Sky could send each other entire emoticon messages, full sentences and paragraphs composed of electronic cartoon characters.

He stuffed the phone back into his pocket. I closed my eyes and pretended to be waiting out the count and Eddie, whose giggles suggested a nearby hiding spot.

"Ten!" Sky announced abruptly, jumping from eight and three quarters.

I opened my eyes to see Celia and Emilie strolling down the flagstone path, books in hand. Both smiled sweetly. Gary, panting, brought up the rear. He saw me and chuffed ahead.

"I didn't lose them," he said, so defensively that I suspected he had.

Celia and Emilie exchanged a pleased look.

"What have you been doing?" I asked, knowing I wouldn't get the truth.

"Reading," Emilie said, holding up a vintage Nancy Drew.

Celia held another volume. "Nancy Drew kicks—"

I held up a cautionary finger.

"Kicks butt," Celia said, causing boyish snickers to erupt from a nearby sagebrush. Celia and Sky launched an elaborate fake hunt for Eddie. After a few minutes, he could contain himself no longer and sprang from his not-so-hidden spot.

"Let's go inside and warm up," I said, feeling

sorry for Gary with his red ears and uncovered bald head.

The kids and Gary bounded ahead. I kept to the middle, with Sky and Celia trailing behind.

"Jackpot," I overheard Celia say. The sound of hands slapping followed. I imagined a celebratory high-five.

At least I knew what the gold coin cartoon image meant. Once inside, Sky and Celia announced they were going to the kitchen to get juice for the kids. I considered following them, but instinct told me that would only put Celia on guard. I decided to start with the weak link. Gary.

He'd plunked down on a long leather sofa against the far wall of the spacious workroom. Two cushions to his left, Emilie sat and opened her Nancy Drew. Eddie took up a place directly beside Gary and began regaling him with the details of his model train set and what engines and cars he asked for—and expected—since he'd been "really, really, extra-good."

"Trains sound fun, Eddie," I said, standing over the duo.

Gary grunted affirmatively. "I didn't lose her," he said again.

I beamed at him. "Great job! Super. Time to debrief, then. Where did you go?"

Gary shot a look at Emilie, who scowled and made a subtle, but surprisingly threatening, lip-zipping motion.

"Oh, all over," Gary said quickly.

Two could be threatening. "Gary, I'm Celia's mother. I need to know exactly where she went.

It's a matter of safety. As her bodyguard, you're obliged to tell me. It's part of your code, right?"

Gary mouthed the word *code*. "Yeah," he said, scratching his bald noggin. "Yeah, okay. The girls played Nancy Drew and the mystery of the hidden something or other."

"The Hidden Window Mystery," Emilie corrected, jabbing at her book's cover. "We were playing a made-up mystery in the storage room and outside in the yard."

And I didn't believe her one bit. Still, I couldn't very well accuse Dalia's granddaughter of fibbing, especially since Celia probably had a key role in it. I told Emilie that the game sounded exciting. "So you looked in some of the storage boxes?"

She and Gary nodded.

"Did you go anywhere else?" I asked.

Her smug look suggested they had. I narrowed my eyes at Gary.

He shrugged beefy shoulders. "We ended up in the caretaker's garage. The girls went inside. I kept watch of 'em real close."

"The blue angel under the daggers holds the key," Emilie said cryptically. She smiled slyly, hands primly folded over the book. On the cover, Nancy, wearing a red bathrobe, shined a flashlight on a peacock.

What would Nancy Drew do? She'd follow the clue. "Stay here," I instructed Gary. "Watch the kids, and especially those teenagers when they return."

He gave me a three-fingered salute, Girl Scout style.

Shasta, rooting through boxes, didn't look up

when I slipped out the door again. I cut through a dry garden of spiny cactus and agave to a small adobe structure with a slanted tin roof. The windows and doors were cottage-style glass, and all were locked. Cupping my hands to the glass, I peered inside. Shovels, pots, and lots of boxes and ski equipment filled the space. What had Emilie said about a key?

I scanned the area around the shed. Francisco's casita was several yards away, looking cold and deserted. The garden he'd cared for was designed for any season. Ornamental grasses, some spiky and upright, others softly waving, painted the garden in swaths of yellow to gold. Evergreen cactus and junipers added color, as did scarlet rose hips the size of kumquats. Other than a few boulders, there was little ornamentation. With one exception. A small cement angel stood under a thorn-tipped agave surrounded by blue glass marbles. *Aha! The blue angel under the daggers . . .*

I lifted the statue and found a key box taped to her underside. The key fit the garage doors, which swung open on their own once unlocked. The air inside smelled musty and earthy, and I wondered if the kids had exaggerated the intrigue. From the looks of it, Francisco and Trey had shared the space for their respective gardening and ski bum supplies. Boxes of snowboard wax stood among bags of potting soil and fertilizer.

I was about to write the garage off when I noticed a feather under a low, curtain-covered cabinet. The feather wasn't the type to poke free from a down jacket. This feather originated from a big bird, and it wasn't alone. Lifting back the curtain,

I discovered a gorgeous headdress decorated in more feathers and myriad minuscule beads. Crowded beside it were various kachina dolls, a wooden cross, and a dark, velvety cloth. Were these some of the missing objects? I reached for the velvet and lifted a corner before recoiling in horror. The empty eye sockets of a partial skull stared back at me.

My yelp was stopped short by a sound outside. A man's voice, talking loudly, almost yelling. My stomach pitched as I peeked out the dusty window and confirmed what my ears already knew. Trey Crundall was outside and coming this way.

I shoved the skull and its velvet back into the cabinet and frantically looked for a way out. There was no back door that I could see. The front doors hung open, only a few inches, but enough that Trey might notice. Crouching in the shadows, I tugged the doors shut, praying a gust of wind didn't blow them open again. Perhaps Trey wouldn't come in. Or if he did, he might think that he'd forgotten to lock them. *Right.* He wouldn't think that if he found me, huddled in a corner.

I needed a better hiding spot. No way was I crawling into a cobwebby cupboard with bones, especially if Trey was coming to inspect his stash. Snowboards and skis were propped up in the far back corners. Hoping spiders and other creepy-crawlies went dormant for the winter, I slid behind a row of tall snowboards and held my breath.

"What the—" Trey interrupted his own loud phone conversation to curse at the open door. "And they blame me for troubles around this

dump," he grumbled as the doors creaked open.
"My storeroom door is open. Man, if I got robbed,
I'm going to be ticked." He drew out the last word.
I cringed at the sound of him stomping in and
banging boxes.

"Yeah," he said, to the sound of boxes tumbling
to the floor. "Yeah. Dude, there's eighteen inches
of fresh powder up at Breck. We should go."

If he was the bone and headdress thief, he sure
had other priorities. Fluffy new snow in Brecken-
ridge, Colorado? Sounded nice, and an unlikely
place to unload skulls. His voice and footsteps approached my hiding spot. One of the snowboards
moved, enough to make my heart pound and give
me a sliver of a view. Trey was decked out head
to toe in sports gear, from a bulky UNM football
hoodie and Denver Broncos hat to ski pants with
a horrifyingly large spider logo on the side. Yuck!
My skin crawled, and I had to stop myself from
swatting at imagined arachnids.

"Yeah, man," Trey said, still too loud. "Aspen
would totally rock. Awesome. I'll bring my Never
Summer Proto. It shreds."

I assumed he was talking snowboards. I prayed
he wasn't talking about a board I was hiding behind.
As a backup, I tried to come up with plausible excuses for lurking in his garage. Absurdities came to
mind. Looking for a lost pet? Hiding from the holidays? Meditating on the meaning of life, spurred
on by his hippie auntie Dalia? Going the distance
with hide-and-seek? Hide-and-seek seemed like
my best chance. Or I could tip the boards onto him
and run. If I was lucky, I'd make it to the house and

the questionable protections of Gary. However, all Trey would have to do was question the little kids or Gary and I'd be found out.

I decided to count to ten before making any rash moves. Like Sky, I dawdled on fractional numbers. I'd hit nine and three-quarters when I heard Emilie yell, "Marco!"

"Polo!" Eddie yelled back. Light, bouncy footsteps entered the garage.

"Yo, little dude," Trey said enthusiastically. Presumably to his phone companion, he said, "Bro, I've got kid company. . . . Yeah, it's my kickin' nephew-cousin, whatever he is. Call you later."

Eddie chatted happily about the game he and Emilie were playing with their best-ever babysitters. "Trey, come outside," he begged. "Come play."

"Okay," Trey said agreeably. I heard their voices getting softer in the distance, alternatively calling Marco and Polo.

I let out my breath and was about to risk sneaking out when the doors creaked again. My heartbeat bounced into panic mode. Perhaps the bone thief wasn't Trey, but the burglar. Maybe he'd been hiding here. I'd be stuck all night. Or worse.

"Come out, come out wherever you are," a familiar voice sang.

Red-faced, I emerged from the snowboards.

"Hi, Mom," said my daughter, raising an eyebrow in feigned surprise. "Whatcha doing?"

Chapter 23

Did you girls have a nice day?" Mom asked later that night. She passed a steaming bowl of mashed potatoes around the tiny table. She'd made the potatoes just the way I liked them as a kid, with lots of butter and sour cream and sprinkled with her secret ingredient: ranch dressing mix. She'd also roasted a chicken, seasoned with more of the ranch dressing spices, as well as asparagus dressed with butter and garlic. The little casita smelled homey and divine. Hugo thought so too.

The cat sat by my feet, alternating his unblinking stare between the carved bird and Celia, who was covertly dropping him scraps. Since Celia knew my secret, I couldn't mention her minor infraction of cat treats at the table. Besides, roasted chicken was Hugo's favorite thing. Along with tuna from a can, nondairy cat milk, soft cat treats, catnip dried and fresh, melted ice cream, and—strangely—cantaloupe.

"We got a lot done this afternoon, didn't we, Mom?" Celia said, helping herself to two extra-large scoops of potatoes.

"Sure did," I said keeping my voice neutral. "Celia and Sky are *ingenious* babysitters."

"We played Nancy Drew and hide-and-seek and Marco Polo in the garden," Celia told her grandmother, who said that was all very nice.

"I read your mother Nancy Drew when she was little," Mom told Celia. She passed the salad and muttered, "Perhaps I should have stuck to *Anne of Green Gables*."

I couldn't blame Nancy Drew for my mix-ups in mayhem. "I remember loving *The Hobbit* too," I said, in indirect defense of Nancy. It's not like I'd become a Tolkien reenactor, although Flori occasionally bartered with one. She provided free desserts. He taught her the ways of elfin sword fighting.

"Little Emilie and I were in charge of finding the clues," Celia was saying, edging into dangerous territory.

I maneuvered my foot around purring Hugo to nudge her shoe.

She ignored me, re-passed the potatoes, and said, "Yep, we gathered lots of information."

We sure did. Now what to do with it? Soon after Celia and I rejoined the Marco Polo charade, I'd made excuses for the teens and me to leave. Sky had wanted to head straight for the Bureau of Indian Affairs.

"The BIA are the feds," he said. "They work with the FBI. They can get a search warrant, right? A raid? Take 'em down!"

"We could go to Dad," Celia suggested. "He was first on the scene. He should get first dibs on catching that sicko Trey Crundall."

Sky generously said that the BIA and Manny should go in as one. "And us too. We should get to come along. We caught him, right, Ms. Lafitte?"

I'd told the teens that I'd be happy to take down Trey, if we had firm evidence that he'd stolen the items. I'd pointed out another problem. Judith hadn't filed a robbery report. Over moans and groans from the teens, I'd added, "Say Trey did take items. How can they be considered stolen if they're still on Judith's property and she won't say they're missing?"

"They're stolen, all right," Sky had said darkly. "Stolen from their people."

There was no arguing with that. I told the teens they'd done their part. "No more sleuthing. No more Nancy Drew, and no getting Emilie and Eddie involved either. Celia, I'll talk to your father. I'm going to say I stumbled on the items, or else we'll all be in trouble, okay?"

Both teens had agreed, a little too quickly for my liking.

"Absolutely," Celia said, turning to the backseat to look at Sky. If I hadn't had my eyes on the road, I'm sure I would have seen a blatant wink.

Back at the dinner table, Celia was talking about her friend. "Sky knows a *ton* about his relatives," she said, picking up a piece of asparagus with her fingers and nibbling the end. "He can go centuries back, thousands of years, really, to the time of legends. We've been to see some of the ancient settlements. They're awesome."

Mom frowned, possibly at Celia's asparagus manners or the implication that Celia knew relatively little about her origins.

"Well," Mom said. "You should come to Illinois next summer, Celia, and we could visit relatives. My sister Karen is working on the family tree and photographing gravestones. She's traced our mother's side of the family to Cornwall and our father's side to western Germany, as far back as the 1700s."

Celia failed to look impressed, but then she regularly walks by buildings older than that. "Cool," she said politely. "What about Granddad's side of the family?"

Mom waved her fork, a table gesture she would normally frown on. "Canada," she said, adding to the faux pas by speaking through a mouthful of potatoes. "A flat, chilly part of Canada. Not very interesting."

Since Mom had dropped her vague bomb about Dad being "swayed," I hadn't gotten a chance to speak with her alone. I wondered if she would open up. She sounded downright evasive now, a quality I should know.

Mom shifted in her seat and began clearing the table. "I need to debone the chicken and get it in the fridge," she said. "Heaven knows, we don't want to get food poisoning before the holidays. My tummy is already feeling a bit unsettled from that hot pepper I accidentally ate. On a cookie! It was in that tray of *bizcochitos* you brought home, Rita. It looked like red cinnamon."

I grabbed the chicken before she could haul it off. "I'll do this. You tell Celia about Kathy's latest e-mail. Tell her about the alligators and zip-lining."

Celia picked up on my cue and expressed enthusiastic interest in gators.

I plucked chicken off the bone, dropping Hugo tastes as I went. What had Dad done? Once, when Celia was assigned a middle school project on family trees, I'd searched for Dad's name online. I'd printed out his obituary and stared at it, hoping that memories would spill forth. Barely any had. I recalled a man with wildly messy dark hair and a big laugh. There were vague memories of swimming at a lake and a stuffed pink cow won at a fair.

"Rita? Will you get the fruit salad out when you put the chicken away?" Mom asked, bringing me out of my thoughts.

I rejoined the table, thinking that every family had some secrets. A family with a collection like the Crundalls'? They probably had darker secrets than most.

After dinner, Mom again called dibs on the dishes. I called Dalia, who raved about Celia and Sky. "What lovely babysitters, sent from the heavens. The kids simply love them."

"Did Shasta ever find those missing pieces?" I asked.

She hadn't, Dalia reported with a heavy sigh. In fact, Dalia's own efforts to search and rectify the books had revealed even more confusion. "Rita," she said. "I feel like a fool. I tried to organize the boxes by acquisition number years ago, but I'm no expert. I couldn't confirm what was inside. I've made a mess of things."

I decided to play one of my cards. "The missing items, did they include part of a skull? Wrapped in velvet?"

Dalia gasped. "Yes! Exactly! How did you know? Did you see it in a vision?"

I liked the thought of conjuring objects' locations. I'd never lose my car keys again, or the corkscrews that Mom had helpfully reorganized into oblivion. "No. No vision," I said. "What about a headdress with feathers?"

"Rita, this is extraordinary. How did you know? Were you detecting? Are you on the case? Oh, you should be! Someone needs to think of Francisco. With all these awful bones and threats, I'm afraid we haven't grieved him properly. We'll hold a ceremony. A wake and a séance."

I felt a jolt of worry, and not only about the séance. I'd blown my cover. However, Dalia was my friend and neighbor. I trusted her. She rescued heirloom garden plants and hung out with pacifists and believed she could cure her ailing sister with positive thoughts and amulets. She wasn't a killer. Besides, I assured myself, she had an alibi for the time of Francisco's death. A stubborn one. Mr. Peppers. I imagined Jake dragging Peppers into court and nearly laughed. Thinking more seriously, I didn't want any rumors getting around. I denied sleuthing.

"I was interested in the garden," I said. "You know I'm always looking for a good gardener."

This was true. As the onsite manager of my mostly absentee landlord's large property, I'd had a terrible time finding and keeping gardeners. The first guy I hired had exhibited a pathological zeal for destroying flowers. Another liked to whack fruit tree limbs in the wrong season. The others hadn't shown up at all. *And Barton complained he had bad help!* At least Shasta mostly showed up and she wasn't destroying anything. I wondered how he'd found her. She was from Albuquerque, practically local. A darker thought struck me. Could she have known Francisco? I'd ask Flori to have the Knit and Snitchers check her out.

"Yes, so you were viewing the garden," Dalia said, obviously trying to hurry me on to the point.

"Well, I saw that cute garage in Judith's back garden. It was unlocked and I couldn't resist peeking in. I was checking out what rose fertilizer Francisco used when I noticed the feather. There was the headdress, under the cupboard, and the bit of skull, wrapped in a box."

"The stars align!" Dalia exclaimed. "Those are important pieces." She paused. "What will I tell Judith? Trey uses that garage for storage. Selfish boy. He must have taken them. He's been so mad at his mother. I'll say it was me, that I misplaced the items in the storeroom."

"I don't think you should do that," I said. "Wouldn't lying invite—I don't know—bad vibes?" Bad vibes sounded cheesy at best, a mockery at worst.

Dalia, however, told me that I was absolutely right. "But a secret isn't a lie, is it? What if the objects suddenly reappear? It'll be our secret, Rita. We'll act surprised. Acting's not a lie."

"I don't know, Dalia . . ." I said. "Wouldn't Judith want the truth?"

My neighbor disagreed. "It's for her own good. She's so feeble. She can't take more hurt and disruption from her disappointing son. You haven't seen her grow ill like I have. First it was pneumonia. Then, ever since we started meddling with this awful collection, she's gotten sicker and sicker."

"It's not up to me to tell Judith," I said. "The police might, though. And if they connect Trey to the thefts, they might link him to the threatening letters and murder."

On the other end of the line, Dalia was silent. Then she said. "Murder? No, that would kill Judith."

Chapter 24

P ie," Lorena Cortez said, stating the obvious. She and Wyatt stepped into Tres Amigas the next morning along with a blast of winter wind during a particularly busy breakfast service. "Cherry cranberry," she continued, waving a hand over a gorgeous creation. Scarlet red fruit gleamed under a golden pie crust sparkling with sugar crystals and shaped like overlapping pine trees. The pie was truly a work of art, almost too pretty to eat. Not that prettiness had ever kept me from devastating a pie.

"I have a cranberry cheesecake at the shop, if you'd prefer," she continued. "Oh, you should have both. Wyatt, run back to the shop and get that other pie."

"No, no," I said quickly. "This pie is gorgeous, Lorena. You shouldn't have." She *really* shouldn't have. I felt bad enough already. Here she thought Wyatt was in the clear, and I was digging up evidence that he might not be.

Wyatt put a hand on his wife's back. "Looks like Rita's busy, darling."

I told myself not to read too much into the pointed edge he landed on "busy." Flori always says I'm a horrible liar and even worse at hiding guilt. Could Wyatt sense my feelings? Had he spoken with Dolores at the spa? According to Flori, who aced the Senior Center's ill-advised workshop on blackjack bluffing, my "tell" was being extra nice. I dialed down my cheerleader smile and agreed that I was busy. My case was helped by the five empty coffee cups in my hand and the stack of menus slipping out from under my arm.

"Feel free to stay, if you want," I said. "Take a seat wherever you'd like." I'd like it if they stayed in the dining room.

"I'll just put the pie in the kitchen for you," Lorena said.

So much for keeping them in the dining room. Wyatt followed her, greeting acquaintances on the way. Lorena waved through the pass-through and was beckoned in by Flori.

"Ah, miss? I think that's my water glass." A customer looked up from his breakfast.

I looked down and realized I was pouring hot coffee over ice cubes. "Sorry!" I said, to his polite chuckles about "vacation-itis." At least I hadn't aimed for the guy's lap or head . . . this time.

"Too cold for ice coffee today," the customer added kindly. "Looks like it might snow."

We made small talk about the weather. I picked up bills and checked on other tables. Then, with no other excuse to delay, I returned to the kitchen.

Flori was standing at the sink, smoothing an apron printed in festive red and green chile peppers. "Rita!" Flori exclaimed in a jovial tone that let me know she meant business. "I'm so glad you're here. I was just asking Wyatt where I could get a Santa costume. I called the costume shop and they're fresh out. How many did you say you got for your hotel, Wyatt?"

At the griddle, Juan shook his head and twisted the corner of his lip. Flori's gambling "tell" was sounding too innocent.

Wyatt shrugged. "Bit late for finding Santa costumes," he said. Then, as if remembering his festive campaign, he quickly added, "But I sure hope you can snag one! Lorena and I are dressing up as Mr. and Mrs. Claus and going out on the town tonight. It'll be a barrel of fun."

Flori said that was a lovely idea. "Rita, Juan, and I should be elves. Wouldn't that be a hoot?"

"Fun!" I said, in a cheerleader burst. Juan groaned and cracked an egg on the grill with a shaky hand.

"You got the costumes at Zia Dave's, didn't you, Wyatt?" Lorena said. "They called yesterday, in fact, to ask if you needed a replacement costume after . . . well . . ."

After he got the first Santa suit covered in blood?

Wyatt squeezed his wife's hand. "Good thing I got some backup costumes," he said, going to look at the simmering pots on the stove.

"Ah, *posole*, my favorite holiday treat," he said. "Lorena, honey, why don't you go rustle us up a table and we can have a bowl."

Lorena, frowning, left without a word. I doubted

she was upset about the stew, with its rich red-pepper broth, tender chunks of long-simmered pork, and the namesake ingredient, *posole*, lye-treated dried corn that puffed like underwater popcorn.

Wyatt reached for a clean spoon and helped himself to a bite of the stew. "I got a strange call from my lawyer yesterday," Wyatt said after praising the stew.

When neither Flori nor I responded, he said. "Yep, Mr. Strong tells me there's a question about whether some visiting British women know their Santas."

"Oh?" I said with what I hoped was a tone of pure incredulity. Flori said the same thing. Coming from her, it sounded a whole lot better.

Wyatt paced the kitchen. "Mr. Strong said those ladies were changing their story, imagining some shorter, Spanish-speaking Santa." He reached over and patted Juan on the shoulder. "Wasn't you, was it, my friend?"

Juan flipped an egg and didn't deign to answer. Instead, he slid the egg onto a plate of cheese enchiladas, one side bathed in green chile, the other red. "Enchiladas, Christmas," he said, passing the plate to me.

"Ho, ho, ho," Wyatt said. His round face spread into a smile, yet chills went up my arm.

"So much Christmas festivity at your hotel, Wyatt," Flori said. "You've really outdone yourself this year. Didn't I see a few other Santas over there? Perhaps that's what caused the confusion. Oh yes, now I remember. My friend's nephew-in-law was one of your valet Santas. Well, you never can have too many Santas, can you, Rita?"

I'd had about enough of Santa. "Nope, never enough," I lied.

Wyatt's cheeks went rosy. "Lorena wants a festive holiday and that's what I'm going to give her. It's already bad enough that that nosy Francisco got himself killed." He stared into a vat of red chile simmering on the back burner. When he looked back up, his stormy gaze had morphed into a smile. "Well, there's a positive side to everything, isn't there? Lorena says she can't bear to lose me now. We're going to counseling and out on dates and I still have my other alibi. Mr. Strong assures me that as soon as the police arrest another suspect, the pesky charge against me will be dropped."

He started toward the kitchen door. As he passed me, he said, "Rita, take it from me, you have nothing to worry about. Your family is precious. Enjoy every moment with them. Savor time with your mother and daughter. Eat pie! Live it up!"

All fine advice, except one thing. I had a lot to worry about.

What if the killer and threatening letter writer are two different people?" I asked Flori. She'd invited me out for a walk, destination undisclosed.

Flori punched the crosswalk button. Above the button, the typical crosswalk image of a figure walking had been stenciled over in bones. A skeleton crossing.

"See?" Flor said, pointing at the skeleton. "Graffiti art can be fun."

I liked the bones well enough, although they reminded me of the real bones cropping up in boxes and garages. Another thought occurred to me. "What if there are three people involved? Killer, writer, and thief?"

"Don't forget the witch," Flori said. She looked like a padded gnome, right down to her puffy snow boots. The walk sign blinked on, a normal stick figure crossing.

"Where are we going?" I asked as we cut a long diagonal across the street and the Plaza.

"It's a surprise," came her scarf-muffled reply.

We walked a few blocks farther, into a quiet neighborhood of little adobe homes. Some remained family homes. Others were tourism rentals going for rates way beyond a café worker's means. Still others were small businesses, including a dentist, a lawyer specializing in water disputes, a yogic healer, a fabulous Indian restaurant, and a small German/French bakery. I hoped for the bakery, but assumed the dentist. If he was single and Mom found out, she'd probably try to set me up.

"Here we are," Flori said, stopping within buttery scent range of the bakery. Beside us, the dentist's front gate swung open, announcing his holiday special on tongue scraping treatments for fresh breath. Was Flori trying to tell me something?

To my amazement, Flori headed down the driveway leading to the back of the bakery. I trailed behind her puffy coat, past a Dumpster and a stack of cardboard boxes to a back door. Flori rapped three times.

"We don't need any more baked goods," I said righteously.

"We're not here for sweets," Flori said, banging again. "We're here to inquire about a witch."

The door opened a crack, and Angel Ortiz, grandson of our missing witch, poked his head out. His goatee was as threadbare as ever. The black apron he wore was nearly white with flour and hung below his knees. "You weren't followed?" he asked.

"Absolutely not," Flori said, a bold claim, seeing as how we openly strolled across town on a sunny winter's day. She reached into her cloth knitting bag and drew out a walkie-talkie. "Ten-four," she said. "The eagles have landed."

"The runway is all clear, Night Knitter," said a scratchy voice I recognized as Miriam's. "Silver Purl, ten . . . ah . . . ten-five and out."

"See?" Flori said to a baffled Angel.

Now I understood why a vintage red Toyota had kept driving by us. Miriam had been our lookout. My eyes were adjusting to the dark room where we stood. A storeroom, I guessed. The air was thick with flour dust.

Angel shuffled and studied his feet and said he didn't have much time. "I need this job. This police trouble with Nana seeing the murdered devil, it got me fired from my good job. The boss didn't like cops coming round asking for me."

"Are you a baker here?" I asked, hoping to calm him with pleasantries. "I love this place. The poppyseed cake is wonderful."

Angel shrugged. "They don't let me bake. I haul

flour and mix and wash dishes. The job won't last. They only need holiday help."

"Sorry," I said. I meant it. The young man had too much talent to be wasted on dirty dishes.

Flori had more pressing matters. "Your grandmother, Angel. We need to speak to her."

He shook his head so vigorously that flour dust billowed. "No. I'm keeping Nana safe. She didn't hurt anyone, no matter what she says."

"Rita and I know that," Flori said, as I wondered whether I believed that or not. "If you let us talk to her again, we can find a way to help you both."

"How?" Angel demanded.

How indeed?

"We're already steps ahead of the police," Flori claimed boldly. "If Josephina can help us solve the crime, you won't have to worry about them bothering you anymore. And maybe we can find you a better job in a nice café or pie shop."

A squawk from her knitting bag interrupted Flori's rousing speech. She dug out a ball of yarn, needles, and a pair of black gloves before extracting the walkie-talkie. "Night Knitter," she said.

"Silver Purl, on the prowl. Black-and-white headed your way," Miriam said. "Moving to rendezvous site now."

"Cops?" Angel sputtered, interpreting knitter code faster than I could. In between bilingual curses, he expressed regret for ever agreeing to meet.

"Now, now, dear, such language," Flori said. "My associate is on her way. Gather your things and remember your coat. It's cold outside."

Chapter 25

We hurried to the back end of the bakery's lot, squeezed through a coyote fence of rough-cut branches, and cut across the garden of a tax accountancy office. Getting to the accountant's driveway required pushing our way through a pitchy pine tree and sweetly scented sage. As I was shaking conifer needles and globs of resin from my hair, the accountant looked out his window and frowned. Flori waved pleasantly. Angel continued to mutter curses. I didn't blame him or the befuddled accountant. Just as we reached the street, Miriam swung around the corner and we all clamored into her Honda. Angel and I jumped in the back, finding space amid enough yarn to outfit a flock of sheep. Flori took the front seat and buckled in.

Breathlessly—and anticlimactically—Miriam stomped on the gas and announced a false alarm.

"It was only that nice Deputy Davis going into

the bakery," she said. "I waited a tick and saw her come out with a poppyseed cake."

"Lovely choice," Flori said, as if she and Miriam hadn't just made us flee through shrubbery and fluster an accountant for no reason.

"I punched out fifteen minutes early," Angel said. "My boss is going to kill me. He'll fire me."

"He won't, dear," Flori said. "I happen to know that man's secret hobby. I could call him on it, if you like. It's not something he'd want out there."

"Leather," twittered Miriam, sounding happily scandalized. "And masks."

"No!" I said, "No, no, no. We are not getting involved in whatever that baker does in his free time. It's Christmas, remember?"

In the front seat, Flori's puffy-shouldered coat rose and fell. She twisted but couldn't quite face us because of the enormity of her winter wear. "He won't fire you anyway, Angel. Everyone's hard up for help around the holidays. I don't know what I would have done if Rita had gone back to Illinois for Christmas."

"You wouldn't be investigating a murder," I said glumly. I wouldn't be either. Nor would I be thinking of devils and witches and bone collections. What would I be doing right now? Sorting through my boxes of old high school stuff, like Mom was always after me to do? Suffering through tea with Mom, Aunt Sue, and Albert the dentist? Figuring out what Dad had been up to? Now that would be intriguing. Or too close to home. Like the baker and his leather, some things might be best unknown.

"Nonsense," Flori said. "You didn't start this.

We're only helping out, in the spirit of holiday giving. Now, Angel, since we're in the car, let's go see your delightful grandmother. Does she like to knit? We could bring her some yarn."

Angel had slumped down among the skeins. Seemingly resigned, he said, "*Sí*. Nana knits. But she won't be happy to see you. She thinks you brought the cops to our house. She blames you. She's been making spells . . ."

There was another thing I wouldn't be doing in Illinois. Getting cursed.

Angel directed Miriam on a winding route through pretty adobe homes tucked among junipers, pines, and sagebrush. Boulders and walls further disguised the homes, which were coated in earth-toned stuccos. After driving up a short but steep dirt road, we arrived at a cluster of upscale townhomes perched on a hill.

Angel sighed. "We didn't think anyone would discover us in a place like this." His tone suggested that he wasn't happy to find himself here either.

"You did quite well hiding," Flori said. "I only found out because your grandmother put a curse on the UPS man, and he told the relative of an acquaintance who knew I was looking for Josephina."

"I told her not to curse him," Angel said glumly. "I said, no cursing or spells or potions."

Miriam brought the Honda to a jolting stop at

the edge of a rather precipitous drop-off, and we all got out.

"It's gorgeous up here," I said, hoping to perk him up. "What a view!" Before us, plains dappled in snow stretched out for miles, punctuated by gray-blue ridges darkening into charcoal purples. Their names still sounded exotic to my Midwest ears: the Sandia, Ortiz, Jemez, and lyrical and dark Sangre de Cristo, the blood of Christ.

Angel seemed unimpressed. "I like home better. They have all sorts of rules here and it's too high up and exposed. I feel like we're being watched."

I could see why he felt that way. A woman getting into her Cadillac stared at us, her pinch-faced expression likely a commentary on Miriam's beat-up ride and Angel's droopy pants. Or maybe it was me and my wind-whipping hair, or Flori, sizing up a statue of a somewhat grotesque horse by the entry gate.

Angel punched in the code and walked us through a lovely, dry-landscaped courtyard to a small patio enclosed by an adobe wall. "My great-aunt owns this place. She's out of town for the holidays and let us stay, as long as Granny doesn't cook up certain stuff on her new stove."

He tapped lightly before unlocking the door.

Josephina sat on a coral-colored sofa watching a blaring infomercial for an electronic quesadilla press. Her grandson greeted her with a kiss to her leathery cheek. "Nana, look, I brought your school friend by," he said. To Flori, he whispered, "She might not remember seeing you. Sometimes, she'll only speak in Spanish."

"*Hola*, Josie," Flori said heartily. "It's been a while."

Josephina cracked a toothless smile. "Florita! Where have you been? Did you run off with Robert Peña?" She cackled.

"No. You put a spell on him," Flori said. "I married that fool Bernard. He was in the newspaper club. Remember him? He played football too, and the violin."

I tried to imagine young Flori, Bernard, and Josephina, decades ago. Flori would have been pretty and dark-haired, like her daughters and granddaughters. And devious.

The elderly witch chuckled. "I remember. You rode the horse to school. In pants." She patted the seat cushion beside her, inviting Flori to sit.

Miriam and I took two uncomfortable straight-backed armchairs in the corners of the room. Angel went to the kitchen to get drinks.

"Scandalous, as always," I joked to Flori.

"Nothing wrong with pants," Flori said. "Or alternative forms of transportation."

She and Josephina chatted about a handsome chemistry teacher and Josephina's cursing of the gym instructor before Flori got down to business. "I hear you were up on the roof of the Pajarito the other night. The night Francisco Ferrara was killed," she said casually.

Josephina grinned and said something I couldn't catch in low, fast Spanish.

Angel, returning from the kitchen with a tray of clinking glasses and a pitcher of apple cider, said, "She says that the devil got what he deserved." He poured and distributed glasses while Flori teased out details.

"It's good you were there, Josie," Flori said.

"Of course I was there. I made the spell. I put the spell on the devil," Josephina said reasonably.

"Nana," her grandson cautioned. He gave her a glass and told her to drink. "You didn't do that. Tell the ladies what you saw."

"*El diablo,*" Josephina declared, sending my thoughts back to that night. The dark roof, the stench of sulfur, the howling wind, the body. Santa in devil's blood. Josephina fixed her dark eyes on me and cracked a gap-toothed smile.

I shook the thoughts away. "There was a man dressed like Santa," I said. "Did he kill the devil? Stab him?"

Waving a gnarled hand as if this were a silly question, Josephina said, "Santa? No, no. Santa was too frightened. Useless. It was the *lobo* who did my bidding."

Now this was new. I looked to Flori, but she seemed as perplexed as I was.

"A *lobo*?" Flori asked. "Do you mean a wolf?"

"*Sí, el lobo,*" Josephina said with a pleased cackle.

"They say a witch can take many forms," Miriam said, helping herself to a cookie. "That's what my grandmother used to tell us kids. She once saw a witch turn into a fox. She said she heard La Llorona too, and that water witch almost pulled her into the river."

Josephina nodded knowingly. Angel crossed himself at the mention of the "Weeping Woman," La Llorona, said to haunt waterways. Even my macho ex had confessed to childhood nightmares of the spirit, known for her unearthly wails and snatching of children. In Santa Fe, she was said to haunt the river near the offices of the

Public Employees Retirement Association. I often thought of her as I crossed the nearby bridge.

I'd never heard her weeping, though, or been yanked into the water. I reminded myself that I didn't believe in such lore. There had to be a more earthly explanation, one that Manny could arrest and Jake could cross-examine. "What did the wolf look like?" I asked.

Angel repeated my question in Spanish. I deduced that he was urging his grandmother to help us so they could leave the condo and get home.

Josephina watched the now-muted infomercial pensively. Then she waved her hand to her grandson. He leaned and she spoke rapidly.

"She says the one who killed the devil wore a big coat. Puffy. Like a parka, I guess you'd say. And she saw the face of the *lobo*. Red eyes and big teeth. Snarling teeth. Like it was smiling before killing. She said she had often wished for that fate for Francisco Ferrara and it happened." He reached over and patted his grandmother's gnarled hand. "Mr. Ferrara tried to help us too, remember, Nana? He gave me the tuition for those culinary classes. He wasn't all bad."

I wanted to know more about Francisco and culinary school, but something else was bubbling in my mind. "Wait . . . a red-eyed wolf? Could she mean a logo on the coat? Like a sports logo, like the wolf mascot for UNM?"

Josephina scowled at me as if I was the one who was loopy. "Sports?" she said in perfectly clear English. "I have no time for sports." She glanced at a grandfather clock in the far corner of the room and chuckled. "The mailman will be here soon."

Angel's shoulders slumped below his usual slouch level. "Nana, I told you, we can't keep bothering him. They'll kick us out."

To us, he said, "Sorry. I need to go get my truck so I can get back here before the mail."

He looked exhausted. I felt for him. It must be hard to juggle his grandmother and whatever work he could find. We left Josephina watching a Spanish-language soap opera.

"She's bored here, without her herbs and routine and stuff," he said as we drove back toward Santa Fe.

I thought of my mother. She was likely bored and missing her routine. Now that she'd organized my kitchen, what did she have to do? Mom loved to read at night. She kept busy with errands and chores during the day. I should be home entertaining her, not visiting with a witch. However, the trip hadn't been wasted. I felt we'd gotten an important clue.

Angel once again slumped in the backseat beside me. I asked him gently, "About Francisco . . . you said he gave you money?"

Angel grunted in affirmation. "Ever since I was a kid. For school supplies and stuff. When I wanted to go to the community college, he paid. My grandmother cursed him, but she does that to a lot of people. He felt really bad for what he did."

I stored this information away, vowing to tell Manny. Francisco's generosity gave Angel little incentive to hold a murderous grudge. "And your grandmother called you the night of the murder?" I asked.

He reached into his layers of jackets, pulled out

a phone, and scrolled through its screens. "You want the exact time? Here." He pointed to a call at 7:28. "I was at work, washing dishes." He named the fancy steak restaurant the Knit and Snitchers had known about. "My grandmother called and said that the devil is dead. I didn't know what she meant, but I was worried and got in big trouble for leaving. Ask the jerk manager who fired me if you don't believe me."

I tended to believe him. Whether Manny would was another story. Flori pulled up near Angel's beat-up truck. As he was getting up, I asked, "Where did you and your grandmother disappear to the night we visited your house?"

He flashed a broad smile. "Why, do you think we flew away?"

"Stranger things have happened," Miriam said.

He laughed. "Sorry to disappoint you. Nana sensed something was wrong, so we walked over to a neighbor's house."

"Josie always had the sixth sense," Flori said appreciatively as Angel slouched to his car.

I decided to test Flori's sense and powers of observation. "You know who wears a Lobos coat?"

Miriam named someone I'd never heard of with "one heck of a dunk." "Those Chicago Bulls should have picked him up," she said.

Flori tried—and again failed—to turn fully in her puffy coat. "Who?" she asked.

"Trey Crundall," I said triumphantly. Yet a small part of me hoped I was wrong, if only for Judith's sake.

Chapter 26

W hat does it take to get you to stop?" Manny said. He sat on a metal stool in the kitchen of Tres Amigas. The seat came with a sparkling stainless steel prep surface, easy access to the cookie jar, and a view of the back garden, yet my ex was predictably grumpy. "Our daughter is threatened. You and that other devil are threatened. Your mother's in town. Yet you and Flori keep poking around. Can't you two find another hobby?"

Flori already had way too many hobbies, and it's not like either of us did this for fun. I maintained a calm front, except for my twitching right eye. Manny wasn't acting properly appreciative, either for my hot tips or for the steaming green chile stew I'd just served him. He was grouchy out of habit and because he was a Grinch.

Miriam and Flori had dropped me off at the café and continued on to an unnamed "appointment." I'd bitten the proverbial bullet, called Manny, and asked him to meet me.

"I wasn't poking anything," I said. "Flori found out where Angel and his grandmother—a key witness in your case—are staying. We went to visit and discovered what could be a big clue."

"I'm looking for Angel Ortiz all right," Manny mumbled. He stopped grumbling long enough to eat some stew. Green chile stew seems humble when putting the ingredients together. First, simple stew meat—beef, pork, or lamb—simmers until tender with broth, onions, and garlic. Toward the end of cooking, waxy potatoes join the mix. It's the final ingredient, though, that takes common stew to extraordinary: roasted green chiles and a whole lot of them. At Tres Amigas, we use a mix of mild and spicy chiles for a truly warming stew.

Manny tore a corner off a *sopapilla*, triangle-shaped bread puffed in a deep fryer. New Mexicans tended to save their *sopapillas* for dessert, coating them with the honey that's provided as a tabletop condiment. Manny used to chide me for eating *sopapillas* with my main meal. More evidence of me being an outsider, he'd claimed. Now he dunked some in the stew and ate it before returning to his rant.

"I should pick both of them up," he said. "Angel and his weird granny."

"On what charges? Francisco Ferrara helped Angel out financially, ever since Angel was a kid. Why would Angel kill him?"

"Maybe the old lady did," Manny said. "I'd want to do some significant harm to anyone who hurt my daughter."

I would too. Still, Josephina had said that someone had done her "bidding." "Josephina's an odd-ball, but who isn't a little quirky around here?"

"That's for sure," Manny said with a sniff. "Does the health commission know you're keeping live-stock?" We had a clear view of Mr. Peppers and Sidekick. Sidekick balanced on a trash can, hooves pointed together like a goat ballerina. Mr. Peppers stared intently toward our window, flicking his big ears and twitching his velvet nose. Could he smell the rewarmed fried treat?

"They're visiting actors," I said, a rather grand description of the gluttonous donkey and goofy goat. "I believe Angel when he said that he was working. You should check his alibi, though. And his grandmother is a bit . . . ah . . ." I struggled for a nice synonym for off her broomstick. "Intense," I said. "But she did see something that night. A person in a bulky jacket. 'A wolf,' she said, but I think she saw a wolf logo." I reiterated the trail of circumstantial crumbs leading to Trey Crundall. "He's mad at his mother for giving away that col-lection and keeping him from the family money. Plus, Judith doesn't want the police to know, but pieces from the collection have gone missing. I found some in a garage both Trey and Francisco used. Maybe Francisco found out."

Manny, showing culinary prowess unheard of in our married years, got up and served himself more stew. When he sat back down, he said, "So, in your theory, rich guy kills the gardener who caught him stealing the family bone collection, even though rich mother won't admit that any-thing's missing. What about the letters? And why bother with the devils?"

"A distraction?" I said, knowing it wasn't the solidest of theories.

Nubby horns appeared at the lowest corner of the window ledge. Wide eyes with alien-slit pupils stared in. Sidekick flashed his eerily humanlike teeth. Manny grumbled that holidays were a distraction, along with goats and criminals.

"Deputy Davis is looking for Trey Crundall," he said, not admitting that my theory was pretty good. "I'll tell her to get some backup. I'll go out and see the old lady."

"You might want to take someone sensitive with you," I said dryly.

"Women love me," he said, flashing his best soap-opera smile. "I should check on that red-headed assistant again too."

I beamed back. "You do that. Be careful with Josephina, though. She could put a curse on you. She gave Flori's high school beau a skin disease. He had to move to Minnesota."

Manny's grin dimmed.

Since I was at the café, I prepped some sauces and a soup and lined up ingredients for the breakfast service tomorrow morning. An hour later, the sun was setting and I was eager to head home. However, as I passed Judith Crundall's house, I noticed a police cruiser in the driveway, alongside a rust-splotched red truck I recognized as Sky's. The truck was Sky's pride and joy, a gift from his father for his sixteenth birthday. Did that mean Celia was there too? I was running out of excuses to drop by, other than the real one. I wanted to check on my daughter.

I pulled in, got out, and was greeted by a near-miss between my nose and the front door. Barton Hunter stepped out.

"Oh, sorry," he said, looking harried. "I'm saying that to you a lot, aren't I?"

I admired his staying power. Other consultants, faced with death threats and a disappearing collection, might pick up and go home.

"Is something wrong?" I asked, my own anxiety rising.

He managed a weak smile. "No. Nothing for you to worry about, at any rate. Your daughter and her friend are babysitting when they should be working for me. The police are here looking for the lord heir of the manor," he joked, assuming a faux British accent that would have delighted Addie.

"Looking for?" I asked. "They haven't found him yet?" I caught myself sounding too in-the-know and reworded to "Why do they want Trey?"

Barton, who was checking his cell phone, waved his free hand. "Beats me. They claim they simply want to talk to him. Judith and Dalia haven't seen him. The ski bum shop is closed. You ask me, he's off on the slopes enjoying himself while the rest of us sort out this mess." He scowled and said, "Some of us, that is. My assistant, Miss Moon, has been enjoying a lengthy teatime in the drawing room with that lead detective. Seems he's extremely interested in her safety."

Right. Sure that's what Manny was interested in. I

held my tongue, not wanting to upset Barton any more. "How did you find her, anyway?" I asked. "I mean, to work for you."

Barton rolled his eyes. "The wrong way, apparently. I contacted local colleges with anthropology programs and she was the only one to e-mail back. I might have done better with a temp service." He ran a hand through his blond locks, which magically fell back into the carefree ruffled look of male catalog models.

"I'm sure you'll sort this all out soon," I said.

He made a scoffing sound. "I'm not."

I excused myself and walked toward the archives wing to look for Celia. On the way, I found Dalia, digging in the yard.

"Crystals," she said, before I could ask. "Judith's having a bad spell, so I thought I'd try this. I've buried healing crystals in all cardinal directions *and* in a mandala shape aligned to the setting sun." She straightened and tucked her trowel into her coat pocket. Dusting off her hands, she said, "Are you looking for Celia?"

The midwesterner in me felt the need to apologize. "Sorry if she and Sky—well, and me too— keep getting in the way."

"Nonsense!" Dalia took the type of breath that yoga instructors deem cleansing. "Honestly, I'm not much of a grandmother's grandmother, if you know what I mean. Phillip's even worse as a grandfather. My daughter's always fussing at us to do something 'normal' with the kids. Celia and Sky are doing wonders to keep the little people happy."

I turned to go. Dalia called after me. "Your mother is here as well. She's a wonder!"

I entered the archives room, expecting chaos. Instead, I found Celia quietly reading, a kid on either side of her. Gary the bodyguard slumped in a chair. His dark glasses were on but his head bobbed, suggesting futile resistance to napping. Mom and Sky stood at a drafting table flipping through ledgers.

"Rita," Mom said. "There you are." Her tone suggested I'd been out playing while everyone else was hard at work. What were they doing anyway? I asked, and Mom said she'd walked down with Dalia, who wanted to cross-check random archival items and make sure they were actually in their boxes. "She had something pressing to do involving crystals and the solar horizon," Mom said, frowning at the inexplicable chore. "I told her that I simply love to check and organize." She beamed. "Sky's helping too, but neither of us is touching any bones." She and Sky shared a look of understanding and then dipped their heads to the ledgers. I felt like the odd person out.

"What are you reading?" I asked Celia.

"We're reading about the twin Zuni war gods," she said, holding up an academic journal that was hardly standard holiday reading material for kids.

"They're awesome," Emilie said. "They keep the world safe. Like superheroes, but really ancient and all-powerful."

Celia pointed to the journal. "Did you know they're carved every year? Representations of them. The carvings hold the war gods' powers and should never leave Zuni lands. It says here, some were bought or stolen in the past. They're worth mega-money. Most have been given back, but you know there's a jerk out there keeping 'em for himself." She scowled in the direction of the storage room.

"Good thing that Judith's giving sacred items like that back," I said.

"Good thing," Celia reiterated. "Because this article says what Dalia's been telling us all along. These war gods bring misfortune to anyone who keeps them away from their home."

"Misfortune," Emilie echoed darkly.

Eddie, bored, slid off the couch and changed the subject. "Let's play Marco Polo. Let's play hide-and-seek."

Sky wrote something on a scrap of paper and obliged. "Okay, let's go," he said. "We'll play hide-out in the storage room." Eddie ran off in front of him. I tailed a few steps behind.

"Sky, what are you and Celia *really* doing?" I asked in my best threatening but cool mom voice when we reached the room.

Eddie ran down the aisles, issuing excited instructions for us to close our eyes. Sky, eyes still open, started a countdown from thirty.

"Sky," I said. "If this was Celia's idea . . ." I said "if," but I was pretty sure it was. Celia had led Sky astray in the past. There had been the cactus painting episode and the time they honored a deceased friend with his favorite beer and got nabbed for driving with an open alcohol container on Pueblo lands.

He shook his head. "This is all my idea. Look, Ms. Lafitte, I don't want to get Celia in trouble. We've got Gary here, watching out for everyone. We're safe. I just wanted to look for some things." He held out the scrap of paper. Numbers and letters presumably matched an archival box. "There's a hide robe from the early 1800s, used in our Pueblo's dances. My uncle described it to me. It should be here."

"If it's here, it'll be going back soon," I said.

"Yeah, but what if it gets lost or stolen before then?" Sky countered.

He had a point. Looking up a box seemed safe enough. Sky and I ran our fingers along the boxes until we found the right shelf. A long, skinny box matched the number on Sky's note.

"Keep hiding," Sky called to Eddie, whose panting was audible from a row over. Carefully, Sky slid out the box and lifted the lid. "This is it," he whispered. The box was filled with archival tissue paper. And nothing else.

Sky removed the tissue and stared into the empty box. "We're too late," he said, sounding heartbroken.

"There could be another explanation." I felt through the paper, hoping to feel fabric.

The sound of small feet running, a shriek, and a deep male voice announcing "Gotcha!" made both Sky and me jump.

Barton Hunter strode around the corner, a laughing Eddie draped over his shoulder. "Let's see that," he said, peering at the box number and the slip of paper Sky held. "Mmm . . . this could be one of the pieces we sent out for cleaning. Shasta should know. We'll ask her when she's done socializing."

"Shasta and Trey are sitting in a tree, K-I-S-S—" Eddie, the singing tattler, began.

Baron scowled and interrupted the ditty. "Who's

up for another round of hide-and-seek?" he said. "Back to the archives room."

Eddie ran off with Barton striding behind him.

Beside me, Sky was silent. His skeptical look said it all.

"Let's wait and see what Shasta can find out," I said to Sky. "If she can't locate the robe, we'll tell Celia's dad."

"Tell me what?" Manny appeared in the doorway, grinning. He always enjoyed startling me.

"Is Shasta with you?" I asked. "Sky and I are hoping she can help us find an item."

Manny, sounding aggrieved, reported that Barton had rudely interrupted his "witness interview" and sent Shasta to get shipping supplies and Indian take-out.

Sky's shoulders slumped and he headed back to the main archives room.

"Sorry about your date," I said to Manny.

My ex flashed a wolfish grin. "I'll manage. Redheads can't resist me. I've got to get back to the station anyway. Davis located Trey Crundall. He was up at the family ski chalet in Taos, drinking himself stupider. She's bringing him back down."

"You've got your man!" I said with forced cheer.

"Yeah, but what can we charge him with? Being a loser?" Manny peppered in some curses and added, "It'll be a Christmas miracle if we get a search warrant for any Crundall properties. We can't go on your wild theories and a crazy old witch's ramblings about devils and wolves. According to Davis, Trey claims he never put those feathers and bones in the garage. He's blam-

ing everyone he can think of. The postman, his
mother, those kids. Well, he was blaming everyone. I'm sure he'll clam up once he gets back here
and meets his lawyer. Want to take a guess who
his wealthy mama hired?"

I didn't have a chance to say my guess. If I had,
though, I would have been right.

"Yep, your pal Jake Strong," Manny said.

Chapter 27

The next evening the sun set in rosy gray hues, and the Plaza sparkled under colorful lights and glittery snow. Strains of Christmas carols warmed the chilly air as the musicians of *Las Posadas* made their way up the street.

Jake wrapped his arm around my waist. He wore a black felt fedora and rust-colored scarf tucked into his parka. "I sense I'm in the doghouse with your mother again," he said. "It's my own fault. I kept you out too late and the police caught us."

Winston, a pampered pooch who's likely never stooped to doghouse levels, shook his wrinkly head. He had felt reindeer horns around his broad noggin, compliments of Celia. A jingle bell adorned the tail end of his fleecy red coat. He looked downright adorable, just like his human dad. Or at least I thought so.

I'd invited Jake to join Mom, Celia, and me

as we followed the caroling *Las Posadas* crew, minus the devils, through downtown. Most of the group was moving slowly, stopping to sing and prod on Mr. Peppers. Mary and Joseph were far ahead, under the devilish influence of Side-kick. The feisty goat cleared their way by butting knees and anything else in his path. Shasta, the usual goat handler, hadn't shown up. I didn't blame her for taking a night off, or maybe Barton had her working.

"No, nothing's wrong," I lied to Jake. "Mom's, ah, dehydrated." We both knew that wasn't true. If anything, Mom was overhydrated *and* overoxygenated. I'd given her the oxygen canister as an early gift, hoping to soften the news of Jake not only representing Trey Crundall but also getting him released without charges. As Jake had said, any lawyer could have done the same. The police had no real evidence, and hanging out drunk in the family ski chalet was hardly a crime.

Mom loved the canned air, and while I was glad, I was also afraid it was making her emboldened and belligerent, like Flori after a sip of beer. When Jake met us earlier, Mom issued a tight nod before aiming her greetings at Winston. Even the bulldog hadn't escaped unscathed, though. Mom asked Winston if he was being a good boy for Santa. Looking guilty, he'd lifted his leg on a snowman. Not his best move.

"Oh, I understand," Jake said, squeezing my arm. "Your mother's worried about you and Celia. It's okay. We criminal defense attorneys have thick skin."

Jake might have a thick skin against prosecutors and arresting officers, but Mom's reaction was personal. And how could he understand if I didn't?

"Mom has this silly idea that Santa Fe's dangerous." I sighed, thinking I sure hadn't helped dispel that image. I'd hear about this next Christmas, when I'd have to return to Illinois. I imagined Mom recounting Wild West horrors over Jell-O surprise.

"Danger does tend to follow you," Jake said, a teasing twinkle in his eyes. "Here I had no clients, now I've got a full plate. I'll have to start turning people away if you and Flori keep going." He grinned and nodded toward a tall, skinny statue, reaching for the sky and clad in a green-and-red-striped loin cloth. "Tell Flori, I won't turn her away when she gets nabbed. I've never defended a rogue knitter before. I'll take free meals as payment."

"That could be someone else's knit graffiti," I said, practically making his case for him.

Jake picked up an embossed calling card reading "SILVER PURL and NIGHT KNITTER—knit the night!" He tucked it into his jacket pocket. "Best to be proactive," he said. "Like keeping the devils out of the performance. I think Judith Crundall made the right call on that one."

We'd caught up with Mom and Celia, who'd stopped to watch three Wise Men and Dalia try to maneuver Mr. Peppers past a bakery. The donkey pressed his lips to the window, blowing kisses—or raspberries—to the horrified workers inside.

"It's boring without devils," Celia grumbled. "Police cars are on every corner. Nothing's going to happen, just like nothing happened last time. I don't see why we devils have to sit out."

Sensing I was about to issue maternal platitudes, she said, "I know, better safe than sorry. Whatever." She rolled her eyes, yawned dramatically, and patted Winston, who was wiggling at the sight of Mr. Peppers.

"I'd better hang back," Jake said. "Winston here gets a little too emotional about hooved animals." Winston whined yearningly at the donkey, now being lured away by a Wise Man with a muffin.

Mom tartly said that was a good idea and took a hit of her oxygen.

Mr. Peppers took off at a trot, following the fleeing robed man with the muffin. Mom and Celia followed. I was torn. Should I hang back with Jake or go with my mother and daughter?

"Go on ahead," Jake said. "Winston and I will pop into the bakery. I need some coffee if I'm going to finish my paperwork tonight." He offered to get me a cup. I declined. Since my thirties, the merest drop of caffeine after dinner kept me jittery all night long. I was having enough trouble with sleep as it was. Since Manny had calmed down about devil threats, Celia was back home, which was great, except I was back on the pull-out torture device.

I caught up with Mom. She puffed more canned air. "Such a thoughtful gift, Rita," she said. "You should get yourself some. You know that low oxygen is dangerous. You can become disoriented."

I let Mom wax on about the joys of oxygen. "Imagine, though," she said. "What kind of place is this if you have to buy air in a canister? I told

your sister all about it over Skype. I told her, I
hope I don't use it all up before I go."

"We can get you more anytime, Mom," I said. If
Trey Crundall could keep his lackluster ski store
open. "Or you can go to the oxygen bar. Remember how fun that was?"

I'd sent Mom to the downtown oxygen bar the
first time she visited me. She'd loved it, except for
the price and the idea of splurging on oxygen and
the word *bar* in the name.

We caught up with Mr. Peppers. The donkey
had stalled again, attracted by a manger scene in
a storefront window. Dalia was whispering in his
big ears.

"I was telling him to listen to the spirits of his
hardworking ancestors," Dalia said with exasperation.

Mr. Peppers yawned, showing off a mouthful of
grass-stained teeth.

"It's that foolish Wise Man's fault," Dalia went
on. "He let Peppers eat the entire muffin. And
where are Mary and Joseph? It's like they're running a race! It's just as well Judith isn't here to
watch. This *Las Posadas* isn't up to her standards."

"The singing is lovely," I said. "Look at the big
crowd. Everyone's having fun."

Dalia shrugged. "It's not the same without devils.
They bring a certain joy." She patted the donkey's
furry neck. "Or maybe I'm imagining it because I
feel bad for Judith. A few of the carolers said they'd
go up to the house later and serenade her. I hate to
think of her missing out on Christmas."

Judith Crundall might financially support *Las
Posadas*, but she didn't strike me as the holiday

sentimental type. Still, caroling was a nice gesture. So was the bouncy song the carolers were singing to Mr. Peppers: "El Burrito Sabanero," the little donkey from the savannah. Celia had learned the lyrics in elementary school when we'd come to visit Manny's relatives.

"Remember this?" I asked Celia.

She shrugged in teenage nonchalance, stifled a smile, and sang a few lines. Mr. Peppers perked up and started walking again, lifting his hooves high in a proud prance.

"One more street," Dalia said. She let out a breath that I interpreted as relief. I felt relieved too. Sure, the evening hadn't gone the way I'd hoped between my mother and Jake, but Mom seemed happy enough now, chugging her oxygen and humming along. The carolers led the way to the south side of the Plaza. Ahead, the Cathedral and the towering pine tree beside it sparkled in white lights. The snow was picking up too, falling in thick flakes that coated the park benches and branches. Some of the audience gazed upward, mesmerized by the swirling white. Others took cover under porticos. I spotted the British ladies huddled under a summery parasol, and Lorena and Wyatt, holding flickering candles and wearing Santa hats.

"Beautiful," Mom said. "How lovely."

It was lovely. The three Wise Men had gathered beside Mr. Peppers, who was contentedly chewing on a tortilla. I found myself swaying with Celia and Mom, singing along to "Silent Night."

Except the night wasn't silent much longer. We'd just sung "all is calm" when a scream pierced the melody, sending the crowd and Mr. Peppers scattering. Dalia yelped and bolted after the donkey until she saw what had caused the chaos. A woman backed away, yelling for help as Barton Hunter, holding his bloody head, staggered forward and collapsed at the feet of the Wise Men.

Mr. Peppers bolted. One of the Wise Men went pale and started to wobble. Another whipped off his robe and pressed it to Barton's head.

"Call an ambulance!" Dalia yelled, rushing to Barton's side. He lay on his side and groaned.

"Let's get out of the way," I said to my mother and daughter, taking a step back as a good example.

Mom dutifully followed me. Celia held her ground and whipped out her phone. "Dad!" she exclaimed after tapping a speed dial number. "It's the other devil, Barton. He's been attacked. He's all bloody." Celia paused to answer questions. "No, I'm okay. There are some Wise Men with him and Dalia. Yeah . . . Mom's right here." She held out the phone to me.

I took it along with a deep breath and then told my grumpy ex to get here fast. Down the street, Mr. Peppers trotted away, head high and wheezing like a steam train. A tall figure holding on to his hat sprinted after him. Even through the filter of snow, I easily recognized Jake and the antlered bulldog and galloping goat running along beside him.

Chapter 28

The ambulance skidded around the snow-slick corner and out of sight. "I wish they'd let me go with Barton," Dalia said. "He's all alone here, no family."

"He'll be okay," I said, with optimism I didn't feel. "It's best that the officer goes with him and can take his statement immediately. With head injuries, people sometimes forget later on."

I was actually glad that officer was Manny. He knew the case. Plus, I didn't need to hear any more of his accusations about me putting Celia in dangerous situations. I told myself he was wrong. From what Dalia understood, Barton hadn't been at the abbreviated *Las Posadas*. He'd been suddenly attacked while walking down a nearby street and "staggered toward the light," as he'd put it.

The sirens faded, and the gawkers, shaken actors, and carolers dispersed. Mom and Celia waited on a bench under a portico. Mom clutched her oxygen and Celia kept her head down, texting furiously. It was cold and snowing more heavily. I knew I should get them home. After one more question. "Did Barton see who attacked him, Dalia?"

She shook her head slowly, in what I interpreted as a negative.

I put a hand on her shoulder and told her, "It's okay, the police and EMTs will take good care of him—"

"Trey!" she said. "He managed to say 'Trey.'" She reached under her layers of scarves to grasp one of her crystal necklaces. Rubbing the clear stone, she said softly, "What if Trey did this? Oh, I can't even think of it! I have to get back and be with Judith." She patted her pockets until she found keys. Then she looked heavenward. "Oh stars! How could I forget? That donkey! I have to find him and the goat."

I felt my phone buzzing in my pocket. The text was from Jake. I read it and said, "I've got a lead on Mr. Peppers and Sidekick. Jake and I can get them safely back home if you'll do me a favor. Will you drop my mother and Celia off at my place before going to Judith's?"

Dalia gratefully agreed. "I want to check on Phillip and the kids first anyway. It's no trouble at all."

Mom eyed me suspiciously when I told her the plan. "I'm just going to help Jake get Mr. Peppers corralled," I said. "I'll come home right after."

"I won't wait up," she replied.

followed a trail of prints—hoof, paw, and cowboy boot—to an appropriate meeting spot. Burro Alley. The name originated long ago, when wood collectors and their pack burros hauled firewood in from the hills and sold it along the block-long lane. Today, the alley features donkey murals and statues, including a life-sized bronze donkey forever draped in logs. Mr. Peppers stood by this taller, thinner, and more industrious version of himself, nuzzling the statue's nose. Sidekick leaned his horns into the bronze donkey's knees.

"Good choice of spots," I said to Jake, who was holding the leads of all three animals, as well as Winston's discarded antlers. The bulldog panted at the donkeys adoringly.

Snow had accumulated on Jake's hat and broad shoulders. He stomped his boots. "I didn't want to take these two escapees too far away in case Dalia wanted them back. Peppers seemed happy to stop here."

I patted Mr. Peppers and told him he was a chicken to run off. The donkey, unrepentant, shoved his nose at my purse. I realized I had some old *bizcochitos* in there—Addie's vegan variety. Vegan wouldn't wreck his nonexistent diet. I gave Peppers and Sidekick a half cookie each and filled Jake in on what had happened.

"Barton Hunter, eh?" Jake said. "And Dalia says he pointed the finger at Trey? Wish I'd gotten to drink that coffee before Peppers took off. Do the police know what Barton said?"

I told him that Manny was in the ambulance

with the stricken man. "If they don't know already, they will soon enough. Let's get Mr. Peppers back and you can hunt down Trey."

Jake patted the donkey on his haunches. "I can't say I'm eager to get him out of trouble again. If he's truly the one who sent you and Celia those threats, I won't be keeping him on as a client."

Mr. Peppers was reluctant to leave his new metal friend. However, his devotion faded when I held out my last cookie.

Jake patted the donkey and asked about my mother and Celia. "If they're waiting for you, Winston and I can herd these two back to their paddock."

"Dalia's taking them home before heading to Judith's." I glanced over at Jake, who was looking extra-handsome bundled up against the snow. "Mom said she's not waiting up for me. Pity . . ."

Jake put his arm around me and agreed that it was a shame. "You know what I want for Christmas?" he asked, the smile lines flaring around his eyes.

Looking up at him, I felt snowflakes melting on my cheeks.

"Time alone with you," he said, and leaned down to kiss me.

Flori announced the capture of Trey Crundall late the next morning, right when I was attempting to balance three platters on my wrist.

"They got him!" she crowed. "He went right back to Taos, the fool."

My load of cheese enchiladas, Christmas-style, tipped precariously. The bowl of piping hot *posole* wobbled.

Flori saved me from brunch collapse by taking the *posole* and accompanying me to the packed dining room. Tomorrow was Christmas Eve, meaning today was the last day before Tres Amigas closed for a holiday break. Our regulars had shown up, eager to fill up on Flori's Christmas *posole* and gossip. The Knit and Snitchers were out in full force. Needles and tongues clacked. The British ladies had also returned and were filling in Addie's vocabulary with words such as *gob-smacked*, *beastly*, and *blimey*.

"Sloshed, Trey was," Addie said when we all convened back in the kitchen. "Drunk as a lord."

"Under some kind of influence," Flori agreed. "The Taos police nabbed him but not in the Crundall ski chalet like before. He was in a cabin rented under the name Shasta Moon, but she wasn't there."

Before I could follow up about Shasta, Flori continued. "One of my friends has a great-niece who cleans over at the police station. No one ever pays any attention to the cleaning staff, so they get the best info. Well, the niece said that Trey was ranting on with the wildest story that he was the victim. Said he went to a bar in Santa Fe to have a drink and blacked out. Claimed he had no memory of getting to Taos and only came to when the police pounded on the door." Flori shook her head in disbelief. "Your Mr. Strong ordered extensive drug tests, just in case."

Addie muttered, "Poppycock," and I had to agree.

Flori said, "There's more. I heard that Judith allowed the police to search her house, garage, and Trey's ski business too. It looks like Trey's been selling off pieces from that horrible collection for years and picked up his thieving recently. Some of the most important objects are gone. He must have panicked, seeing that it was all going to be repatriated."

I thought of Trey and his interests in pot, snowpack, and board wax. I could see him pawning a few baskets or bowls for extra cash, but connecting with a hard-core underground black market for bones? He would have needed help.

"So where is Shasta?" I said. "She didn't show up to walk Sidekick in *Las Posadas* last night." Was she on the run like Manny suggested? Or was she another victim? I shuddered, thinking of all the deep canyons and remote landscapes between here and Taos where a killer could dump a body. Or perhaps she'd simply gone home. "Surely Manny checked down in Albuquerque," I said.

Flori was filling a tortilla with slow-roasted pork in red chile sauce. "Now that's one of the best parts," she said. "I was saving it for last. Bill Hoffman heard that Deputy Davis went down to Albuquerque to look for Shasta Moon. Get this, she found her!"

"That's great!" I said.

"Not so fast," Flori said. "I didn't get to the interesting bit. Shasta Moon never left Albuquerque."

"What?" Addie and I said in unison.

Flori loves telling a good story. She made us wait as she tucked in the ends of the burrito, draped it in the red and green chile sauces, sprinkled on cheese, and slipped it under the broiler. Looking over her Harry Potter–style bifocals, she said, "The Shasta we know is a fake."

When Addie and I appropriately gasped, she said, "Deputy Davis and the UNM police located a graduate student by that name. She's been working on a bone study in her lab for the entire winter break. She'd never heard of the Crundalls."

I pondered Flori's revelations throughout the lunch rush. Had Trey and the fake Shasta known each other previously? Or had she seen the temporary job and Trey's lax morals as opportunities to steal from Judith's collection? Who was she? *Where* was she? I was so consumed by questions that I mixed up orders and was more inept than usual with the cash register. Customers kindly joked off my mishaps as "vacation fever."

"Go home!" Flori finally ordered at ten minutes to two. "It's Christmas Eve eve! We're officially on vacation. I have to get going too and start my holiday meal preparations. I certainly miss Linda's tamales."

I knew she missed having her eldest daughter home for Christmas most of all. We promised to keep in touch.

"I'll find you tomorrow night for the Christmas Eve *farolitos*," Flori said. "If you want to bring your mother and Celia over, we're having a big feast on Christmas Day." Flori had already invited me several times. I hated to turn her down, but

I knew Mom would prefer her traditional meal. I was already pushing Mom's limits by inviting Jake to celebrate with us because his parents were in Wyoming visiting his sister.

"I'll do my best," I said to Flori. So far, my best hadn't worked out very well at all.

Chapter 29

On Christmas Eve day, Celia again headed down to the Crundall mansion to babysit. I was suspicious but not all that worried since Trey still languished in jail. The drug tests Jake had ordered were delayed by the holiday, and Judith Crundall was teaching her thieving son a lesson by refusing to post his bail bond. Mom and I stayed in and cooked, preparing her favorite cranberry-orange relish and mixing up the dough for her wonderful savory monkey bread, which tastes like stuffing in bite-sized, buttery bread form.

As fat snowflakes fell outside, we took a baking break for tea and family gossip. "Remember when Aunt Sue used to play the drums?" Mom said. "Uncle Carl would walk around town for hours until she was done practicing. Then she'd start up again right when he got back, to show him how well she was doing."

I grinned. "I remember her bringing down the house at the Lutheran church."

Mom agreed that Sue might have missed her calling in percussion. "I'm glad for your little friend Addie," she said. "She's a bit odd, but she's pursuing her passion, isn't she?"

She sure was. Mom, Celia, and I had gone to see Addie perform an early show at a downtown lounge last night. Addie's soulful Christmas carols earned a standing ovation from us, her British friends, and the rest of the crowd.

"You liked your job, didn't you, Mom?" I asked. I'd always assumed that she did. Mom had a passion for organizing and shelving, as my spice drawer, pantry, and closet could attest to.

"Oh yes, it was fine," Mom said. "I love libraries."

We certainly shared that in common. "I always liked meeting you there after school," I said. When I was little, I'd been allowed to walk the few blocks from my elementary school to the public library, where I'd read until Mom got off work. I thought how difficult it must have been for her to juggle work and two kids.

Mom was reminiscing about watching out the library window, waiting for Kathy and me to appear.

"You did a great job on your own, Mom," I said, meaning it.

Mom reminded me of Dalia, studying her teacup for a message. Except her clear herbal tea had no leaves to read.

"Rita," Mom said, suddenly serious. "Do you remember much about your father?"

Memory's not my best trait. Flori can recall what she wore for each first day of school and what cake she ate for every birthday celebration. My memories were foggier.

"Not too much," I admitted. My heartbeat sped up. Was Mom about to drop something big?

Mom went to the stove and poured more water from the kettle over her teabag. "About your father, I've been meaning to—" My phone, blaring "Jingle Bells," cut her off.

"Oops, sorry!" I said, grabbing it. I intended to turn it right off, but then saw it was Celia. I mouthed her name to Mom, who gestured for me to take the call.

"Everything okay on the babysitting front?" I asked.

"Fine," Celia said offhandedly. In the background, Eddie was talking loudly about trains. His sister told him to shut up and read.

My suspicion shot up, and not because of the squabbling kids. Celia's "fine" sounded too cool. "What's up?" I asked, trying to match her nonchalance.

"Not much," Celia said, lowering her voice so that I could barely hear it over Eddie's siren screech. "It's just that . . . Sky and I . . . we think someone's trying to kill Ms. Crundall."

Sky's excited voice came over the line. "We know it!"

I told them to stay where they were. "I'll be right down." I apologized to Mom while struggling to zip my parka. In the end, I left the coat open. "Celia and Sky are . . ." I paused, wondering how much to tell Mom.

"They need you," Mom said. "Go."

I was halfway to the car when she called out the door. "Zip your coat up, Rita. You're no good to anyone if you catch a cold."

found the kids and teens in the archives room. "Arsenic," Sky said in an incongruently merry voice. He sat at the long table beside Eddie, who was occupied with a coloring book of trains.

Emilie looked up from her Nancy Drew and frowned. Eddie took no notice other than to sing out the word *arsenic*.

Arsenic? I mouthed so that Eddie wouldn't continue caroling about poisonings.

Sky got up and walked to the far side of the room, with Celia and me following. "I was researching NAGPRA," he said. "That's the law about returning sacred objects and human remains to First Nations."

Emilie, presumably still reading her book, flipped several pages in succession.

"You tell," Sky said to Celia.

She said, "In the gross old days, archeologists and collectors treated feathers and fur and other materials with arsenic as a preservative."

Sky wrinkled his young face in disgust. "Sacred objects, poisoned. When museums give stuff back, they're supposed to make sure it's clean so it doesn't hurt the recipients."

I was beginning to see their point. "You think those kachinas and good-luck charms Judith has been holding are poisonous?"

The teens nodded. Sky listed off symptoms of arsenic poisoning that matched Judith's many complaints. "And there's more," he said.

Before he could tell me, Barton Hunter entered the room. A thick bandage ringed his forehead. He gave a weak high-five to Eddie and came over to greet us. "Rita, I fear I didn't say hello properly the other night."

"You were kind of busy," I said. *Busy collapsing from a head wound!* I smiled sympathetically and asked, "Are you okay?"

"Flesh wound," he said. Then he said, self-mockingly, "Dalia keeps following me around watching for signs of a concussion. I feel like a duped fool more than anything else."

I yearned to ask him what happened, yet the little kids had sharp ears. I said instead. "You're not working, are you?"

He leaned against the table. "Someone has to fix this mess. Anyway, I'm not supposed to lie down and fall into concussive sleep unsupervised. More than that, I'm not sleepy, and I'm the one who hired you-know-who."

"Who?" Eddie said, showing off his keen kid hearing. He then declared that he wasn't sleepy either.

"Good man," Barton said. "Now, what were you saying, Sky? You found something?"

Celia started to say, "We found—"

Something made me cut in. "We found a great coloring book for Eddie," I said, going over to the table. "He was telling us all about trains."

Trains was a magic word to get Eddie talking. He chatted on about the caboose he was sure he was getting for Christmas tomorrow.

Barton said he was off to find things himself. "Off to the room of messed-up boxes," he said.

When he'd left the room, the teens and I huddled. "If Sky's right about the arsenic, we don't know who's involved or if it's an innocent accident."

"Trey," Sky suggested. "Or that fake Shasta person or . . ." He stopped, his face conflicted.

"No way," Celia said, shaking her head violently. "If you're thinking Dalia, she'd never do such a thing. She's Ms. Crundall's sister. Right, Mom?"

Right, I wanted to say. But Dalia was also the half sister who didn't get the Crundall name or fortune, the person who plied Judith with possibly poisonous objects and treatments. "Let's keep this all to ourselves for now," I said.

Standing in the hallway with the archives room door shut, I called Manny. My ex added a few choice words between "Merry" and "Christmas."

"Happy holidays to you too," I said, forcing a beaming smile at the phone for the sake of Celia, hovering nearby. I decided flattery was the best route. "You know how Celia takes after you, how she's confident and determined and . . ."

Manny sighed. "What's going on now, Rita?"

I told him the teens' theory. "Arsenic poisoning fits with Judith's symptoms," I said. "What we don't know is if the objects Judith carries around are actually contaminated. And even if they are, maybe no one realized. I wouldn't have known they contained arsenic."

"Someone familiar with her house might," Manny said. He was silent for a few beats. "We found a bunch of old chemicals back in what Ms. Crundall was calling her grandfather's 'laboratory.' Some in that garage too. I'll send the lab techs over to collect samples. Christmas Eve. They'll be thrilled." He uttered a few more unholy words and ordered me to take Celia home. "I don't want her in that house or turning into a snoop like you," he grouched.

"You're welcome," I said, in lieu of true sentiments, and hung up. To Celia, I said, "Your father's going to send tech people over. Let's find Dalia and tell her we're going home, okay?"

We went back inside to tell Sky. Cass's tall son perched on a metal stool, staring down at spreadsheets and mailing lists. To my surprise, he readily grabbed his coat.

"Sure," he said. "Let's get out of here."

I told the teens I'd go look for Dalia. I found her near the kitchen, in a cloud of smoldering cedar and sage.

"I've been purifying," she said. She held a clump of herbs and announced that she was off to Trey's quarters. "Judith thinks I'm silly," she added. "It can't hurt, I keep telling her."

Unless it could. "Dalia," I said carefully, "How did you choose the . . . ah . . . healing objects for Judith?"

She waved the sage toward the ceiling. "They called to me. I found some of them last year in Granddad Crundall's laboratory. They looked so lonely and sad. Shasta picked out some others. Oh, but she's not Shasta is she? What should we call her? In any case, she said they'd be perfect, since they were uncataloged." Dalia smiled serenely. "They're doing Judith a world of good. I know they are."

Shasta said . . . I covered my shiver with a cough and told Dalia we'd drop the kids off at her place to hang out with their grandfather. Judith Crundall's rambling old house seemed suddenly ominous to me. I wanted to get out as soon as possible, and especially before the crime scene techs showed up.

Chapter 30

Thousands of *farolitos* glowed across the adobe city on Christmas Eve. Bonfires crackled in courtyards, and throngs of revelers strolled the streets. Mom—after noting that the falling snow might hold down mass conflagrations—acknowledged the beauty.

"I've never seen anything like it," she said. "You were right, Rita. It's gorgeous, and so nice that the streets are shut to traffic."

Of course, a few drivers were still flouting the rules. Their cars crept at the pace of the crowds, who resisted parting for motorized annoyances. I'd parked a few blocks away from the main *farolito* extravagance of Canyon Road and the surrounding east-side neighborhoods.

"How are we going to find Flori?" Celia asked, standing on her tiptoes.

"She said she'd be by the elementary school," I said. We were weaving that way. The paper kites powered by candlelight were once again taking to the skies, and Flori wanted to get in on the action.

"There!" Celia said, bending to peer across a big bonfire. She pointed to two figures decked out in matching puffy tundra wear. Flori and her husband, Bernard, held steaming paper cups and stood dangerously close to the fire. I headed their way. Celia veered left. I spotted Sky, tall amid the crowd. "I'm going to say hi," Celia called back. "We'll catch up with you."

I wanted to hold her hand and keep her close. *Like that would go over well.* And she'd be right to be grumpy. We were literally surrounded by happy, festive people.

"Keep your phone close," I said instead.

"Sure, Mom," she said with an eye roll and a smile. "You too. I'll catch up with you and Gran soon."

I watched her go. She'd be fine with her friends, I told myself. Safer than with the snack-obsessed Gary, who had the night off anyway. Poor Judith, hiring bodyguards for others when she was the one who needed protection.

"I heard," Flori said, when Mom was busy greeting Bernard. "Judith Crundall checked into the hospital and is getting tested for arsenic poisoning. Dalia always said that collection was toxic, didn't she? Do you suppose she knew all too well? Judith did get the family fortune . . ." She waved a mitten-covered hand. "I can't see it, though."

I couldn't either. I told her how the missing imposter-Shasta had selected some of Dalia's "healing" objects. "And there's Trey too. He clearly resents his mother and wants to have free access to the family fortune."

"That boy doesn't seem smart enough," Flori said.

I had to agree, somewhat. "But he went to college and minored in anthropology. Plus, he's been around that collection all his life. He could know more than he lets on."

Flori and Bernard decided to stay by the fire awhile longer. "You and your mother go stroll and take in the *farolito* displays. By the time you do the loop around the main streets, the kites will be going up."

I texted Celia to let her know which way Mom and I were heading. She wrote back promptly, saying that she and Sky would catch up with us later.

"Stunning," Mom said as we walked. *Farolitos* lined pathways, walls, and rooftops, casting a golden glow over the silvery, moonlit night. Carolers and musicians gathered around the crackling bonfires. Some residents even offered up bowls of hot *posole* and invited strolling strangers into their kitchens.

"It's all so different," Mom said, taking a slug of water. She'd filled her dual hip holster with essentials: water and oxygen. "But what marvelous old traditions. I *can* see why you like it here, Rita."

Her words warmed me more than a bonfire. We walked and gazed and for a while, I forgot about the dead devil and Judith Crundall's troubles. I didn't forget about Celia, though. I occasionally glanced back. Far down the street, I saw a car pushing through.

Rude, I thought, which turned my mind to another irritation. Namely, Manny, griping that he didn't want Celia turning into a snoop like me. *Typical Manny*. Gazing into an ember-spitting bonfire, I chided myself. Tonight was a special night, not a time to get dragged down by my ex. Still, something I couldn't quite grasp gnawed at the edges of my memory.

Behind us, the pesky car had crept closer. I hoped the driver wouldn't take Gormley Lane, my planned shortcut over to Canyon Road and its glittery art galleries. The short, unpaved lane cut across remnants of the pastures and orchards that once existed in this part of town and felt like an insider's secret.

"Let's turn here," I said to Mom. "I'll text Celia."

A few yards down, Mom said, "Wouldn't you know it? That car is turning too. Why anyone would try to drive here tonight . . ."

Mom and I kept walking. The car hovered in a parking area near a house and turned its lights off. *A resident, getting home late*, I thought, until I heard the crunch of tires on gravel.

"Ugh," I groaned, as we stepped off to the side, waiting for the car to pass.

However, the driver stopped a few feet ahead of us and rolled down the window. In an instant, I recognized Barton Hunter. In another instant, my mind wrapped around the foggy memory that had been bugging me. *Shasta, at Barton Hunter's door, upset by the bloody devil doll in the mailbox. Barton, usually a smooth flirt, grumping at her to calm down and have some of her favorite cookies. The red silk and lace on his bed.* Shasta was supposedly a temporary assistant, someone unknown to Barton. Or so she and Barton claimed. Now we knew that Shasta wasn't who she said she was. What if Barton wasn't either?

I backed up a step. His eyes followed me, and in the lowered lids and upturned lips, I glimpsed something my sister also encountered this Christmas . . . an alligator sizing up its prey. Adrenaline spiked through my temples. I tried to cover with perky Christmas greetings.

"Merry Christmas, Barton! Aren't the *farolitos* gorgeous? Canyon Road should be amazing, although you might want to go park somewhere else. Probably back that way." I gestured wildly in pretty much all directions but here. I grabbed Mom's elbow and began moving us in the direction we'd come from.

"No need to hurry off," Barton said. "We should talk."

"We should talk too, Rita," Mom murmured at my side.

Barton tilted his chin toward the backseat. "Get in."

No way was I getting in. "Come on, Mom," I said in a low but urgent tone. "Hurry."

Barton leaned out the window. "Don't you want to take a ride with your daughter?" With a mean smirk, he nodded again toward the backseat, then slowly drove forward.

I lunged and grabbed at the rear door. Yanking it open, I saw a blanket-covered figure writhing on the floor, moaning in a high, feminine pitch. I couldn't tell if it was Celia, but I couldn't take a chance.

Mom stood frozen a few feet away. "Go, Mom! Get help!" I yelled, clinging to the door. I leapt in and Barton sped up, but not before Mom landed heavily on top of me.

"Mom, no!" I cried.

"I'm not leaving you, Rita," she said breathlessly.

I wanted to push her back out. Before I could, she yanked the door shut, and I heard the sickening thud of automatic door locks behind her.

While Mom sputtered about rudeness, I struggled to uncover the figure at our feet. I loosened the blanket and pulled it back to reveal the bruised face of the woman who called herself Shasta Moon.

Mom gasped. The fake Shasta groaned and tried to sit up.

"Surprise," Barton said lightly. "Now, hand over your phones. We're all going on a little holiday drive."

I didn't have a chance to call for help. Barton twisted in his seat and waved a gun. "Hand them over," he ordered. "Don't try anything stupid, or I'll shoot you all."

Shasta called him a foul name. He responded with a mean chuckle and more unpleasantries.

I gave Barton my phone and the travel phone Mom carried for safety. *Some safety.* Hauling Shasta up on the seat beside me, I saw her hands were pinned behind her back with plastic tie cuffs. Flori probably would have had a knife handy, or a knitting needle shiv. I had nothing. Mom buckled up and told me to do the same. I did as she said, thinking that car safety was the least of our problems.

At the end of the lane, Barton turned away from the revelers, and we passed one of my favorite landmarks, a giant sculpture of a horse's head. Even through my fear, I noticed the red and green knit mask the horse now sported. A clutch of people snapped photos. Flori and Miriam's "big surprise," I guessed.

"Cute," Shasta murmured.

Barton's scornful snort set off bickering between the two. *Like an unhappy couple.* I should have noticed. Barton hadn't been pleased when Eddie sang about Shasta kissing Trey, or when Manny flirted with her in the name of police work. The consultant and his assistant, as was now apparent, were a lot more acquainted than they'd let on.

Shasta accused Barton of being a fake and a bully. "I'm so sick of you," she said. "You're a fraud and always will be. You only married me to shut me up and make me do all the work."

"A lot of good it did me," Barton countered. "You're a terrible assistant. Plus, did you really think you could double-cross me? *Any of you?*"

Mom reached over and gripped my hand.

"This is between you two," I said. "My mother and I should get out of your way." I said this lightly, as if we'd just stumbled into an awkward breakup luncheon.

Neither of them took any notice. "At least Trey's *real*," Shasta said. She nudged me and raised her chin toward Barton. "*He* grew up a nothing. He still is. A thief and con, like his daddy, trying to swindle his way into class."

They resumed bickering, hurling insults at each other's families. I leaned into Mom, both glad she was here and desperately wishing she wasn't.

"Rita," she said quietly. "About your father . . ."

"We can talk about this later, Mom," I said.

Barton stopped insulting Shasta's mother and

said, "You have something to say to your daughter, you should say it now. Could be your last chance . . ."

All of us in the backseat went quiet. I didn't want to ask what Barton had planned. There were three of us. Good odds, except for the gun and handcuffs and my worries about Mom.

Mom sat up straighter beside me. Her voice was strong. "Rita, heaven forbid, if this is our last chance, you should know. I've been trying to find a way to tell you the entire time I've been here. Your father . . ." She paused. Shasta leaned forward, eyeing Mom expectantly.

"Yeah? Spit it out," Barton said.

"Your father's alive!" Mom stammered. "He didn't die when you were in kindergarten. He left us and then faked his death. There. I've told you."

"Nice one," Barton said, sounding truly appreciative.

My head spun. All I could manage was, "Alive?"

"Great," Shasta said sarcastically. "Let's hope he's not a loser and a con like Barton here."

"He was," Mom said.

"Better to stay dead then," Shasta said, suddenly an advice columnist.

Mom nodded thoughtfully. "That's what I thought. I honestly did believe he'd died. Years later, he reappeared when Rita was thinking of leaving college and going to culinary school. She was already so confused. I thought it best to keep the shock from her."

"Hey!" I said, forgetting my terror long enough to be indignant. "Culinary school's one of the best decisions I ever made." Then the full implications of Mom's words struck me. "But what about his grave and the obituary?"

Mom squeezed my knee. "Your father got involved in shady financial dealings with a dishonest client, Rita. He was a restless man. He wanted a new life and lifestyle. When he left, his client had just gone to jail. I thought he was scared of jail himself. Honestly, I was rather relieved he'd saved us the embarrassment. My mother said I should consider him dead, but I couldn't until we saw his obituary in the Bucks Grove paper a year later."

"People always believe the obituaries," Barton said. "And the morgue? So few people take the time to actually verify a body. It's almost too easy. Except when your partner double-crosses you!" In the rearview mirror, his glare fixed on Shasta.

"Yeah?" she countered. "How about I get the glamor role sometime? Why is it me who always has to play the assistant? Why not you?"

"Because I have a reputation built up," he growled. "And the old ladies love me."

Shasta writhed beside me. "I'm through with your games," she said again. To me, she said, "Did you see how he had me playing a nerdy vegetarian grad student? Lucky for me, Trey thought my glasses were hot. So did that hunky policeman."

I realized another clue I'd missed. "Wait . . . you ate *bizcochitos* without asking if they had lard in them!" I exclaimed. "Barton said they were your favorite too!"

"Lard? What?" Shasta said, perplexed, proving she was definitely not New Mexican.

Mom said, "Even I learned that pretty quick."

"Clever," Barton said, turning the car in the direction of Fort Marcy overlook. I'd watched many an incredible sunset from this ridge perched above town. It would likely be deserted now. However, I knew the area well. If Mom and I could make a break for it, we could hide among the stubby pines or run for a nearby house. Except Barton kept driving, turning on a road leading to the ski resort high in the mountains and, before that, witchy Josephina's borrowed condo.

Mom was saying in an apologetic voice, "I'm sorry I didn't dig into your father's death, Rita. I was busy trying to keep a stable home for you girls. I'm not a sleuth like you."

"Healthier that way," Shasta said.

Barton agreed. "You're right about that. We wouldn't be in this particular mess if it wasn't for you, Ms. Lafitte."

I started to protest. "I wasn't—"

He cut in with a list of all I'd done wrong. "I heard about you. And I saw you snooping around the night Judith landed in the hospital."

"Dalia sent me down to check on Trey!" I protested. "I thought I disrupted the burglar. How was that you? You called me when I was chasing the guy."

"I called after I was far enough away, to cover my tracks," he said. "I sent you those nice home-made death threats too. Which you disregarded. And sending your kid and her buddy to babysit?"

I stopped breathing. What if he suspected Celia and Sky? Would he go after them next?

He continued with a sneer. "Like I believed *that*. I saw through that ruse. You using those kids for an excuse to come by and snoop."

I let out the breath I'd been holding, relieved but only momentarily. This was my fault. I had to make the situation right. Slowly, I unzipped my coat and loosened my belt. The belt was tight from too many Christmas goodies, but comfort wasn't my aim. I planned to loop it around Barton's neck. And then what? Strangle him? Could I actually do that? And what about the gun and the car possibly spinning on the snow-slick road?

"I love you, Rita," Mom said. "I only wanted the best for you and your sister."

"I love you too, Mom," I said, and started inching out my belt.

Chapter 31

Where are we going?" I asked Barton, keeping my tone light.

"Where do you want to go?" he replied.

Anywhere without him. I'd happily go to the Japanese-style hot spring for some steaming ramen, cool sushi, and a hot soak. I imagined Mom's reaction to raw fish and nude bathing, but then even Mom would choose those over Christmas Eve with a madman.

The headlights lit a tunnel of windswept snow edged by jutting junipers. On a tight curve, I felt the tires skitter and Mom's knee pressing on her air brakes. Barton and Shasta had resumed their argument.

"All you had to do was ship out the good stuff," he said. "No one looks twice at the hired help. Easy."

Shasta sputtered. "Easy? You try dealing with your sicko clients." She turned to me. "The ones who want the bones are the worst."

I nodded. I could certainly imagine that.

She kept going, addressing me. "I didn't even know he was going to kill that gardener. He wrote those letters too and put the creepy doll in the mailbox." She turned back toward the front. "You jerk! You could have told me!"

Barton said, "Calm down. You should be grateful I killed that guy. He was poking around. He *knew!* I daresay, I handled it pretty well too. You never did fully appreciate the long con, darling."

"Yeah?" Shasta sputtered. "Is that what you think? I had my con with Trey going fine until you dragged me away. He said I was perfect. He'd have married me."

Barton snorted. "You're already married. Anyway, old Mother Crundall might not kick it for years. What were you going to do? Play housewife daughter-in-law for a decade? You're not the type."

"Mama Crundall was going quicker than you think," Shasta said. "I made sure of that."

"With the arsenic?" I blurted out.

Shasta scowled at me. "You know?"

Uh oh. Her expression suggested that Barton wasn't the only one ready to do away with me.

"Ah, the police think that some of Judith's collection was contaminated," I said. "Arsenic was an old-fashioned preservative. No one's to blame." Unless Shasta had added some extra.

She turned a flirty voice and southern accent on Barton, and I knew I'd made a big mistake. Make that another big mistake.

"Sweetie doll," she drawled, "I've got an idea. Once we get rid of these meddlers, let's go on to

California like we planned. There's that awful mummy collection in Monterey. You'll have that old couple eating out of your pretty hands."

He wasn't fooled or flattered. "So you can do me in later? Pack a little poison for the road? Call to the police as you hightail out of town? No, doll, I have a new plan. I've already written your suicide note. You'll confess to skimming off the collection with Trey and killing the nosy gardener. Oh, and doing in Ms. Lafitte and her mother here. Don't worry, you'll say you're sorry. I'll express terrible shock."

Shasta's urgent pleas didn't help my nerves. "We can split up! We'll get a divorce. You'll never see me again. I'll go to—"

Barton cut in with a mean laugh, "I prefer to be a grieving widower. I'll be fine. Look how well I'm recovering from my head wound."

Shasta grumbled to me, "He did that himself. Probably didn't even hurt. A little blood and moaning for the ladies. He drugged Trey too, you know. Framed him. Poor Trey . . ."

"It did hurt," Barton said. "I whacked myself a good one. I had to make it look real. Know what inspired me? Imagining all the trouble I was about to inflict on your snooty boyfriend."

"I suppose you also faked your migraine," I said, since he was confessing.

"Sure," Barton said. "I do get them and had a legit prescription. People around here are so kind and trusting, like that nice pharmacy tech who drove me home. All I had to do was wait a bit, then sneak over to that hotel and take care of Francisco." He caught my eye in the rearview mirror.

"Rita, did you notice the sulfur smell when you found the body? See my attention to detail? That was a sulfur bomb. Nice touch, don't you think?"

I didn't answer. We drove in silence for a few minutes until Mom said, "I grieved your father, Rita, even after he'd deserted us so callously. Then when he turned up all those years later, with a new life, he was still dead to us. My mother was right."

"Amateur," Barton said. "Never go back or get stupid and sentimental."

I had my belt off. I gripped the ends, waiting for my moment. Barton had picked up speed. If he veered off the road, we'd crash into a rocky hill or tumble into an icy ravine. I stared ahead into the tunnel of snowy white, frozen with fear. I didn't want to crash. I didn't want to strangle anyone, even Barton Hunter.

"Where are we going?" I asked again.

"Ski Santa Fe," Barton said pleasantly. "I have a car parked up there. Planning ahead. Like I said, no one does the long con better than me."

I gripped the belt so hard my nails cut into my palms. I willed myself to act. I'd do it. I had to . . . on the next straight stretch.

I was steeling myself, when what had to be a mirage appeared. A figure in black jumped into the center of the road, waving a stick. Barton jabbed the brakes, sending the car into a tail-spin. We skidded toward a pine. Metal scraped branches and the car hurtled down the ravine.

Mom's arm and my lap belt stopped my forward lurch. Shasta's scream mingled with the crunch of metal and the front airbags bursting. My knee slammed painfully into Barton's seat. Except for my pounding heart, though, I felt okay. I checked on Mom. Her eyes were closed. My pounding heart seemed to stall. *No . . .*

I reached out to touch her just as she murmured, "Amen" and unbuckled her seat belt. Relief swept over me, but only momentarily. Barton was struggling to extract himself from the airbag.

The window beside Mom was shattered. "Quick, climb outside," I urged Mom.

Beside me, Shasta was attempting her own escape by rubbing her wrist ties against the broken window. The glass was the safety kind and crumbling.

"Help me," she begged as I guided Mom's foot out the window. "Get these ties off, and I'll deal with *him*. There's a penknife in my purse."

The old fable of the scorpion and frog crossing a river came to mind. Would she—like the scorpion—turn on me as soon as she was safe? Mom reached a hand in for me. Barton had slithered out from the airbag and was pushing open his door.

Mom and I couldn't outrun him, especially not in the snow. I made a decision and reached for Shasta's purse. As I hacked at the tough bands, I told her, "Listen, I don't care about what *you* did. Leave town. Go. No one knows who you are."

"He does," Shasta said darkly. I scrambled out the window and clamored up a small embankment with Mom. Frigid gusts howled down through the canyon, and when I managed to press on my key-chain flashlight, all I could see was a blizzard whiteout. Turning in the direction I hoped was toward home, Mom and I made our way down the road.

We were panting hard, neither of us daring to say a word, when a shot rang out. The sharp crack echoed, seeming to come from all directions. A scream followed but quickly disappeared into the howling wind. Was it male? Female? I craned my head backward, terrified of who might appear behind us.

"Look," Mom exclaimed, and my heart flip-flopped. But Mom was pointing ahead, toward headlights dimly shining through the snow.

I ran as fast as I could up the slick road, waving my arms and my flashlight. An old truck with a sputtering motor slid to a stop.

Shielding my eyes, I approached the driver's side. Angel Ortiz cranked down the window. His witchy grandmother Josephina, dressed in black robes and gripping a crooked stick, sat on the bench seat beside him.

"Nana thought someone needed a ride," Angel said, over Josephina's cackle.

On Christmas Day, we didn't eat at noon, as Mom's tradition demanded. We didn't have Aunt Sue's gelatin surprise or marshmallows on the sweet potatoes, and the gravy came spiked with red chile.

Flori, the gravy spiker, raised a toast. "To all

those we love, near and far, here and beyond," she said.

Bernard kissed her, glasses clinked, and the friends and family squeezed around Flori's massive dining table sang out, "Feliz Navidad."

Mom and I touched glasses, hers sparkling water, mine wine. Celia stretched her cranberry juice across a centerpiece mound of tamales.

Celia had sounded the alarm last night when she saw Barton drive by. There was something in his eyes, she'd said. A bad feeling that made her shrink back into the crowd as he passed. When she couldn't reach me or her grandmother, she and Sky rushed through the revelers searching for us. She then called Manny and Jake, who, together with Flori and her pals, launched a wider search of Judith's properties and the main roads leading out of town. It was Deputy Davis who found us first. Or, rather, we found her. Her patrol car was creeping down the snowy road with its lights flashing, when Angel stopped and beeped. The deputy had been overjoyed.

"Looks like I won the betting pool," she'd said.

I was too relieved to care that I was still the subject of a police betting pool. "For finding us, right?" I asked.

"Yeah," she said. "Unless you found another dead guy out there, in which case Jean-Marie on dispatch wins."

I'd since learned that there was no dead guy. Only a wounded Barton Hunter, or whatever his real name was. The would-be widower had been shot in the gut by his wife, real name also unknown. She'd disappeared into the blizzard.

Deputy Davis predicted that they'd find her body by Three Kings Day, January 6. I bet she'd get away and transform into someone else.

A warm hand drew me out of my dark thoughts. Sitting beside me at the table, Jake sneaked a peck on my cheek and asked me to pass the mashed potatoes.

"You make fine mashed potatoes, Ms. Lafitte," he said, leaning forward to compliment my mom. "And that monkey bread is absolutely delicious. Even better than my mother's sage dinner rolls, although I won't admit to that in front of her." His parents were due back from their trip around New Year's and he'd invited me to go meet them.

"We'll stay one night, tops," he'd promised. "Otherwise, they'll grill you forever. You think your mother is an interrogator. Wait until you meet mine." On the way back, we planned to stop at his cabin on the Pecos River. Our long-awaited weekend getaway finally seemed like a reality. And a priority.

I leaned my head on his shoulder for a moment and then praised Mom for her green bean casserole.

Mom blushed under the compliments, or maybe it was the spicy gravy. Our brush with death had emboldened her. She'd tasted a little bit of everything on the table. Flori's Christmas enchiladas with cheese and onion, the red *posole* stew, tamales filled with *carne adovada* and green chiles, and a traditional New Mexican Christmas salad made with crunchy jicama, juicy orange slices, and ruby red pomegranate seeds. Mom had declared some dishes dubiously "interesting," taken second help-ings of tamales, and was surprisingly hooked on the salad.

For my part, I was still shocked by Mom's secret. She'd revealed more when she, Celia, and I were safely back at home last night. Celia had taken the news a lot more calmly than me.

"The jerk walked out on you, Gran," she'd said. "He tricked you and ran off with dirty money and started another family and made you think he was dead. Of course you didn't want to have anything to do with him. We get that, right, Mom?"

Did I get that? After a night of tossing and turning, I supposed I did. When my father had appeared at Mom's door years ago, begging to contact my sister and me, Mom had said she'd think about it. By the time she had, he'd disappeared again. He'd been drawn to adventure and the Southwest, she said. *Like me.* That was one of the reasons she'd worried when I moved here. Would I, like my father, disappear from her life?

Dad had contacted her again a few months ago. He'd sent a postcard with a scene and postmark from New Mexico. That's what compelled Mom to break the news. She didn't want me to be shocked by a stranger, or upset at her, if he found his way to my door.

Flori passed a plate of savory empanadas down the long table. I wanted another, but I had to save room. The dessert table was practically sagging, laden with Jake's yummy mincemeat empanadas, a half-dozen versions of *bizcochitos*, Mom's soft gingerbread cookies, and two pies from Lorena Cortez: chocolate cream dusted with red chile and her holiday special, pumpkin pie in a wonderful gingersnap crust.

I'd called Lorena early Christmas morning and told her about Barton's confession, as grudgingly shared by Manny. The so-called consultant had actually repatriated some items, enough to make himself seem legitimate and build a reputation. The best pieces, he'd been selling to shady contacts.

Francisco, with his background in archeology and history, had figured out what was going on but made the mistake of trying to gather more evidence. He'd quizzed Shasta, who'd guessed his suspicions and told her con-man husband. Barton couldn't resist bragging to the police about his elaborate murder scheme. He'd planned ahead for several weeks, sending the death threat letters. He'd then faked the migraine, knowing that Francisco would be around to fill in as the devil. As extra flair, he snagged Trey's UNM Lobos coat from the ski shop, in case he was seen. He would have been happy to have Wyatt, the panicked Santa, take the fall. However, when Wyatt's alibis came forward, Barton resumed his original plan of framing Trey by planting incriminating evidence in Trey's garage and workspace.

Barton had also easily figured out Shasta's scheme to double-cross him by romancing Trey, who had been pilfering the collection for years. Little Eddie had blabbed about kissing. Barton had also heard the couple through the thin door between his rooms and the ski shop. Shasta's ultimate plan, he claimed, was to knock him off and set herself up as future heiress, after getting rid of Judith Crundall.

I'd called Lorena to tell her the news. She'd been grateful to confirm her husband's innocence and her friend's good nature. Francisco, she reported, had bequeathed all his assets to Angel, supporting the young baker in death as he had in life. Angel and Josephina had come to the Inn of the Pajarito for the will reading the day before. "Francisco didn't have much," Lorena said, "But I'll try to help out in his memory." She'd offered Angel a job at Pie in the Sky. "I need a good assistant baker," she said. "It'll free up time for all the dates Wyatt wants to take me on. I swear, it's like someone put a romance spell on that man." *Maybe someone had.*

Dalia was horrified that she'd inadvertently pushed poison on her half sister. On their own, the contaminated pieces wouldn't have caused illness. Shasta, however, had doused them in extra arsenic. A search of Judith's kitchen also revealed arsenic in the teas Dalia had hoped would cure her sister. Dalia planned to purge the house and hire a local expert to repatriate the collection properly.

Judith took the news in her usual crusty stride. According to her, she never fully trusted the flirty Mr. Hunter, calling him way too pretty. Trey, meanwhile, was stunned by Shasta's deception and his mother's reaction to his thefts. Judith was evicting her son from the house until he could prove that he was capable of making an honest living. Tough love, Judith called it. Just deserts, I said.

Dishes went around the table again, and I couldn't resist a few more tastes. By the end of the meal, I'd discreetly loosened my belt by a notch. I leaned back in my chair, gazing into Flori's living room, where her great-grandkids played with old-fashioned Lincoln Logs, and Winston snuggled up by the fireplace with Flori's big orange cat and a niece's shivery Chihuahua.

Mr. Peppers and his friend Sidekick had returned home for the holidays, but not before taking an encore walk around the Plaza on Christmas morning. We'd all gone to see them off. Peppers had mostly behaved. He'd only stolen one hat and a croissant. Sidekick had eaten a wreath.

"I'm so glad we did this," Mom said, later, as some of us bundled up for a brisk walk around the block before tackling dessert.

"Me too. Flori makes a wonderful holiday meal," I said.

Mom agreed that the meal was wonderful. "I meant, I'm glad we had this time together, Rita. Time to bond and share."

We'd bonded, all right, under the worst of circumstances. I started to apologize for the holiday that wasn't filled with peace or goodwill or even a proper molded gelatin salad.

Mom stopped me. "It's been lovely. Let's hope next time I visit, though, there's less excitement."

"You'll come back?" I asked, surprised.

Mom smiled. "Of course. But I'll need more of that oxygen. And I still can't tolerate beans for breakfast or hot chile and you really should consider getting a larger place with a real guest bed and . . ."

Ahead of us, Jake and Celia lobbed snowballs to Winston. Flori modestly pointed out a knit-embellished stop sign, and the adobe walls were iced with picture-perfect snow. I still hadn't decided whether I'd seek out my wayward father. Part of me thought he didn't deserve it. Another part was curious about the man who disappeared. What I did know was that I had some of the best Christmas gifts ever. Mom and Celia were safe, a murderer languished in jail, and I was the proud owner of a brand-new, hand-knit ski mask.

Flori's Holiday Posole

Servings: about 6

INGREDIENTS
  1 onion, diced
  2–3 cloves garlic, minced
  1½ lb. pork, cut into bite-sized cubes
      (pork shoulder or loin, trimmed of fat)
  6 c chicken or vegetable broth or water
  1½ c frozen *posole* (rinsed several times in warm
      water) or canned hominy (rinsed)
  1 bay leaf
  1 c red chile sauce (recipe below)
  Red chile sauce
  1 T olive oil or lard
  1 T flour
  1 clove garlic, minced
  3 T powdered red chile, preferably New Mexican
      (start with mild and add heat as desired)
  1 c water
  Pinch of dried oregano
  ¼ t salt (or more to taste)
  Dash of red wine or cider vinegar

TOPPINGS
  Choose your favorites: Chopped cilantro, diced avocado, thin radish slices, crumbly Mexican cheese, sour cream or Mexican *crema*, toasted tortilla strips, lime wedges.

DIRECTIONS
  In a large soup pot, sauté the onions until tender.

Add minced garlic and stir for a few minutes. Add the cubed pork, broth, rinsed frozen *posole* (if using canned hominy, wait until the final step and add with the chile sauce), and bay leaf. Bring to a boil, skim off any froth, and then lower heat and simmer until the pork and *posole* are tender, about 2 to 3 hours. Note that some stew meats may take longer, so it's best to start early or a day ahead.

While the pork and *posole* are cooking, make the red chile sauce. Heat oil in a small saucepan. Add flour and stir until it's golden. Next, stir in garlic, then the red chile. Mix the paste around for a minute or two to bring out the flavor. Whisk in the water until smooth. Add oregano and salt and simmer for about 10 minutes, stirring occasionally. Stir in dash of vinegar. Set aside.

When the pork and *posole* are tender, add the red chile. If using canned *posole*, add it now. Simmer for another 15 minutes. Taste for seasoning. Serve with warm tortillas and the optional toppings.

Quick options: This stew can also be made with leftover rotisserie chicken or roasted pork. Use canned hominy and combine all ingredients. Simmer for about 15 minutes, season, and garnish as above.

Noche Buena Salad

Noche Buena, or the Good Night, refers to Christmas Eve and is often the night of the biggest feast in Spanish-influenced cultures. There are a lot of variations of this salad, so feel free to improvise with a colorful mix of fruits and vegetables.

Servings: 4

INGREDIENTS

- 2 oranges, sliced with pith removed as much as possible.
- 1 crisp apple, sliced thinly
- 1–2 firm bananas, sliced (slice and add to salad immediately before serving)
- 1½ c jicama, peeled and cut into matchstick slices
- ½ c thinly sliced radishes
- 1 jalapeño pepper, deseeded and thinly sliced (optional)

DRESSING

- ¼ c fresh lime juice (about 1 large lime) and zest (about 1 t)
- 3 T sour cream or yogurt
- 3 T mayonnaise
- 1 T honey
- Salt and pepper to taste

TOPPINGS

- 3 T chopped cilantro
- 3 T chopped salted or unsalted roasted peanuts (optional)
- 3 T pomegranate seeds

BASE
 Bibb lettuce leaves, washed and dried

DIRECTIONS
 Make the dressing by whisking all the ingredients together. Taste for balance of tangy, salty, and sweet. Prepare the fruits and vegetables. The radish, jicama, pepper, and oranges can be prepared ahead. If preparing the apple in advance, dress with lime or lemon juice to prevent browning. Slice the bananas at the last minute. When ready to serve, arrange the fruits and vegetables on top of the lettuce. Drizzle with dressing. Top with cilantro, pomegranate, and peanuts.

Note: The ingredients are flexible. Try red grapefruit in addition to orange, or add thin slices of red onion or juicy mango.

Mom's Monkey Bread

One bread, two flavor options: savory mustard herbs and cheesy green chile

Makes one big Bundt loaf

INGREDIENTS
BREAD
4 T butter
1½ c milk (any sort) or water
1 T honey or sugar
1 envelope active dry yeast (2¼ t)
1½ t table salt
~3½–4 c all-purpose flour

CHEESY GREEN CHILE FLAVORING
~½ c roasted green chiles, diced. You can use freshly roasted, frozen (thawed), or canned (drained; use one 4½ oz. can). If using whole roasted chiles, remove charred skin and seeds before chopping.
3 T butter, melted
2 c shredded cheese (a mix of cheddar and
    Monterey Jack works well)
2 cloves garlic, minced (or more or less to taste)
3 T chopped cilantro (optional)
2 T chopped chives or green onion (optional)
1 t dried oregano

SAVORY MUSTARD AND HERBS FLAVORING
4 T butter
1 small onion, finely diced

2 cloves garlic, minced
2½ T whole grain mustard
1 T chopped fresh parsley OR 1 t dry parsley
    flakes
1 T chopped fresh sage OR 1 t dry sage leaves
½ T chopped fresh rosemary OR ½ t dry
    rosemary leaves
½ T chopped fresh thyme OR ½ t dry thyme
    leaves

DIRECTIONS

Make the dough first so it can start rising. Melt butter in a saucepan. Add milk and gently warm. Pour into a large mixing bowl. Test the temperature. The milk should be warm, about 95–115°F, or comfortable to touch to the inside of your wrist. (If the milk is too hot, it could kill your yeast). Sprinkle in the sugar and dry yeast. Whisk and set aside. In five or ten minutes, the yeast should be bubbling and frothing on the surface. If nothing happens after 15 minutes, your yeast could be dead. Start over with a fresh batch.

Next, stir in salt and then half of the flour. Keep adding flour until you have a soft, shaggy dough. Tip the dough out onto a lightly floured surface and knead, adding more flour as necessary to keep the dough from sticking to your hands or the surface. The amount of flour can vary depending on the humidity of your kitchen. Knead for about 10 minutes until the dough is elastic and supple. You can also knead using a KitchenAid with a dough attachment.

Clean and butter the bowl. Place the dough in the bowl, turning it over once to coat in butter.

Cover with plastic wrap and place in a warm, humid place to proof. A good proofer is your microwave. Boil a mug of water, then push it to the back of the microwave and tuck in the dough bowl. Let rise until doubled in size, about 1 hour.

While the dough is proofing, make the flavoring mixture of your choice.

Cheesy green chile flavoring: Make sure the green chiles are drained and as dry as possible. Keep butter aside. Mix all other ingredients in a low, flat bowl (such as a pie plate). Store in the refrigerator until you're ready to assemble.

Savory mustard and herbs flavoring: Melt butter in a skillet. Add onion and sauté until translucent. Mix in garlic and stir for a minute or two. Stir in mustard and then herbs. Season generously with salt and pepper. Set aside to cool. When ready to assemble the bread, reheat slightly to melt again, if necessary.

To assemble and bake: Prepare a tube or Bundt pan by coating in oil or butter. Turn the dough out onto a lightly floured surface. Cut into quarters. Roll each quarter out into approximately 1½-inch-wide, 12-inch-long logs. Then cut into approximately equally sized pieces (about the size of a large walnut). You can either form the pieces into balls or use them as they are. For the cheesy green chile option, melt the butter. Roll each dough ball in butter and then the cheese mixture. For the savory herbs option, roll each piece in the mustard, onion, and herb mixture. It'll be a little messy but worth it.

Arrange the coated dough in the pan. Don't worry if the level or coverage is a bit off; the dough will fill in gaps as it rises. If it looks like you're going to have extra flavoring mixture, sprinkle it on top of the dough balls as you go. Cover with plastic wrap and let rise again until nearly doubled, about 45 minutes. Toward the end of the proofing, preheat the oven to 375°F.

Bake approximately 35–40 minutes, until golden. Let rest in the pan for about 15 minutes. Tip upside down onto a rack. If you like, you can then flip the bread right-side up. Cool for at least half an hour before serving. Serve on a plate and let guests tear off individual pieces.

Note: If you don't have a Bundt pan, you can use regular bread pans or baking tins and adjust the baking time (a little less time for thinner or smaller breads). This is a great bread to take to potlucks since it's so pretty and diners can serve themselves.

Bizcochitos

Bizcochito traditionalists swear by lard for proper flavor and texture. If you don't have lard or prefer not to use it, shortening or butter can be substituted. You can also spice up your cookies by adding some chile powder to the cinnamon sugar.

Makes approximately four dozen cookies (depending on size)

INGREDIENTS
    1½ c lard (or substitute shortening or butter)
    ¾ c sugar
    1 egg
    1–1½ T anise seeds, crushed lightly
    3 c all-purpose flour
    1½ t baking powder
    ½ t salt
    ¼ c brandy, sherry, or other sweet wine or anise-
        flavored liqueur, OR apple or orange juice

CINNAMON SUGAR TOPPING
    5 T sugar
    3 t ground cinnamon
    ¼–½ t powdered red chile (optional)

DIRECTIONS
Preheat oven to 350°F. Line a baking sheet with parchment paper. Using a stand or hand mixer, cream the lard, shortening, or butter until it is light and fluffy. Add sugar and continue to mix. Next, mix in egg and anise seed.

In separate bowl, mix the dry ingredients. Gradually add flour mixture and brandy or orange juice to the creamed egg mixture until you have a soft but not sticky dough. If you're baking in a dry region and the dough seems too stiff, add a little more orange juice or brandy.

Knead gently and form the dough into a disc. Wrap in plastic and refrigerate for about an hour (or longer) for easier rolling. When ready to bake, mix the cinnamon, sugar, and powdered chile (if using). Roll out the dough on a lightly floured surface to about ¼ inch thick.

Cut the cookies using your favorite cutter. Round or rosette shapes are popular. You can also simply cut the dough diagonally to form diamond shapes. Excess dough can be re-rolled; try to handle it as little as possible to keep the dough tender.

After cutting, press the top of each cookie into the cinnamon sugar and place on the baking sheet. Sprinkle with a little extra cinnamon sugar.

Bake until lightly golden, about 8 to 10 minutes. Cool on a rack. *Bizcochito*s store well in a sealed container, if you can resist eating them all.

Lorena's Gingersnap Pumpkin Pie

Makes one pie

INGREDIENTS
CRUST
1⅔ c gingersnap cookie crumbs (whirl in a food processor, or place in a bag, cover with a tea towel, and pound lightly with a rolling pin)

5 T melted butter or margarine

1 T sugar

Pinch of salt

PIE
15 oz. can of pumpkin

1 c dark brown sugar

2 t ground ginger

2 t cinnamon

¼ t freshly ground nutmeg

¼ t allspice

¼ t ground cloves

½ t salt

½ c heavy cream

⅔ c milk (any kind)

4 eggs, whisked

1 t vanilla extract

Crust: Mix all ingredients and press into a pie dish (use the back of a spoon or metal measuring cup to press in the buttery crumbs). Chill until firm. Heat oven to 375°F. Bake for 6 to 8 minutes. Set aside.

Raise oven temperature to 400°F. Make sure a

rack is available at the lower third of your oven. Prepare filling.

Pie filling: If you have a food processor, whirl the pumpkin, brown sugar, spices, and salt together for a minute or two. Alternatively, use a blender or whisk. Transfer the mixture to a saucepan and warm to a simmer (be careful of sputtering pumpkin, and don't bother to clean the mixing bowl since you'll reuse it). Simmer for about 5 minutes, stirring frequently. Whisk in cream and milk and gently warm. Remove from heat.

In the mixing bowl, blend eggs and vanilla. Add a little of the warm pumpkin mixture to the eggs to temper them. Then add the rest of the pumpkin (or half if you're about to overflow your food processor bowl) and blend. Combine all the filling if you haven't already.

Place the pie pan on a cookie sheet for easy handling. Pour the warm filling into the crust and bake on lower rack for about 40–45 minutes, until edges are puffed and set and middle is still a little jiggly. Turn halfway through baking. Be careful not to overbake, or you'll get cracking (though whipped cream can cover that!) Let cool for several hours. Serve with whipped cream.

Southwest Spice Mix

Use as a dry rub for poultry, a seasoning for roasted potatoes, or a spice for soups.

Make a big batch and put in small spice bottles for holiday gifts.

Makes about ⅓ cup

2 T red chile powder (mild, medium, or hot,
    to taste)
1 T coriander
1 t cumin
1 t garlic powder
1 t dried oregano
1 t kosher salt
1 t cracked black pepper

Mix all ingredients and store in a sealed jar or plastic bag. When using for turkey or chicken, carefully loosen the skin and rub spice mixture and butter under and over the skin before roasting. If using hot chile, be sure to wear plastic gloves.